AMELIA'S JOURNEY

MARTHA ROGERS

REALMS

Most Charisma House Book Group products are available at special quantity discounts for bulk purchase for sales promotions, premiums, fund-raising, and educational needs. For details, write Charisma House Book Group, 600 Rinehart Road, Lake Mary, Florida 32746, or telephone (407) 333-0600.

Amelia's Journey by Martha Rogers
Published by Realms
Charisma Media/Charisma House Book Group
600 Rinehart Road
Lake Mary, Florida 32746
www.charismahouse.com

Scripture quotations are from the King James Version of the Bible.

Cover design by Nathan Morgan
Design Director: Bill Johnson

Visit the author's website at www.marthawrogers.com

What Others Are Saying About the Winds Across the Prairie Series...

Becoming Lucy offers readers a powerful message of love, hope, and transformation. Highly recommended to all readers who are on a journey to "becoming" all they are meant to be in Christ.

—JANICE HANNA THOMPSON
AUTHOR OF *LOVE FINDS YOU IN POETRY, TEXAS*

Set in the Oklahoma Territory, bits of historical truths are woven into this story about a young woman from an affluent background and a young man carrying a burden too large to bear, who finally find their God-chosen place of belonging. Treat yourself to a step back in time—you won't be disappointed.

—KIM VOGEL SAWYER
BEST-SELLING AUTHOR OF *MY HEART REMEMBERS*

In *Finding Becky*, Martha Rogers ushers you into the past where her characters take your hand and invite you into their lives. Martha's attention to historic detail is a treat for the senses, her endearing story a balm for the troubled soul.

—MARCIA GRUVER
AUTHOR OF THE *TEXAS FORTUNES* TRILOGY

Martha Rogers masterfully portrays characters in the early twentieth century. They're firmly attached to the way of life they've always known, yet reaching toward the changes brought about by increasing technology and transitioning ideology.

—LENA NELSON DOOLEY
AUTHOR OF *WILD WEST CHRISTMAS, WILD PRAIRIE ROSES,* AND *LOVE FINDS YOU IN GOLDEN, NEW MEXICO*

Full of characters that stay with you long after the last page is turned, *Finding Becky* is Martha Rogers's best book yet!

—KATHLEEN Y'BARBO
AUTHOR OF *THE CONFIDENTIAL LIFE OF EUGENIA COOPER* AND *BELOVED COUNTERFEIT*

Caroline's Choice is a delightful tale of adventure and romance, of coming of age and making choices.

—KATHI MACIAS
SPEAKER AND AUTHOR OF *VALERIA'S CROSS* AND THE *EXTREME DEVOTION* SERIES

Caroline's Choice brings home the intense need of forgiveness. Martha Rogers has written a compelling story of love and redemption.

—DIANE LESIRE BRANDMEYER
AUTHOR OF *HEARTS ON THE ROAD*

Library of Congress Cataloging-in-Publication Data:
Rogers, Martha, 1936-
   Amelia's journey / Martha Rogers. -- 1st ed.
      p. cm.
   ISBN 978-1-61638-582-8 (trade paper) --
   ISBN 978-1-61638-667-2 (e-book) 1. Young women--Fiction.
I. Title.
   PS3618.O4655A84 2012
   813'.6--dc23

                                        2011032845

First edition

12 13 14 15 16 — 9 8 7 6 5 4 3 2 1
Printed in the United States of America

Delight thyself also in the LORD;
and he shall give thee the desires of thine heart.

—PSALM 37:4

Chapter 1

Saturday, August 19, 1876

*A*melia Carlyle's face ached from the smile pasted on it for the last three-quarters of an hour. Would this ceremony never end? She balanced first on one foot and then the other to relieve the pain caused by the white satin pumps Amanda had insisted Amelia must wear.

Amanda's face glowed with the radiance of the love she had for Charles Scott Bishop, the man who became her husband today. If that love ever happened to Amelia, and she decided to marry, it'd be a small and simple wedding without all this pomp and circumstance.

At last the minister pronounced them husband and wife, and Charles leaned forward to kiss his bride. Amelia's thoughts went immediately to the buffet to be served at the reception. Mama and Papa had spared no expense for their oldest daughter's wedding, and Amelia anticipated the spread of lobster, roast beef, croissants, and wedding cake.

Amanda and Charles made their way back up the aisle, and Amelia dreaded walking even that short distance in her shoes, but she put on another smile and made it to the front steps of the church where carriages waited to take them to the hotel for the reception.

Once they arrived, guests mingled and greeted the bride and groom, but Amelia found the closest table and sat down to slip off her shoes. Her white-stockinged toes wiggled in great relief to be free of their bindings. She turned her back to the room to hide her most unseemly behavior, but comfort won over decorum. She lifted her skirts to run her fingers along the arch of one foot, which relaxed in contentment. Of course if anyone asked her to dance later, she may not be able to squeeze her feet back into the slippers, but she had seen no one with whom she cared to dance anyway.

"Excuse me, Miss Carlyle?"

Amelia snatched the hem of her skirt and yanked it down to cover her legs and feet. She whirled around to find herself looking up into eyes so dark brown, they were almost black. The man towered over her with broad shoulders that blocked any view of the room behind him. A tingling started in her toes and progressed its way to her heart. Why had she not noticed this handsome young man before? "Yes, I'm Miss Carlyle, but I do believe you have the advantage." His smile sent even more tremors through her bones. "I...I don't recall having met you before."

"Of course you don't. You were twelve, and I was a skinny fourteen-year-old. Neither of us paid much attention to the other when we last met at my grandparents' home for dinner after church one Sunday. My name's Benjamin Haynes."

Benjamin Haynes, of course, the son of her parents' best friends of school days, but what was he doing in Boston? His family lived in Kansas. "Oh, yes, that was a few years ago. Have you moved back here?"

He grinned, and his eyes sparkled with amusement. "No, but my parents found your sister's wedding to be the perfect opportunity for a return trip, and I must say now I'm glad I came along."

Heat rose in her cheeks, and her tongue turned to mush. She simply stared back at him with what she hoped was not a stupid smile. What if he asked her to dance? Her feet crossed and rubbed against one another beneath her dress. She'd never get her feet back into those shoes.

"May I get you some refreshment?"

Amelia nodded. "A…a cup of punch would be nice." As he turned to carry out the request, she groaned. Another thing she'd forgotten, no buffet table without her shoes. If she dared walk across the floor without them, her skirt would drag and give away her secret. As if in protest, her stomach grumbled and sent a wave of hunger pangs to her brain. All that food so near, yet it may as well be in another town for all the good it did her seated across the room.

Her gaze landed on Benjamin at the serving table. Although she vaguely remembered him from his last visit, he appeared much taller and was certainly more handsome than he had been then. His dark brown hair even curled slightly at the neckline. Of course she hadn't been truly interested in boys at that time. Being noticed by him created a bit of delight in her now.

Benjamin returned, not only with a cup of punch, but also with a plate filled with some of her favorites from the buffet array. "I thought you might not want to cross the floor to the serving table without your shoes, so I brought it to you. I hope you like what I selected."

Heat again filled her face. He'd noticed her shoeless feet and had sought to save her further embarrassment by being so polite. For that her stomach thanked him. "Thank you, Mr. Haynes. This will do quite nicely, but what about you? When will you eat?"

"If you'll allow me, I'll get my plate and rejoin you."

"I'd like that very much, thank you." Her heart beat in double time as he returned to the buffet and made his own selections. His broad shoulders hinted at the muscles and strength that must be hidden beneath the sleeves of the black suit he wore. The evening took on a whole new interest, and Amelia tucked her feet well beneath her skirts to keep them hidden from view.

When he returned, he sat in the chair next to hers. Miracles of miracles, no one asked to join them, and they remained alone. Her father may have a few words about that later, but for the time being, Amelia planned to enjoy every minute she could have with Mr. Benjamin Haynes.

He spread a napkin across his lap. "Tell me, Miss Haynes, what have you been doing since the last time I saw you?"

It had only been a little more than five years ago, but it may as well have been a lifetime for all Amelia could remember. Her mind a blank, she could only stare at him.

He must think her to be a complete ninny. She cleared her throat. "In school, but of what interest could that possibly be to you? I would imagine your life has been much more eventful and interesting."

Benjamin grinned at her and sipped his punch. He set the cup back on the table and cocked his head to one side. "My life has been herding cattle and getting them to market as well as bustin' broncos to have horses to ride."

"Now that sounds a lot more exciting than going to school, taking piano lessons, and learning to embroider." She pictured him herding cattle or riding a bucking horse. An appealing image.

A young man approached the table, and Amelia cringed. The last person she wanted to see wore a determined expression on his face. Rudolph, Charles's brother, wanted to dance, but his surly attitude the night before at a family dinner had frightened Amelia in a way she couldn't quite explain.

He stopped beside Amelia and Benjamin. "Miss Carlyle, may I have the honor of this dance with you?" His dark eyes held nothing but malice even though his words were polite.

She stuck a shoeless foot out from under her dress. "I'm sorry, Mr. Bishop, but I don't have my shoes on and have decided not to dance this evening. I'm sure you understand I can't be on the dance floor in my stocking feet."

He glared at her for a moment, then, without a word, swiveled on his heel and strode across the room. Amelia shivered, thankful she had removed her shoes.

"I must say, that was rude." Benjamin frowned after the man.

Amelia nodded then smiled at Benjamin. "He's Charles's brother, and I'm glad I didn't have to dance with him." She picked up a pastry. "Let's enjoy ourselves and not think about rude men like Rudolph Bishop." Indeed, she wanted to know everything she could learn about Benjamin Haynes.

Ben wanted to know more about this intriguing young woman he'd known in childhood. Until his father decided to pick up stakes and head west to start his own ranch, the Carlyle and Haynes families had spent many weekends together as his father and Mr. Carlyle had been close friends and schoolmates.

How thankful he was now that he had not insisted that he be left behind to help the ranch hands with the herds. If he had, he would not be sitting across from the lovely young woman in a pink dress.

"Amelia, do you remember the week my family left for Kansas? Your parents gave a wonderful farewell party for us. Of course you were only five, but I hoped you might recall that night." If she did remember, he might find himself in trouble as he had delighted in pulling her golden brown curls more than once just to see her reaction, and she hadn't disappointed. She had stomped her foot and hit him each time until his mother corralled him the third time and made him stay by her side.

Amelia chewed a piece of pastry and narrowed her eyes at him. She swallowed and pursed her lips. "Was that the time you kept pulling my curls?"

Heat rose in his face. "You do remember. I apologize for

my awful behavior that evening, but you looked so cute with those long curls hanging down from that big yellow bow."

Amelia laughed. "I forgive you, but it hurt that last time, and I wanted to cry. I wasn't about to let you see me in tears, and I believe your mother took care of you. Mary Beth and I had fun after that."

"Yes, Mama made sure I stayed by her side, and I didn't have much fun the rest of the evening. I'm glad you did though. Then your family came to the railway station to see us off on our adventure westward." That had been some scene with both their mothers crying and their fathers promising to keep in touch.

"Oh yes, I recall how afraid I was of that big engine with its smoke and loud whistle. When it started up and began rolling on the track, I hid behind Mama's skirt, but I saw you wave at us from the window. I thought you were so brave to move away like that with your family."

"It was quite the adventure." And one he would never forget. He held no regret at all for leaving Boston all those years ago.

He glanced up to see his sister headed their way. He didn't often get to see her so dressed up with her dark hair piled on her head. He grinned when she squealed and grabbed Amelia, her brown eyes dancing with pleasure. "I've been looking all over for you. I should have known Ben would have you all to himself."

Amelia hugged the girl in return. "Mary Beth, I'm so glad to see you. I spotted you at the church when we went back up the aisle. Sit down and join us."

Benjamin shook his head and glared at Mary Beth, but she paid him no mind and plopped down in the chair on the other side of Amelia. "I'd be delighted. What has my big brother been telling you? I could reveal a few of his secrets if you'd like to hear about some of his antics."

"We were just talking about one on the night we had that party before you left."

"Oh, yes, that was some fun watching him get into trouble." Mary Beth grabbed Amelia's hands. "How I wish you could have come out to visit us, and I wish we could have come back to Boston more often. Ben almost didn't come with us, but Pa persuaded him. I'm really sorry we haven't kept in closer touch."

Amelia glanced at him and grinned in a way he could only call wicked. "To think we might have missed reminiscing about old times if you'd stayed back with the cows. What a shame that would have been, Mr. Haynes."

Again heat rose in his cheeks, but he would not let her teasing get to him. "Since we're such old friends, call me Ben; everybody else does."

"All right, Ben it is." Then she turned back to his sister. "Now, tell me what it's like living on a ranch with all those cattle and horses."

Ben groaned. Once Mary Beth started, he'd never get a word into the conversation. He may as well just enjoy his food and listen to their prattle. At least he could sit back and show interest in what Amelia had to say without being obvious with his attraction to her.

Her chestnut hair sat piled on top of her head in an elaborate arrangement that must have taken hours to accomplish. Two long curls like those of long ago hung down in the back from the curls amassed atop her head. His fingers itched to reach over and pull one of them as he had when she was five. Now seventeen, she had become a beautiful young lady with a sense of humor and a smile that could melt the heart of any man in her presence.

He blinked his eyes and shook his head as Amelia squealed with delight and clapped her hands. He stared at his sister. "What was that you said about staying in Boston?"

"Ma and Grandmama talked with me last night, and Pa agreed. I can stay here for the social season this fall."

"Isn't it wonderful, Ben? Mary Beth and I can do so many things together and have fun, and I'm sure there will be lots of parties."

Ben narrowed his eyes. "I'm sure there will be." This was the first he'd heard of any desire from Mary Beth to come back here. She loved the ranch, or at least he'd thought so.

"What will Ma and Aunt Clara do without you?" She'd been such a big help to them that he couldn't imagine life without her around.

"They'll get along just fine. After all, there aren't any more babies to care for. Gideon, Grace Ann, and Billy are old enough to care for themselves, so they don't need me looking after them all the time."

That was true. With his youngest brother now eight years old and in school, no more children stayed at home needing care. Ma and Aunt Clara would manage just fine. Still, he had a difficult time believing his pa would let his oldest daughter live so far away.

Amelia and Mary Beth sat with heads close together discussing all the things they wanted to do in the coming months when Mary Beth would be presented to society just as her mother and grandmother had been before her. Then a bright side occurred to him. With Mary Beth here, that could mean Ma taking more trips to see her. Pa wouldn't want to leave the ranch, so that would leave Ben to accompany Ma on such trips.

More trips to Boston meant more opportunity to see Amelia Haynes. Of course, he'd have to gain permission from her parents, but that shouldn't be a problem since their families were longtime friends. The future began to look brighter and brighter. This had been the best trip he'd taken in a long time, and he looked forward to many more like it—that is, if Amelia agreed to his calling on her.

Chapter 2

*A*melia dressed with extra care on Sunday morning. Ben Haynes would be at church with his family, and after their meeting last night, she looked forward to seeing him again. After the service, the families planned to dine together at the Carlyle home, which meant even more time together.

"Amelia, quit dawdling. It's time to go. We don't want to be late."

The tone of her mother's voice left Amelia with no choice as she pushed a pearl-tipped pin into the crown of her hat. "Coming right down, Mama."

At the bottom of the stairs her mother greeted her with a frown. "Must you always come bounding down the steps? You're a young lady now, and you should act like one." She turned on her heel and headed for the door. "Come along, your father is waiting with the carriage."

Amelia sighed and shrugged her shoulders. Why should being seventeen make such a difference in how she walked or came down the stairs? She didn't feel any different, but Mama and Papa certainly expected her to act like a lady. Of course with Amanda gone to her own home now, Mama would be paying much closer attention to Amelia and her behavior.

In the carriage her parents talked while Amelia dreamed about the tall young cowboy, Ben. His appearance spoke of his life on the ranch, but his manners revealed the background of his family and their position in society. With her height, finding young men to whom she could look up and not eye to eye was difficult, but last night she'd had to raise her head to look into his eyes when they stood to say good-bye.

Her fingers reached to touch one of her curls, and a smile formed in her heart at the memory of his tugging on them so many years ago. The last time she'd seen him as a young teenager, he'd spent most of his time with his male cousins and had very little to do with the girls, but it looked like that had changed. For that she could only be grateful.

As they drew up to the stone structure of their church, Amelia's toes itched to jump out and run inside to see if the Haynes family had arrived. Respect for her parents bade her to control her desire and sit still until the carriage stopped for her family to alight.

Once on the ground, she hurried with as much sedateness as she could muster. Stepping into the dim foyer, she blinked to allow her eyes to adjust from the bright sunlight.

Mary Beth hurried toward her. "Amelia, I'm so glad you're here. Mama said I could sit with you if it's all right with your parents."

"Of course it is. They'll be delighted." Mary Beth's dark

hair was arranged in a most becoming style that set off her tanned complexion and brown eyes. Amelia had wished often enough for either dark hair or blonde instead of the somewhere-in-between brown that she had been given.

Mary Beth followed Amelia to their pew. Out of the corner of her eye she spotted Ben and his family in the row directly behind where the Carlyles were to sit. His smile sent the heat rising in her cheeks, so she focused her eyes straight ahead as she took her seat.

During the music, Amelia fought the urge to turn her head just a bit to see Ben. Instead she concentrated on her surroundings. Being in the Lord's house called for reverence, not fanciful imaginings of the handsome young man seated behind her.

Light filtered through the stained glass windows, casting a rainbow of colors across the congregation. Amelia fixed her gaze on the one to her left. The picture of Jesus holding a lamb always brought peace to her. Whenever she stumbled and fell, Jesus would be there to pick her up, and she'd done quite a bit of stumbling in the past few weeks. Not that she didn't respect her parents, but lately she had found herself at odds with them more often than she should.

When they were seated and the sermon began, Amelia forced herself to concentrate on the message about the feeding of the five thousand. The Lord had provided for the needs of the crowd, and He had never failed to provide for her needs. She must rely on Him now. If her attraction to Ben was to go anywhere, it had to be the Lord's doing.

A discreet glance at Mary Beth revealed her grinning as though she read Amelia's thoughts. Heat rose in her cheeks, but she couldn't resist an answering grin, which brought a tap on her thigh from Mama, who had eyes in the top, back, and sides of her head.

Amelia reached down between her and Mary Beth and grabbed her hand to squeeze it. Having Ben's sister here for their coming out would be fun. Most of the girls of Amelia's acquaintance were much too stuffy for her tastes and fun-loving spirit. Perhaps in the process of renewing their friendship she could learn more about Ben.

Ben's gaze had never left Amelia from the time she had walked down the aisle to the pew in front of his family. The sermon seemed to go on forever, and Ben tuned out the minister's words to concentrate on the girl before him. She had grown so tall in the years since they'd last seen one another. When she stood last night at the reception, the top of her head had been even with his eyes. Finding a girl whose height fit in with his so that he didn't tower over her delighted him no end.

He stifled a chuckle when Mary Beth and Amelia grinned at each other and Mrs. Carlyle reprimanded Amelia. Looked like Amelia was just as feisty as he'd remembered her. Apparently finishing school had not been able to subdue her spirit.

At last the sermon ended and the families made their way outside. Before Ben could invite Amelia to ride with his family to the Carlyle house, Amelia asked her parents if Mary Beth could ride with them. So much for that idea. He'd have to wait until dinner to have any conversation with Amelia.

At the table Amelia sat across from him while he sat between Mary Beth and his younger brother, Gideon. Several times during the course of the meal, his gaze locked with hers in silent communication to seek out time to be together later in the afternoon.

As the parents discussed how things had changed in Boston in the years since their last visit, Mary Beth spoke up. "I think it would be lovely if Amelia and I could ride around the city this afternoon so she can show me some of the sights. It will also give me an opportunity to become more familiar with the city since I'm going to be living here with Grandmama and Grandpapa. Of course Ben should accompany us."

Amelia's face lit with her smile. "That's a grand idea. We'll be safe with Ben as our escort." Her eyes sparkled as she glanced in his direction.

Bless his sister for thinking of a way he and Amelia could be together!

Mr. Carlyle nodded in their direction. "I think that will be quite suitable. It will also give you the opportunity to renew your friendship." He signaled to the young woman who served the table. "Inform Toby that we will need the carriage brought around."

Amelia and Mary Beth could hardly contain their excitement, and Ben anticipated the excursion with pleasure. As soon as manners permitted, he and the girls excused themselves from the table.

The girls ran up the stairs to freshen themselves, but Ben remained in the foyer. His parents and the Carlyles went into the parlor, and his younger siblings headed for the library and the games set out for them there.

Amelia and Mary Beth descended the steps, and Amelia's beauty once again robbed him of breath. He'd already seen the lively spirit of nonconformity in her last evening and eagerly awaited what more he would learn today.

Both wore large-brimmed straw hats decorated with ribbons and bows. Since they would be in an open carriage, they both carried parasols. Ben offered his arms to the girls, and each one placed a hand in the crook of his elbows. "I think I may be the luckiest man in Boston to have two such beautiful young ladies on my arms today."

Mary Beth laughed and patted his arm. "He wouldn't be saying that if we were at home. He'd be pushing me along and telling me to hurry up and get in the buggy."

He couldn't deny that fact. At home he spent much more time teasing her than he did paying her compliments. After he assisted Amelia into the carriage, Mary Beth climbed up and sat on the opposite seat, leaving him his choice of her or Amelia. His appreciation for his sister grew by leaps and bounds this afternoon as he settled in beside Amelia.

The carriage moved forward, and Amelia smoothed her skirt. "Father told Toby to take us through the historic section. After all, we've just recently celebrated the centennial of the birth of our nation."

All the scenery Ben needed sat next to him, and he hoped to make the best of his time with Amelia today. As the horse clip-clopped over the cobblestone streets in the older sections of Boston, Amelia pointed out the places of interest. He remembered many of them from his last visit, but Mary Beth wanted to know more about each place.

"I loved American history in school. I wish I'd been living during the Revolutionary times." Mary Beth pointed. "Oh, I remember Faneuil Hall."

Amelia said, "That and the old State House are two of my favorite buildings. When I look up at that balcony on the end, I can just imagine the crowds there listening to speeches." She turned to face Ben. "What was school like in Kansas?"

"Nothing like the Latin School here, I can assure you. We did reading, spelling, arithmetic, and history, but no Latin, and none of the classics they had here. I don't regret my schooling, but the last time I was in Boston, the sons of some of Pa's other friends talked about the courses they took, and I envied them."

Amelia twirled her parasol and grinned. "I did too, as there's no equivalent like it for girls. I attended a private school to study the classics, but I have no desire to go on to college."

That suited Ben just fine. If she went off to Wellesley or Smith, she might meet someone else and forget him.

Then the two girls began conversing about the coming social season and all the parties and cotillions that would be planned. Ben shook his head. Another obstacle in his hopes of winning Amelia's favor. Amelia would be meeting many eligible young men, all with college degrees and family connections. But he had chosen the path of ranching for his life. His visions for the future included a place of his own with his own herds and ranch hands, but would Amelia fit into that lifestyle? His mother had, but then she'd been so in love with Pa that she would have followed him anywhere in the world. He hoped to have that kind of love for and from a woman sometime.

Amelia touched his arm. "Ben, you've certainly been quiet for the past half hour. Are we that boring?"

Heat rose in face. Thankfully she couldn't read his thoughts. "No, I enjoy listening to the two of you having such a good time."

Amelia folded her parasol. "Well, we're home, and I'm ready for something to drink. I hope Lettie has saved some of that delicious cake from dinner."

The carriage stopped, and Ben hopped down to assist the ladies. When they entered the house, his parents were gathered with his brothers and sister in the foyer. His mother mentioned having luncheon with Mrs. Carlyle before the family headed back to Kansas.

Their train was to leave in five days. He must have some time alone with Amelia, but how could he manage it? He stepped over to Mr. Carlyle. "Sir, since my mother is having luncheon with Mrs. Carlyle, may I have permission to tour the city with Miss Carlyle during that time? There were a number of sights that we missed on our ride today."

Mr. Carlyle studied him with narrowed eyes and pursed lips. "Mrs. Carlyle and I will discuss your request and send word to you."

"Thank you, sir." That was not what he had hoped for, but at least her father hadn't said no. Of course he'd expect a chaperone, and he knew the perfect one, Aunt Clara. Being only fourteen years older than he, she would have a better understanding of his purpose. "Excuse me, I might add that I will ask my aunt Clara to join us."

"I see. That will be satisfactory. We'll send a message to you with our answer tomorrow morning."

Ben bowed slightly and backed away to join his brothers. He would pray tonight that the answer would be a yes.

Chapter 3

*A*t breakfast on Wednesday, Isaac Carlyle stirred his coffee and glanced at his wife. "Do you think we're doing the right thing by letting Benjamin and Amelia spend the afternoon together?"

"I see no harm in it. They will only be here until Friday. It's not like they are courting. Of that I would not approve at all, even if their background is on an equal footing with ours. Kansas is too far away, and I would never want Amelia that distance from home."

"I totally agree, but I noticed the way he looked at her Sunday both at church and at dinner. There is more than a little interest in our daughter." Perhaps he shouldn't have agreed to this outing, but he hadn't been able to come up with a good excuse that would be plausible to his old friend. Clara Haynes would be with them, and she would see to it that nothing happened to cause alarm.

"Maybe so, but Amelia is aware of our plans for her this fall, so after he leaves she will be much too busy to think about him." Lenora took a piece of toast and buttered it. "I still remember when Elizabeth and Matthew left Boston. Her parents were terribly upset, but his were proud of their son for adventuring out west to start his own ranch. She and I cried about being apart, but Elizabeth would have gone to the ends of the earth with Matthew."

"I remember that, and somewhat envied Matthew for the courage to pick up stakes and start out anew." At Lenora's frown, he hastily added, "Not that I wasn't content to be here, my dear, but Matthew did a very brave thing taking his family to the unknown."

"Foolish, if you ask me. He had no idea what he may face on the frontier, but then Matthew was more adventurous than most. Of course, it's none of my business what others have done unless my own children become involved."

Isaac chuckled. "And you'd hiss and fuss like a mama cat protecting her kittens if that happened. I honestly don't think we have anything to worry about. Let the two young people enjoy each other's company while the Haynes family is here." Young people and their emotions could be quite unpredictable, but he preferred to place his trust in Amelia. Even as headstrong as she was, she'd think before doing anything foolish. Still, he'd keep a close watch on her.

With Amanda they'd never had the problems they encountered with Amelia. Her stubborn streak and strong will had led to punishment more than once, but he loved her spirit and wouldn't have it any other way.

Amelia appeared in the doorway. "Good morning, Mama, Papa. I'm sorry I'm late. I had a difficult time deciding what I should wear for our outing today." Amelia sat across from her mother.

"You chose well, my dear. That lemony yellow is perfect on you. With the warm weather today, the shear fabric should be quite comfortable."

"Thank you, Mama." She turned with a smile toward Isaac. "And thank you, Papa, for allowing me to visit with Ben this afternoon. We didn't have time to see as much as I wanted to show him on Sunday."

Papa nodded and placed his napkin on the table. "Then it's good you will have Clara Haynes with you. I'm sure she can tell you what Boston was like when they left." He pushed back his chair. "It's time for me to leave, but I'm sure you and your mother have much to say to each other."

Isaac leaned over and kissed his wife's forehead before leaving. The sound of their voices followed him to the door. He'd decided to ride his horse into his office this morning, and Toby had the roan saddled and ready for him. "Thank you, Toby."

"Yes, sir. Shall we expect you home at the regular time?"

"Yes, I believe Lettie is preparing something special for us tonight, and I don't want to miss it." He climbed up and swung his leg across the horse's back. A hint of the cooler days to come laced the breeze that greeted him as he headed for downtown Boston. In not too many weeks the trees would turn to announce the arrival of fall, and if things went as planned, Amelia would be caught up in the whirl of social activities. She would find a beau just as Amanda had and would settle down here in Boston.

He harbored visions of grandchildren one day filling the Carlyle home once again with the laughter of young ones.

He'd prayed all through their younger years that his daughters would find suitable young men to marry. God had answered that prayer for Amanda with Charles Bishop, and Isaac was certain Amelia too would find a good man, despite her streak of independence and not always conforming to society's convention. Indeed, he had frowned at the fact that she'd gone barefoot at the wedding reception. That was not his idea of how a young lady should behave.

Then he chuckled as he remembered the other times Amelia had done what she wanted to do rather than what propriety expected. What was he going to do with Amelia in the days ahead? One thing for certain, home would be a very dull place without her around to enliven his days.

Amelia stood at her window and peeked through the curtains to watch her mother leave to meet her friend for their luncheon. Almost as soon as her carriage moved away, Ben arrived. She dropped the curtain and grabbed her parasol to make her way downstairs. She reached the bottom of the stairway just as Murphy the butler answered the door. Ben stepped into the foyer and spotted Amelia right away. His smile sent her heart into somersaults as she moved toward him.

"Good afternoon, Miss Carlyle; you do look lovely. Aunt Clara is waiting for us. Shall we join her?" He offered his arm, and Amelia grasped it.

"Thank you, and I truly look forward to our ride around about the city today." She fell into step beside him as he escorted her down the front stoop to the carriage where Miss Haynes sat waiting.

Clara Haynes sat in the middle of the seat with her back toward the driver, so that left Ben and Amelia to sit side by side. A twinkle in Clara's eyes let Amelia know the seating arrangement had been thought out beforehand. For that Amelia was most appreciative.

"Good afternoon, Miss Haynes. I'm so glad you were free to accompany us today."

"I looked forward to it, and please, call me Clara. Everyone else does. After all, I'm only fourteen years older than Ben." She moved her parasol so that it blocked the sun from her face.

Amelia did the same with hers and welcomed the shade it provided. "All right, I will." She turned to Ben. "And remember we're not standing on formality, so I'm Amelia and not Miss Carlyle."

Ben chuckled and shook his head. "I don't think you'll ever be anything but Amelia to me."

The coachman drove them along the street toward the Old North Church, one of Amelia's favorite places to visit. Clara reminisced about the places they passed, then interrupted one of her stories to grin at Amelia. "Here I am going on and on about Boston when you probably know a great deal more than I do since I've been gone for a while."

What a perfect opportunity to learn more about Clara Haynes. "I was wondering, why did you choose to go out west with your brother?"

"I went with the idea of being a teacher and helping with the mission work there, but then Matthew and Elizabeth needed me to help with the children. Five children were a lot for Elizabeth to handle. When Billy started school a few years ago, I went back to teaching the older students in the school. I've enjoyed it."

"Do you ever regret leaving Boston and all your family and friends here?" That would be the hardest for Amelia to do.

"At first I missed my parents and other siblings, but Matthew's household was so lively that soon I didn't have time for missing them. I made many new friends at the church we attend there, so now I don't miss Boston at all, although I still love this city."

"It all sounds so exciting to live on a ranch, but I'm not sure I'd want to leave everything here, even though I do love adventures and new things."

Clara smiled and leaned over to pat Amelia's arm. "Oh, if the right man came along, you might change your mind. Love does strange things to us."

Heat rose in Amelia's face as she caught a glimpse of the smile on Ben's face. Yes, she was attracted to him, but he'd be gone in a few days. And would she be willing to give up her life here for life on a ranch in Kansas? For that she had no answer.

The red spots on Amelia's cheeks shot Ben's thoughts far ahead to the future. He wanted to be that man in her life, but with the distance between them, he had no hopes of fostering a growing relationship. Mary Beth's staying did give him some hope of seeing Amelia again, but with her beauty and spirited personality, she wouldn't remain single long in Boston.

As the two women talked, jealousy for the young men who would claim Amelia for a dance or two at the cotillions in the days ahead wiggled its way into his heart. One of those would most likely win her hand in marriage as well.

He had no right to expect anything more than friendship from Amelia Carlyle, but his heart wished for more, much more. Her animated expressions and use of her hands while she conversed with Aunt Clara fascinated him.

She turned to glance at him. "And what do you find so amusing, Benjamin Haynes?"

Now it was his turn to have heat in his face. "I was admiring two lovely women enjoying their time together."

Aunt Clara clasped her hands and held them in her lap. "Here I've been rattling on like a buggy with a loose wheel. This is supposed to be your time together, and I'm monopolizing it. Please excuse me, Ben."

He laughed and bent over to grasp Aunt Clara's hands. "You're excused. Besides, your conversations are interesting, and I've learned a good deal about our hometown."

"Still, I should keep quiet and let you two have your visit. We'll have to return home soon."

Indeed, the time passed faster than he would like, but perhaps he could salvage what was left. Before he had the chance to speak, Amelia shifted her parasol and gazed directly in his eyes. His breath caught in his throat at the depth in those brown pools of color.

"Tell me what it's like living on a ranch."

That he could do with ease. "It's busy. We have a large herd of cattle and lots of land for them to roam. I ride my horse every day while we're checking the herds and repairing fences. I hope to get a parcel of land and begin my own ranch one of these days in the near future."

"What is the weather like in Kansas? I've heard you have bad storms."

He remembered the tornado last year during the springtime and nodded. "Yes, we do have tornadoes, but we also have droughts, and once our creek flooded after a heavy rain. The winters are cold, and we have snow much like Boston." He groaned inwardly. His talk of the weather could turn her against the land. "But the beauty of the prairie and the freshness of the air in springtime and the beauty of the fall more than make up for the few times we have storms."

A glance across at Aunt Clara revealed her twirling her parasol with a satisfied smile. She liked Amelia and would be a good ally to have when he started courting Amelia to win her hand. Wait a minute. What had given him that idea? He couldn't court Amelia halfway across the country, and he had too many responsibilities to remain here. He swallowed hard to quench the desire in his heart.

"Mary Beth has told me a few things about your home there. It sounds quite nice."

Ben blinked his eyes and returned his attention to the girl beside him. "It's a large house with barns and stables and a garden sitting out on the edge of our property. If we didn't have such a large family, I imagine it would get lonely for Ma. Our nearest neighbor is several miles away." There he went again, bringing up the negatives. He'd never win her interest if he didn't bring up some of the good points.

Aunt Clara shook her head. "Don't let him scare you. We go into town for supplies twice a month and to church on Sunday. Sweetwater Springs is a nice-size town, and the people are quite friendly."

"And we have lots of socials and fun events, especially in the spring and summer." If he could make the town sound more appealing, perhaps his parents could convince Mr. Carlyle to bring his family for a visit. He was only kidding himself. If they had any intention of ever coming to Kansas, they would have done it long before now. But he could dream of such a visit—and even pray that it might happen.

Chapter 4

*F*riday morning Amelia spotted the Haynes family at the railroad depot, but she had eyes only for Ben and headed in his direction. Her parents followed behind, and her father called out to Mr. Haynes. Memories of that other farewell at this same station filled her mind. Then the huge engine had frightened her, but today it brought sadness into her heart.

Ben greeted her with a smile and placed his hand on her arm. "Let's go down this way a bit, so we can talk more privately." He led her several yards away from his family and the noise of the train as it prepared to depart.

"We don't have but a few minutes, and there's so much I want to say." Ben grasped her hands in his and gazed at her with his deep brown eyes that glittered with a sadness to match her own. "I can't begin to tell you how much this past week and renewing our friendship has meant to me."

Moistness filled her eyes, and she swallowed hard. "I've enjoyed every minute with you, and I will miss you very much."

"Then we must keep in touch. Mary Beth can give you our address, and she's already given me yours. Please say you'll write to me." His hands exerted a slight pressure on hers as though to plead her answer.

"Of course I'll write." Even if he hadn't asked, she planned to do just that. No matter what propriety may say, she didn't intend for this friendship to fade away because of distance. "I'm glad Mary Beth is staying because now I'll have another way of finding out about what your family is doing besides just your letters." Heat rose in her cheeks, and she dipped her head. He must think her to be terribly brazen, but she meant every word.

The heat from the train added to the heat of the day, and trickles of perspiration formed on Ben's forehead. He released her hands and removed his western style hat. He also wore cowboy boots, and his suit was not the same as those her father and other men in Boston wore. His hair now slipped down over his forehead in a dark brown wave. It added a boyish appeal to his handsome face.

"When do you think you might return to Boston?" With Mary Beth here, surely the family would be back for a visit in a few months.

"I don't know. If Ma wants to visit Mary Ann at all, it'll have to be before November and winter setting in. The weather gets really cold with ice and snow, so travel is pretty much limited until spring." His fingers brushed hers. "I don't want to wait until then to see you again."

Her heart beat with fury beneath the gauze of her bodice. She didn't want to wait that long either. Before she could respond, his mother called to them.

Ben glanced toward his family. "I suppose we must get

back. Ma is ready to board." He grasped her hands again. "Please don't forget me."

"I...I won't. I promise." When he released her hands and turned toward his family, the heat from his touch remained. She walked as close to him as possible without touching him in order not to draw her father's attention.

The months loomed ahead with loneliness even though she would attend many parties and events leading up to the cotillion and her presentation to society. Her friends from school had talked about nothing else before graduation last year, and most of them had made their debuts that fall, but she'd been too ill with pneumonia to participate.

Ben leaned close to whisper, "Don't go falling for any of those fellows you'll meet in the next few months." Then he grinned and winked before picking up his youngest brother.

Heat rose in her face once again. She had no intention of caring about any of the young men she might meet in the coming social season. In fact, if she had her way, there would be no parties or cotillions at all. They were a complete waste of time and money as far as she was concerned. Still, her parents expected it and had already made several commitments.

Clara wrapped her arms around Amelia. "It's been so much fun to be with you and your family." She grinned and added, "Remember, I've been through what you are to experience in the next few months, and it doesn't mean you have to pick one of them for a husband." The sparkle in her eye left no doubt as to her meaning.

Amelia hugged her close. "I do hope I get to see you before another six or seven years go by."

The train whistle screeched through the air, causing Amelia to jump much as she'd done as a child. Clara laughed and picked up a small valise. Mr. Haynes stepped up onto the car platform and waved to her parents. "Let's keep in better touch now, Isaac."

Amelia didn't see or hear her father's response. Her attention focused on Ben, who sat near a window with Billy on his lap. Both of them waved at her.

The train moved down the track at a snail's pace, then as it cleared the depot, it picked up speed and carried Ben out of her life—but only for the time being. He'd be back. He had to, because if he didn't come, her heart would break into a thousand and one fragments.

Ben gazed out the window until he could no longer see the dot of yellow that was Amelia. For the first time in his life, he didn't want to go home, but common sense bade him see otherwise.

The hardest thing he'd done in the past few months was to not kiss Amelia good-bye. He could have reached her forehead if he'd moved just inches closer, but he had really wanted to taste her pretty lips. Only the shocked reaction that would come from her parents prevented him from doing so. He had to do everything right to stay in their good graces, or Amelia would be put off limits faster than he could rope a calf.

The ranch would require much work in the days and months ahead to prepare for the winter season. He and his brother Gideon would help the ranch hands round up some of the herd to take to auction in Abilene, and the rest would be gathered into the winter pastures closer to the ranch house and barns. Pa had purchased two new bulls before they left home and was expecting their arrival on the ranch to coincide with the family's return.

That would mean new calves next spring and more work rounding them up and branding them. If things went well, one more trip to Boston before winter might be possible, but if not, then a return would be put off until early summer.

He settled Billy in the seat beside him. Gideon and Grace Ann sat across from him. Gideon narrowed his eyes and grinned. "I think you would have liked to stay behind with Mary Beth."

Ben jerked his head back. "Whatever gave you that idea?"

"Ha, that look in your eyes every time you're near Amelia Carlyle is a dead giveaway, brother."

Grace Ann sighed. "She is so pretty, and she has such beautiful clothes. I wish I had a dress like that one she wore today."

Ben shook his head and chuckled. "And just where do you plan to wear something like that in Kansas?"

She shrugged and lifted her eyebrows. "I don't know, but if I had a dress like that, I could think of somewhere to go...maybe a church social or one of the dances in town."

Gideon punched her in the arm. "You're not even old enough to go to those yet. Pa said you had to wait until you're sixteen."

Grace Ann blinked her eyes, but a tear still slipped down her cheek as she rubbed her arm. Ben poked Gideon to remind him not to tease his younger sister so much. Gideon shrugged and picked up a book to read.

Ben reached over and squeezed Grace Ann's hand and winked. That elicited a smile. Satisfied she was all right, he turned and gazed out the window as the train sped across Massachusetts. Farm after farm dotted the land as well as trees everywhere.

The white spire of a church steeple lifted its point toward heaven as they passed through a small town along the way. He would see many of those between here and St. Louis, where they would change trains to head across Missouri to Kansas. Many times he'd considered the first families to move west and marveled at the stamina it had taken to travel in covered wagons for such distances. He was thankful his father and mother had chosen Kansas, close to the Missouri border, for their final destination.

Now that he was older, he better understood the generosity of his grandparents who had helped Pa with the funds he needed for the ranch. He glanced now at his parents seated across the aisle. They talked with their heads together. His mother had given up so much to adventure out with Pa. Would Amelia ever do something like that for him?

Pa beckoned to him from across the aisle. "Come and sit with us, Ben. We'd like to talk."

Ben settled onto the bench and waited for his father to speak his mind.

"We noticed that you took quite an interest in Amelia Carlyle this week. Is there something there we should know about?"

Ben gulped. There went his belief that he and Amelia

had been discreet. If his parents noticed, hers were bound to have done the same. "I don't think so. At least not yet." He lowered his head to make his confession. "But I do like her, and we've promised to write to each other."

His father frowned. "Son, I understand how you could be attracted to a girl as pretty as Amelia. But you must understand her life is very different from ours. You are bound to have seen that this week."

"I did, but I also sense a spirit of adventure in her." The memory of her shoeless feet at the reception brought a smile to his heart. Life with Amelia would be one of fun and surprises.

Ma leaned over and grasped his hand. "Ben, it's more complicated than that. Her parents have certain expectations for her and have many plans for her future."

"But you and Pa lived that life, and your parents were willing to let you and Aunt Clara go and have your own life. I just know Amelia would love it on the ranch." He could see her riding across the range with him now, her silken hair flowing behind her.

Pa shook his head. "Her father is much more conservative than either of your grandparents. In addition, I have two brothers who went into business with my father, and a sister who married and stayed here. Your mother was the same, except she had three sisters who all married well. Amelia and Amanda are the Carlyles' only children, and to have one of them move so far away would be unthinkable for them."

His father spoke the truth, but Ben could still dream and hope for Amelia's love to be great enough for her to want to live in Kansas with him. "If it's what Amelia wants, and she loves me, I don't see how her parents could stand in the way of our happiness. I wondered if we could ask her parents to come out to Kansas for a visit, so they could see how good it would be to live there. Then maybe they wouldn't object as much."

Ma pressed her lips together and covered her mouth with the handkerchief she held in her hand. She turned her gaze out through the window, but not before he noticed the glisten of moisture in her eyes. Why would his desires make her so sad?

His father's voice became deeper, a sure indication of his concern. "Ben, you have to be sensible. Consider all the consequences and ramifications of your actions. You have nothing to really offer Amelia now. When you turn twenty next year, you will get a share of our ranch where you can build a house for yourself, and you'll find a girl in Kansas who will be only too happy to share it with you. That's the life you will have to plan for your future."

Ben nodded without meeting his gaze, then rose and returned to his seat next to Billy. He'd expected opposition from Mr. and Mrs. Carlyle, but for it to come from his own parents rent his soul in two. Still, he would not be dissuaded. Only Amelia herself could stop him from pursuing her.

Chapter 5

*A*melia breathed deeply and squared her shoulders before entering the dining room for breakfast. She had no desire to go through the social season and hoped to convince her parents that she didn't need to do so. Most likely she would lose this argument, but she had to try.

If only she could muster up the enthusiasm for such show as Mary Beth, who had talked about nothing else in the week since her family returned to Kansas. All the while Mary Beth talked about dresses to wear and whom she might meet, Amelia had been devising ways to get out of the entire ordeal.

No good plan had materialized, so now she had to face her parents and let them know she didn't really want to participate as one being presented. Attending wouldn't be a problem, but the parading of herself as a young woman now eligible for marriage created a bitter taste.

She pasted on a smile and entered the room. "Sorry, I'm late, Mama, Papa. My hair gave me fits this morning."

Not exactly the truth, but not a complete fabrication either for she had changed hairstyles twice.

Papa eyed her with a smile. "You look lovely, my dear."

Mama didn't say a word but searched Amelia's face. For what, she wasn't sure, but it had happened the past several mornings. It was almost as if Mama was trying to read Amelia's mind.

After bowing her head and saying a short prayer of thanksgiving, she spread her napkin across her lap. Maeleen set a plate with eggs and bacon on the table. Amelia thanked the servant and followed her departure back to the kitchen with interest. Now there was a young woman who would turn heads. Even her servant's uniform could not hide her comely figure and attractive features. Amelia sighed and picked up her fork. Sometimes she believed she'd rather be a servant than a wealthy man's daughter.

Mama buttered her toast as she peered across at Amelia. "Don't forget we are to go for a fitting for your presentation gown this afternoon. I believe Mrs. Haynes is bringing Mary Beth for hers at the same time."

Here was her opportunity to approach the subject of the cotillion. "Mama, do we have to have a presentation for me? Mary Beth could have it all to herself, and then we wouldn't have to be concerned with the cost of so many dresses and parties for me."

If she had dropped a cannonball in the middle of the table, her mother's expression could not have expressed more horror. Even Papa's mouth skewed into a terrible frown. His forehead creased and his thick brown eyebrows formed a straight row across it. "Whatever gave you that ridiculous notion?" he said. "You're seventeen and just graduated from Mrs. Harcourt's finishing school. This is your season."

Mama's hand gripped her napkin until the knuckles turned white. "Amelia Carlyle, I will not even consider such nonsense. You will go to each and every party given, and you will be presented with Mary Beth at the cotillion."

"But it's such a waste of money." No sooner had the words left her mouth than she wished them back.

Mama blinked her eyes and pursed her mouth. "The dates are set, plans are made, and invitations ordered."

Papa pushed back from the table. "You will participate like the Carlyle you are, and I won't hear any more from you about canceling. Understood?"

"Yes, Papa." Oh, she understood all right. The Carlyle name would be sullied if they backed out now. Anything to protect their precious reputation. Amelia pushed away her plate, her appetite gone.

When he had left, Mama leaned toward Amelia. "My dear, I know you don't really care for the social life like Amanda did, but this is what we do, and it's what is expected of you. You'll meet many nice young men who are all good prospects for marriage."

"Oh, Mama, don't you see? It's like I'm being paraded like cattle to auction for the men to assess and evaluate my worth."

Mama's eyebrows raised and her eyes opened wide. "Wherever did you get such a ridiculous notion? What do you know about cattle auctions?"

Heat rose in Amelia's face as she regretted her choice of words. She mustn't implicate Ben in any way. The less they knew about her feelings for him, the less likely they were to forbid a relationship. "I believe Mr. Haynes mentioned something about cattle auctions while they were here. He said they took herds to Kansas City where a price was determined by their size and appearance."

"I see." She tilted her head. "It's best you remove that idea from your mind and concentrate on all that lies ahead in the next month. We're going to be quite busy, and I need your full cooperation."

"Yes, ma'am." She laid her napkin on the table and stood. "I'll be ready when it's time to leave this afternoon." Her sedate exit from the dining room became a mad dash up the stairs once out of her mother's eyesight.

She shoved the door of her room closed behind her and threw herself across the bed. It had already been made up, and she grabbed one of the lavender silk throw pillows and hugged it to her chest. So much for that little idea, but she had tried. When her father had that look she'd just seen on his face, no argument could change his mind.

The next few months loomed ahead as a dark blot on the horizon of her life. If only she could just go about her daily routine of reading, practicing the piano, and taking care of volunteer duties at the church. She had no taste for the luncheons and other social events in which her mother was involved.

In addition, all the other girls looked at the season as a time of competition for the most eligible men, and hurt feelings, jealousy, and resentment often resulted. She couldn't forget some of the things said about Amanda behind her back when Charles Bishop had proposed.

No matter what others had said, Amanda loved Charles

with all her heart. She had confided in Amelia during those days when Charles courted her. Amanda dreamed of her life with Charles and the love they had. One only had to look at their faces when they were together to see that theirs was a love ordained by God. It spoke of purity, trust, loyalty, and faith not only in God but also in each other.

That's what Amelia wanted. God wouldn't show her the man of her future at some fancy dress ball. She'd prayed about it often enough to know that God would give her the best young man for her. Perhaps, just perhaps, Ben Haynes was that young man. One thing for sure, he'd at least get an invitation to the cotillion from Mary Beth, whether he was able to come or not.

Lenora glanced up from her writing when Isaac entered the bedroom and approached her. He placed his hands on her shoulders. "Dear, that little outburst of Amelia's concerns me. She has a free spirit that doesn't enjoy being bound by the duties of her station in life, but we can't allow her to have free rein with her likes or dislikes."

"I know, and we had a little talk after you left. She compared the cotillion to being paraded in front of the men like cattle at an auction." A tiny smile passed her lips. "I never thought of it like that, but we are presenting her to eligible young men to see if they might choose her for their bride." Of course Isaac would never see it that way, but she had an inkling of how Amelia felt as she had experienced her own introduction to society.

"That's the way it's done. And some of us are fortunate enough to find young women we truly love as I did with

41

you and as Charles has done with Amanda." He leaned over to kiss her cheek. "If nothing else, we know that our Amelia will keep us guessing, but I'm sure in the end she'll find a young man who suits her tastes."

Lenora reached up to press his hand against her shoulder. "I do pray that will happen. She's such a special young woman, and God is sure to have great plans for her in the days ahead. I only hope she'll listen to what He tells her and not what she wants." She anticipated many more talks with her self-willed daughter in the weeks ahead, but Amelia was a smart young woman, so perhaps it wouldn't take long for her to settle into the routine expected of her.

"Have faith. Everything will work out for the best." He squeezed her hand. "Now, I must be getting about my business."

He left the room and headed downstairs. Lenora picked up her pen to continue with the invitations for a luncheon planned for several weeks from now. So many of her friends now had daughters the age of Amelia, and all of them looked forward to the coming season with much enthusiasm. Being around them and talking about what they would wear, who would be on the dance cards, and who was the best hostess should help Amelia to be more excited about her role.

Lenora's thoughts clouded. She didn't want to completely squelch Amelia's spirit, but somehow it would have to be bridled in the weeks ahead, or they would all be in for a most trying social season.

Ben stepped off the train, very happy to see the dark yellow and brown depot in Sweetwater Springs. Home at last. He breathed deeply only to start coughing from the soot in the air.

Gideon laughed and slapped him on the back. "Wait until we get away from town before you start trying to breathe fresh air."

"Yeah, I have to remember that. I was just so glad to get off that stuffy train, and I'll be even happier when I can change out of these clothes." He reached up to remove his tie and unbutton the top two buttons of his shirt.

"I can't wait either. It's too hot for so much clothing, but Ma insists we look halfway decent. Not that I see it matters any." He followed Ben's example and tugged off his tie.

Ben waved toward the luggage piling up on the platform. "Let's go get our things and help Pa get it loaded into the wagons."

The foreman of their ranch, Zeke Stone, and Steve Harris, another ranch hand, had brought two wagons to take the family the rest of the way to the ranch. Ben strode to the pile and picked up two bags and carried them to the first wagon. "I'm sure glad to see you. It would've been hard to wait for you in this heat."

Zeke removed his hat and wiped perspiration from his brow. "It's a killer, that's for sure, and here it is September." He glanced around. "It's good your pa had you wear your western hats. It'll help shade your eyes against this sun."

Ben gazed up at the cloudless sky. From the looks of

the dust covering everything around, rain was still badly needed. He removed his jacket and rolled up his sleeves. By the time he finished loading the wagon and sat Billy up on one of the bags, sweat drenched his back. Ma and Pa would drive one wagon with Zeke and Steve on the other one. He climbed up behind the ranch hands, and Gideon joined him. That left Grace Ann and Billy to ride with Ma and Pa.

Getting back to Sweetwater Springs, Kansas, meant getting back to work as well, but Ben welcomed the diversion it would create. It would also put his mind to business rather than on one brown-haired girl with an independent spirit. A smile creased his face at the memory of her.

Gideon leaned over and winked. "That smile isn't for all the work we have to do. I bet it's for one pretty girl named Amelia."

Ben's cheeks burned. "And what if it is?"

"Well, now, I say you'd better forget her. A fancy young woman like her isn't going to fall for a cowboy like you."

"Oh? And why not? Ma came out here with Pa, and they've done very well." That's the hope he could cling to with all his heart. They had come and been happy, so maybe he and Amelia could do the same.

"Ha! I don't think Mrs. Carlyle is anything like Grandma Haynes is. Mrs. Carlyle is a snob."

"Gideon, that's no way to speak of Mrs. Carlyle. If you can't do better than that, then keep your words to yourself, and if you don't, I'll tell Ma." Although the boy spoke some truth, he didn't need to voice his opinion like that, and Ma would never stand for his criticism of her best friend.

"I'm sorry. But I still think you're wasting your time mooning over Amelia."

Wasting time or not, Ben couldn't help but think about her and what it would be like to have her as his wife.

When they arrived at the ranch house, Ben gazed out to the prairie before climbing down from the wagon. Someday, he and Amelia would have a home out there. He believed with all his heart that God would provide the way despite any opposition from his or her parents. No matter how long it took, he'd dream and plan until it happened.

Chapter 6

*A*melia waited while Maeleen buttoned up the back of the blue and cream dress to be worn to the dinner tonight, the first of many parties to come. Amelia didn't look forward to it with the enthusiasm her parents expected. However, out of respect for them, she would smile and enjoy the evening as much as she possibly could. Having Mary Beth along would help, but not enough.

Maeleen stepped back. "Now, ye be all fastened up, and if ye don't mind me saying so, ye be a beautiful lass. And a good time ye and Miss Haynes should be having, but I dunna see the spark in your eyes."

"You're right. I don't really want to go, but Mama and Papa expect it, so I'll go and have an enjoyable evening for their sakes." She pulled one curl over her shoulder and tilted her head to peer into the looking glass. No, that was coquettish. She shoved it back to her neck and patted the waves on the side. There, that was better.

After Maeleen left, Amelia reached over for her letter box and removed Ben's letter. Once again she devoured the words as he described arriving home and resuming his chores at the ranch. She let her hands drop to her lap and imagined Ben in his work clothes and on a horse. A smile played about her lips. What a grand picture that made.

Mama stopped in the hallway by the door. "You look lovely, my dear. Now come, Papa has the carriage drawn around, and don't forget your wrap. The evening air is cool, and we don't want you to catch cold after the first dinner party and miss the season again."

Amelia hid the letter in the folds of her skirt. "Yes, Mama." She waited until her mother left before stuffing the letter back into its box. She picked up the shawl matching her dress and shrugged. A lot of good it'd do if the air were truly cold, but she never again wanted to be as ill as she'd been last year. When Amelia stepped into the hall, Mama was already halfway down the staircase.

Papa helped Amelia and Mama into the carriage. As Amelia smoothed her skirt so as not to wrinkle it during the ride, she remembered her afternoon with Ben a few weeks earlier. How she wished he could be her escort for the evening, but another young man, Stephen Armistead, would have that privilege tonight. At least Mrs. Killingsworth was known for her dinner parties and the food would be good. In addition, her daughter, Isabella Killingsworth, had been a good friend at school.

They arrived at the Killingsworth home and alighted from the carriage. Papa grasped Mama's elbow and ascended the short steps to the entry. Amelia followed close behind. The house windows glowed with gaslights throughout the rooms. The low hum of conversation filled the foyer as they stepped inside.

Mrs. Killingsworth greeted them right away. "Mr. and Mrs. Carlyle, so nice to see you." She nodded to Amelia. "Isabella and the other young people are waiting in the drawing room. Dinner will be served soon."

"Thank you. I'll join them. If you'll excuse me, Mama, Papa." She left them talking with Mrs. Killingsworth and another guest.

The drawing room had been cleared of all furniture except for chairs lining the walls. Floor-to-ceiling windows looked out onto a terrace that was lit with oil lamps and candles for strolling in the fresh air later. Space had been set aside for a stringed ensemble that would play for dancing after the dinner, and cloth-covered tables would hold punch and pastries to enjoy during that time.

She headed for a group of young people at one end of the room. Isabella turned to greet her as she approached. "Amelia, my dear, come and join us."

Stephen stepped forward. "Ah, my lovely dinner partner has arrived."

Isabella handed her a dance card. "As you can see, Stephen has already claimed three numbers with you."

"Thank you, Isabella." She smiled at Stephen. "It's nice to see you, Stephen."

An arm encircled her waist. "I thought you'd never get here." Mary Beth leaned close and whispered, "I don't know anyone except Isabella, and I've only just met my escort."

Amelia hugged her friend. "Don't worry. You'll do fine." She turned to Stephen. "Have you met Mary Beth Haynes from Kansas? She's returned to Boston for the season and is staying with her grandparents."

"Yes, I've had the pleasure. I do hope you will save a dance or two for me later this evening, Miss Haynes."

A handsome young man with sandy hair and blue eyes stepped up. "After I've had my spots filled in, there may be one or two left for you, Armistead." Andrew Farnsworth extended his hand. "Shall we, Miss Haynes? I believe dinner was just announced."

Amelia observed the exchange with delight. She desired for Mary Beth to find a proper young man here and perhaps even marry and stay in Boston. Either Stephen or Andrew would be perfect. She grasped Stephen's elbow. "I'm looking forward to dinner and chatting with you." She cringed inside because she wasn't being completely truthful. The food yes, but sitting with Stephen, not really.

They entered the opulent dining room where a crystal gas-lighted chandelier lent a golden glow to the surroundings and created a sparkle in the crystal and silver appointments. Mr. and Mrs. Killingsworth had spared no expense in entertaining for their daughter. Stephen held her chair until she was seated then slid it slightly forward.

After the blessing of the meal, conversation flowed and course after course of delectable food appeared before the guests. Stephen spoke beside her, but nothing that needed her rapt attention. She replied when necessary and smiled. How tempted she was to slide off her shoes under the table, but Mama and Papa would be humiliated were she to be discovered. Pinched toes were all a part of being entertained during this season.

Her mind wandered to Kansas and what Ben would be doing at this hour. No doubt he'd be having dinner with his family. She pictured him in his home with his parents and siblings. What a wonderful time they must have together.

Envy invaded her heart for Mary Beth having brothers. Sometimes she wondered why her parents hadn't had more children. She swallowed a sigh. If there had been more children, her parents wouldn't have had to smother her so much.

Matt propped his foot on the bottom railing of the corral and leaned his arms on the upper one. The week had been busy with checking the herds. Pa had put his two new bulls in with the heifers and half-heifers, one in the north pasture and one in the south. He hoped for a great number of calves in the spring, which would mean long days of roping and branding.

Ben stared out across the prairie behind the barn and stables. The squawking of the hens getting ready to roost for the night coupled with the gentle nickering of the horse now eating out of Ben's hand brought peace to his soul.

He reached up and ran his fingers through the stallion's mane. Black Devil once lived up to his name, but now he wore a bridle and saddle as if he'd been born with them. Ben had shortened the name to Blackie after the young horse had been saddle broken. That had given Ben a few bruises last year.

"Guess it's time to get you brushed and ready for the night. The chickens know when it's time, so we'll follow their lead." He entered the corral and guided the horse to his stall. Ben picked up a stiff bristled brush and began brushing sand and dust from Blackie's hide with short, brisk strokes.

As he brushed, Ben imagined Amelia on a horse by

his side. Riding across the range was most likely not the number one thought in her mind tonight. Ma had received a letter from Mary Beth yesterday, and tonight was the first dinner party of the social season. Mary Beth had named her escort but not Amelia's, which led to Ben's imagination running wild.

What if she met some handsome young man who swept her off her feet? Would she even remember or think about the cowboy who had visited a few weeks ago? As pretty and spirited as she was, Amelia would have all the young men vying for her attention, and that would most likely boot him out of her mind completely.

Straw shuffled, and he turned to find Clara behind him. Here on the ranch, he called her Clara. Being called aunt by someone only fourteen years younger had made her feel like an old woman, so he had stopped at her request.

She smiled now and shoveled up a few oats with her hand then held it out to Blackie. "I saw you leave after supper. I'm thinking you have a pretty little Boston gal on your mind about now."

Nothing got by Clara, and she didn't hesitate to say what she was thinking. "You'd be right." He continued brushing Blackie's coat. "Mary Beth's letter said tonight was a dinner party at somebody's named Killingsworth. I was thinking about how she and Amelia must be the prettiest girls there."

"No doubt about that. I remember the Killingsworth family. Isabella is the youngest girl. She has two older sisters and a brother. One sister is my age, and we were presented the same year."

Ben laid the brush aside and picked another one to

smooth out Blackie's mane. He'd picked up quite a bit of dust and dirt out on the range today. His hand paused over the horse's neck. "Clara, what was it like when you went through all this business of being presented to society?"

She didn't answer right away, and a faraway look veiled her eyes. A slight smile curved her lips before she breathed deeply and sighed. "It was a wonderful time. Of course we'd heard rumors that a war might begin with the South, but that was of very little concern to us girls."

"Was Tom your escort for all the events?" He had met Tom Hamilton, but it had been when Ben was just a child, and he didn't remember much about the man.

"No, only for the presentation cotillion. He was an upperclassman at West Point training to be an officer. He was able to come only for the last affair, and that's where I most wanted him to be."

From what he'd heard, his aunt had been very much in love with Tom. He hoped that wouldn't happen with Amelia and one of her escorts. "I wonder who Mary Beth will choose for her cotillion."

Clara laughed and shook her head. "Of course your wondering would include Amelia. You needn't worry too much. From what I gathered listening to your mother and my mother talking, the young ladies far outnumber the young men, so she may very well be escorted by her own father and Mary Beth by her grandpapa."

Relief flooded his heart. Now that he could handle without any problem, but the idea of any young man claiming all of Amelia's attention sent pangs of jealousy through his soul. He finished grooming Blackie and put away the equipment. There was one more thing he wanted to learn from Clara.

He gazed at her now. Because of their closeness in age, she was more like a sister than an aunt, but he knew very little about why she had come west with his family. Even now he saw the beauty that had made her a sought-after young woman. He'd heard rumors and stories about why she was still single, but never from her.

"Clara, I'm not being nosy, but since we talked about Tom, can you tell me what happened?"

Her eyes opened wide and then misted over. "You were just a little one when the war started. Tom and I planned our wedding to take place when he graduated from West Point and had it all set for the summer of 1861. Then everything went to pieces." She stopped and blinked her eyes. "I'm sorry, Ben, I haven't talked about this since that horrible summer. That spring states in the South seceded, and then Fort Sumter was fired upon. All the young men due to graduate received their commissions and went right into the army that summer in June. We thought he'd be home and the war would be over by the end of summer, so we went ahead with our plans."

Again her eyes took on that look. Ben could almost see the memories flashing there. She swallowed hard. "Tom was killed in the battle of Bull Run that July."

Ben took her hand and squeezed it. "I'm so sorry, Clara. I shouldn't have asked and brought up such a painful memory."

She pressed his hand in reply. "It's OK. I think I needed to talk about it. After the first few weeks or maybe a month, no one ever mentioned it again. It was as though Tom had never existed."

"But why didn't you marry later?"

She stepped back and swiped at her cheeks with her fingers. "I loved Tom with all my heart, and it broke into a million pieces when I received the news of his death. Then with the war lasting another four years, I didn't want to take a chance and lose someone else."

Ben gazed at her. "You're amazing, Clara Haynes, and I'm so thankful you didn't become bitter and resentful."

"Thank you. Only the grace of our Lord saw me through that painful time. I learned then that I could never get along without His help."

She hooked her hand over his elbow. "I have one piece of advice for you. If you truly love Amelia, let her have her season, and then go after her with everything you have. Life is too short not to be lived to the fullest, and if she's God's choice for you, nothing will stop you from being together. You may hit a few snags along the way, but if it's God's will for it to be, it will be."

No wonder he respected his aunt so much. Her wisdom never ceased to amaze him. After her great loss, she still gave God glory and followed His will for her life. With that legacy before him, he could do no less than be obedient to God's calling, but he prayed that Amelia would be the one for his future.

Chapter 7

utterflies played havoc with Amelia's insides. Tonight on this September 15, her parents were hosting a dinner party in honor of her eighteenth birthday. If it hadn't been for Mary Beth, this event would be as miserable as the rest of them had been. She much preferred Amanda's coming-out parties two years ago. Then Amelia had no worries about escorts or impressing young men.

Maeleen stepped back from arranging Amelia's hair. "There, ye will be the most beautiful young woman at the dinner. I think the yellow is even more becoming to ye than the blue."

"Thank you, but you know I'd much rather be doing something else." She fingered the folds of satin fabric draped into the skirt. "Don't you think all this is a huge waste of money? Think of all the good that could be done with what is wasted on this frivolity."

Maeleen ducked her head. "'Tis not for me to say, miss. Ye parents pay me a good wage, and 'tis satisfied with that I am."

Of course she would think that way. None of the servants would ever criticize those who paid the wages. If only she could trade places with Maeleen tonight.

Maeleen left the room, and Amelia finished her preparations for the evening. The clock on the stairway landing chimed eight times. Guests would begin arriving any moment. She gave one last glance in the mirror and headed down to face those who would attend tonight's dinner.

Mary Beth arrived with her grandparents at the same time Amelia stepped into the foyer. She grasped her friend's hands. "I'm so glad you're early. We'll have a few minutes to ourselves before the others arrive."

Mary Beth handed her wrap to the butler and followed Amelia to the door of the drawing room, which had been cleared of its regular furniture and arranged for the party. "Happy birthday, and I do have some good news that might make your day even better. I had a post from Ma this morning, and she plans to be here for our cotillion in two weeks." She paused for effect, and her eyes danced with merriment.

Amelia's heart soared. "And?"

"Ben will be coming with her."

Amelia squealed and clapped her hands. What a perfect birthday present! Then she stopped and rearranged her features. Mustn't let Mama and Papa see her excitement at the fact Ben would be coming back to Boston. For the first time, true joy filled her, and she was glad now that she and Mary Beth would be presented together.

More guests entered the drawing room, and Amelia now accepted her role as hostess with more graciousness than she would have an hour earlier. Her escort for the evening, Philip Barlow, approached her.

"Good evening, Miss Carlyle. Your home is lovely as you and Miss Haynes are." He smiled and bowed slightly at the waist. "It must be your birthday that puts the extra sparkle in your eyes tonight."

Amelia smiled and nodded. "Thank you, Mr. Barlow." She'd never let on that the sparkle came from thoughts of another young man. She'd play her part tonight, and play it well.

More guests arrived, as did Mary Beth's escort. When Andrew Farnsworth greeted her, his eyes filled with admiration, and he bowed to kiss her hand. In her emerald satin dress, Mary Beth was quite striking. More than one man would think her lovely tonight, and that's the way Amelia wanted it to be for her friend. Better for all the attention to be on Mary Beth.

Amelia turned to Philip. "How nice that the weather has cooperated so we could enjoy a beautiful evening."

"Yes. The mild temperatures have been quite pleasant." He grinned and held out his hand. "May I see your dance card?"

She handed it to him. "As you can see your name is filled in for the first and last sets." He'd want more, and she would gladly welcome his name in the blank spaces, for he was one of the best partners in their group. She'd considered asking him to be her escort for the cotillion, but since Ben would be present as Mary Beth's, Amelia opted for asking her father to escort her for the presentation. That would give him great pleasure and keep her free for more time with Ben. The next two weeks would be the longest of her life.

Dinner was announced, and Philip offered his arm to escort her to the dining room. Mama had gone to great lengths to make sure the table would be one of the most beautiful of the season. Red, cream, and pale pink roses filled sterling silver epergnes placed a few feet apart on table. Candelabras holding six white candles each filled the spaces between the flowers. Crystal and silver gleamed in the light of the gas-lit chandelier hanging above. Name cards in silver holders indicated where each guest would sit. Amelia had peeked earlier and made sure Mary Beth would be next to her and Philip.

As the servants served the meal, Amelia's heart swelled with pride that her parents went to so much time and expense to honor her with this dinner. She'd have to put away all thoughts of the waste and honor them with her most proper behavior this evening. However, even a handsome escort and opulent surroundings would not keep her mind from straying to thoughts of a young man coming soon from Kansas.

Ben pulled his jacket closed and buttoned it up under his chin to ward off the night chill. The first cold front of the season had blown in today somewhat earlier than usual. Clear and cold with stars dotting the inky sky like spilled sugar, the night wrapped itself around him. Moonlight shone down to give him enough light to see his surroundings.

According to Mary Beth's letter, tonight was the dinner party at the Carlyle home to celebrate Amelia's birthday.

How he would like to be there to wish her happiness. He had no idea what he could present her as a gift, but if he was in Boston, he'd surely think of something special.

Despite Aunt Clara's words of encouragement, he had begun to doubt his ability to compete with the wealthy young men of Boston. He couldn't give her all the possessions and social standing her family now afforded her.

He'd been educated here at Kansas University in Lawrence, but it did not hold the prestige of Harvard, where many of the young men of the Boston elite sought their education. Still, he had land and opportunity to offer Amelia if he could entice her away from the life she knew in Boston.

Riding at night like this with the wind whispering through the prairie grass and the lonely howl of the coyote off in the distance gave peace to his soul. The sounds and smells gave testimony to God's great handiwork in nature. The grass beneath Blackie's feet crackled from lack of moisture and reminded Ben of the need for a good thunderstorm. He sniffed the night air but found no comforting scent of rain, and the clouds now beginning to float across the moon gave no sign they held moisture.

Not too far away he spotted the herd as the cattle settled down for the night. Rustling in the grass and thumps as steer hit ground were music to his ears. All was calm and in good shape. Come spring, new calves would increase the herd and bring new life. He loved spring that brought newness to all of God's creation.

Most people would consider this a lonely place, but with the cattle, the coyotes, the winds through the grass, his thoughts of Amelia, and all the stars, he could no more feel alone than if he were in a room full of people. Of course if

Amelia were beside him, it would be all the better.

A noise behind him and the nickering of his horse caused him to turn in his saddle. Zeke, the ranch foreman, rode up beside him.

"I saw your horse gone from the stables and figured you'd come out here. You like the beauty and quiet of the night as much as I do."

"You're right, I do. Something about it gives me great peace."

"Me too. When I'm out here, I wonder how anyone could not believe in God." He pointed upward. "No one can ever tell me those bright stars just happened into space, or the moon or the sun just happened to be where they needed to be to give us light and life."

Being a Christian made all the difference in Zeke's attitude. When he'd first come to the ranch, he hadn't been a believer, but working around Pa and Ma, you either became one, or you moved away in a hurry. Most usually stayed and became strong in their faith. That was Pa's way.

Ben stretched out his hand. "I found a piece of land over behind those rocks down by the old mill. I want to build a house there and bring home a bride. Pa says he'll give me a share in the ranch when I turn twenty next year."

"That's good. You work as hard around here as any of our hands. You'll be a good rancher. Got anybody in mind for that house you want to build?"

"Matter of fact I do, but it's gonna take a heap of praying to get her to leave her home in Boston and come out here. Ma did it, but she and Pa were already married and had a family when they came."

"Is that Mary Beth's friend?"

"One and the same. Ma sent a letter last week telling Mary Beth we'd be attending her coming-out party. Pa won't leave, so I'm going with Ma." He had already started counting the days until he'd be back in Boston. The trip couldn't come soon enough.

The wind picked up and send a bone-chilling gust their way. Ben pulled his hat tighter on his head. "Getting colder out here. I think it's time to get on back to the house. I hope Ma left some coffee on the stove, and a piece of her berry pie will taste good. Care to join me?" He turned his horse back toward home.

"Don't mind if I do. Your ma's pie is about the best around these parts." Zeke followed alongside Ben.

About half a mile from the house, Ben spurred his horse. "Race you to the stables." Blackie took off like a streak of lightning, leaving Zeke to try and catch up.

After a cup of hot coffee to ward off the chill and a piece of pie to fill his belly, Ben would spend the rest of the night with sweet dreams about a brown-eyed girl with curls in her hair.

Isaac laid his robe across a chair and strode to the bed where Lenora already lay. She was just as pretty now with her lacy nightcap on and the covers pulled up over her chest as she was when he'd first seen her almost twenty-five years ago.

He sat on the edge of the bed. "I think tonight went very well. Both Mary Beth and Amelia were quite lovely in their gowns, and their dance cards were full. Amelia appeared to be enjoying the evening more tonight than

I've seen at other events." He reached over and grasped her hand. "You did a wonderful job with the menu and decorations. The house looked beautiful."

Lenora sighed and shook her head. "Thank you, but I'm wondering if part of Amelia's joy was because Mary Beth told her of Ben's coming to the cotillion. Mrs. Haynes said she'd heard from Elizabeth and that she and Ben planned to arrive on Thursday of that week."

"Mr. Haynes told me the same. He seemed to be quite pleased to have his grandson coming back. Ben is to be Mary Beth's escort." With such a shortage of eligible young men, that was probably a wise choice for her. Amelia hadn't said anything yet about who would accompany her, but he hoped it would be Philip Barlow.

"Amelia must make her decision for an escort very soon, or there will be no young men left."

Isaac lay back on his pillow and arranged the covers across his body. "It would please me if she chose Philip. His father and I have become good friends since our firm is handling some of their business."

"That would be nice. He's a fine young man. I've been worried that she is still entertaining thoughts about Ben Haynes, but surely she realizes that such a union would never work out, much less have our approval."

He leaned over and kissed his wife's cheek. "Amelia has too much sense to become involved with a cowboy who lives as far away as Kansas." At least he prayed that was so. The last thing he wanted to do was forbid Amelia from her pursuits, but if they included Benjamin Haynes, he may have to do just that.

Chapter 8

*A*nticipation for the evening sent shivers of delight through Amelia's whole body. In just a short time she'd see Ben at the Farnsworth mansion where the cotillion would be held, and she and her friends would be officially presented to society. He'd been in town since Thursday, but Mama and Papa had kept her so busy she'd had no opportunity to see him before tonight. Would he still be as interested in her now as he had been over a month ago?

With only two letters from him since he'd left, she feared that perhaps he'd lost interest, and the very thought of it filled her with dread. After all, they had only seen each other a few times, which gave them little opportunity to really get to know each other. None of that mattered now. Tonight, the last night of September, she'd find out if what she felt was real or only a fancy cooked up by her imagination.

Despite her usual lack of concern for her appearance, this evening she took extra care with her dress. Maeleen had done wonders with her hair, and Amelia admired the effect of the upswept hairstyle with six perfect curls falling from just below the crown. She secured the silver comb embellished with six small diamonds atop her hair. It had been a gift from her father just for this night.

"Amelia, it's time to go." Her mother entered and stopped. "Oh, my dear, you are beautiful. Your father is going to be so proud to be your escort this evening."

"Thank you, Mama. This is going to be a wonderful night." Not just because of the meaning of the occasion, but also because of a certain Kansas cowboy.

She followed her mother downstairs where Murphy waited with their wraps. Papa grasped her shoulders and leaned forward to kiss her cheek. "You look beautiful, my precious girl. I'll be the proudest father at the ball tonight."

"Thank you, Papa." Amelia pulled her cloak together and fastened it at the neck.

A few minutes later she sat in the carriage with her parents. Once again her thoughts wandered as her parents conversed with each other. If she could see Ben right away, she'd be able to put his name on several of the spaces for dances, that is, if he still wanted to be with her as much as she did with him.

When they arrived at the home, the twelve girls to be presented were escorted to a room where they would assemble before the presentation. Names were checked and places assigned for presentation alphabetically, which meant Carlyle would come very close to the beginning.

Mary Beth made her way to Amelia. "This is so exciting. I'm so glad Ma and Pa were willing to let me stay for this. Of course Mama went through hers years ago and wanted me to have the same experience."

That was fine for Mary Beth, but Amelia wanted to know about Ben. Before she had the chance to ask, Mary Beth said, "And you should see Ben. I must say my brother looks quite handsome in his formal clothes."

Amelia's heartbeat quickened. Only a few more minutes and she'd see him. Everything else paled in comparison to being with him tonight.

Ten minutes later the hostess for the evening lined the girls up and led them to where their escorts waited. Amelia breathed deeply and willed her heart to stop pounding as she stepped through the door to the hallway where her father greeted her.

He grasped her hand and tucked it around his elbow. "Ready, Princess?"

His childhood nickname sent a warm feeling to her heart. Then she glanced behind him, where she spotted Ben. Her breath caught in her throat when his gaze met hers. Amelia sent a quick smile his way and turned her attention back to her father. The whole exchange had lasted only seconds, but her father must have noticed from the frown he now wore.

She turned on her brightest smile. "This is going to be a wonderful night. I'm so proud to have you escort me."

His mouth then turned up to a smile, and he squeezed her hand as music filled the hallway and the line proceeded forward. After each girl and her escort had been announced, the orchestra played her favorite piece of music.

When all had been presented, they headed to their

assigned tables. Amelia picked up her dance card to find it already filled in. She had forgotten that was the custom for this cotillion. The names of all the young men present were listed, including Ben. Somehow his name appeared twice, as did two of the others. Whoever had made out the form couldn't have known Ben was one she wanted as a partner more than once.

During the sets preceding the one with Ben, Amelia's gaze had no trouble finding him and knowing where he was at all times. At the same time she managed to keep her attention focused on her partner. When it finally became her first turn with Ben, her knees shook and she could barely breathe.

Ben smiled and placed one hand at her waist and the other on her hand. "I thought this moment would never come." The music began, and he swept her to the dance floor with a grace and ease that belied his cowboy background.

Heat rose in Amelia's cheeks, but her voice lodged in her throat. She merely returned his smile and nodded. After a minute or so, she swallowed hard and found her voice. "I'm amazed at how well you know this dance. Did you learn on the ranch?"

He lifted his chin and chuckled. "As a matter of fact, I did. Ma taught me. She said if I was going to attend such affairs, I needed to know what to do. Then Mary Beth and I practiced after I arrived here."

"Well, it certainly paid off. You're one of the best partners I've had." The smile remained on her lips, but a grimace filled her heart. What a stupid subject of conversation. She didn't want to talk about his dancing ability, but she couldn't be so bold as to tell him how much she had missed him.

His hand tightened around hers. "I've missed you and wanted to come yesterday to call on you, but Ma insisted you would be much too busy as Mary Beth was getting prepared for this evening."

Amelia's body became light as a feather, and she followed his steps, floating on air. He had missed her. That's all she needed to know. They had no need for words, for his eyes told her how much he cared. The music ended all too soon, and Ben escorted her back to her table.

He bowed toward her. "Thank you for the dance, Miss Carlyle, and I look forward to our next one."

After he strolled away, her heart continued to pound in her chest. Not wanting to see her parents right then, she headed upstairs to the room set aside for the young ladies to check their appearance. When she entered, several of the girls stood around Mary Beth.

Isabella practically swooned. "Where have you been hiding that handsome brother of yours, Mary Beth Haynes? If I'd known men like him grew in the west, I might have planned a visit there."

Mary Beth's laughter filled the room, and the other girls tittered and giggled. "If you had to live with him, you might not be so quick with your praise." She glanced over at Amelia and winked.

Isabella turned around, her eyebrows raised. "Amelia, how did you manage to get his name on your card twice? He's not on mine until later, but I watched him, and he dances divinely." Her sigh and fluttering lashes brought another round of titters.

"I don't know, but I've known Ben and Mary Beth since we were children. That may have something to do with it." Amelia left the girls to their talk and hurried through adjustments to her hair and gown. The time would drag until next he held her in his arms.

Ben headed back to his family's table after leaving Amelia. He wiped damp palms down his trouser legs, his nerves a wreck. So much he wanted to say to Amelia, but all they'd exchanged was that little bit about his dancing. A groan escaped his throat. His tongue had become thick as a slab of beef. Next dance he'd do better; he'd have to, or Amelia would never know how much he wanted her to come to Kansas.

He seated himself next to his grandparents and mother. His mother grasped his arm and leaned toward him. "I can see why you're so attracted to Amelia. She's beautiful tonight."

"Yes, she is." His throat filled, and he could say nothing more.

Ma squeezed his arm. "Please don't get your hopes too high. Like your father said once, Mr. Carlyle won't be inclined to let his daughter become involved with someone who lives in Kansas, even if our families are longtime friends."

"I know that, but if Amelia returns my feelings for her, how can he keep us apart?"

"He will try, my son, he will try, and even as free-spirited as you say Amelia is, she won't go against her parents. She has too much respect for them to do that."

Mary Beth returned with several other acquaintances,

all giggling like schoolgirls, but each one stopped and composed herself before rejoining their families. His sister seated herself beside him, but his line of sight followed Amelia back to her table.

"Can't take your eyes off her, can you? She's been a wonderful friend these past few weeks and has introduced me as though we'd been best friends for a long time."

Ben grinned and turned his attention to Mary Beth. "Well, our families have known each other a long time and been friends, even from a distance."

"All I can say is, I hope you two get together. I'd love to have her as part of the family." She grinned then held her hand toward the young man now claiming her for the next dance.

Ben gasped. How could she have known that's exactly what he wanted too? He blinked his eyes and glanced across the room to see Isabella Killingsworth staring at him. The music had begun, and he realized it was his turn to dance with her. He pushed back from the table and hurried to where she sat. He bowed and extended his hand. "I believe the next dance is ours, Miss Killingsworth."

She placed her hand in his and stood. "Why yes, Mr. Haynes, I believe it is."

He led her to the dance floor where he held her as he had Amelia. Because Isabella was petite in size, he had to keep his chin and eyes downward to talk with her. That kept him from spotting Amelia and her partner.

Two more to go and he'd be with her again. A finger tapped his arm, and he snapped back to attention with Isabella. She batted her eyelashes again and smiled. "Mr. Haynes, it is such a great pleasure to dance with you.

We've enjoyed getting acquainted with your sister Mary Beth. It's nice that you could return to Boston to be her escort tonight."

"Thank you. We've had a good time on this visit." The musicians must have added an extra page or two in this number because it went on much longer than he desired.

"Tell me what it's like living on a ranch in Kansas. Are there still horrible Indian raids and massacres all over the place with girls being kidnapped and men scalped?"

"Farther west the settlers still have some trouble, but for the most part things are quiet around our part of the country. We're about a half hour from town on horseback. Of course Sweetwater Springs isn't Boston, but it's a nice-size town."

Isabella's smile didn't reach her eyes, which held little interest in what he was saying. "How quaint."

Quaint wasn't exactly the word Ben would use to describe the town he loved, but Amelia may think of it in the same way. He must tell her more about the ranch and Sweetwater Springs when he danced with her again.

"I would think that after you visited your sister and saw all that the city has to offer, you would be loath to return to such a primitive setting." Distaste laced her words and sent doubts racing through Ben's heart.

Amelia wasn't the snob that Isabella appeared to be, but he would be asking her to give up a lot if she consented to living in Kansas as his bride. He'd tell her everything, even the harshness of the winters and the spring storms that could wreak havoc in only seconds of time. Then if she came, saw for herself what it was like, and still cared about him, he'd have no qualms about her coming.

Mercifully the music ended, and Isabella returned to her table. He endured two more dances with young women who flirted and cooed with their wiles to draw his attention, but his wish was to be again with Amelia.

When her turn finally came, Ben resolved to make this time count. Despite his body complaining of all the activity in his formal clothes, no discomfort would keep him from his few minutes with Amelia. Then he remembered the night of Amanda's wedding.

"I see you've kept your shoes on tonight. They must be more comfortable than the ones you wore to the wedding."

A grin lit up her face, and she giggled. "Not really, but I wasn't about to let anything keep me from this dance. I'd walk on hot coals if necessary to spend time with you."

He brightened. "And I with you. I'm so sorry I didn't have time to write more before we came back. Pa kept me so busy, and then I wasn't sure how long it would take for a letter to get here. Mary Beth did send letters home, and the one with our invitation took a week to reach us. I promise to do better when I go back."

He proceeded to tell her all about the town and its people just as he had Isabella. Amelia listened with interest that had been absent in her friend. "So you see, Sweetwater Springs has none of the conveniences of Boston, and the ranch is away from town, but it's a wonderful place with friendly people." If she married him, they would have their own place on the ranch. He gulped and his eyes opened wide. He hadn't intended to think along those lines this soon, especially since he hadn't even asked her father permission to call on her.

"Oh, Ben, I'd love to see it."

71

Now he'd opened Pandora's box, and he'd have to deal with the situation sooner than he had planned. "I'll talk to my parents about sending your parents an invitation to come visit next spring. Perhaps your parents will be willing to come west and visit old friends." Between now and springtime, he'd have time to properly show his intentions, albeit by distance. Whenever he returned to Boston for a visit, he'd have to do everything he could to win the approval of Mr. and Mrs. Carlyle.

Chapter 9

*A*ll through the night and even into the Sunday church service, Amelia replayed her time with Ben. He did like her and wanted her to visit his home. But Papa would never accept Ben as a proper suitor as long as he lived halfway across the country. God answered her prayer for Ben to care about her, but no answer came as to what to do with it or how to approach Papa.

The service ended, and Papa hurried Mama and her out to their carriage without his usual long conversations with other elders. After she and Mama were settled in their seats, Papa peered at her over his spectacles.

"We are headed to the Haynes's home, where we have been invited to have dinner. Mrs. Haynes and Ben will be leaving on Tuesday to return to Kansas." He grasped Mama's hand. "This will give you time to visit with Elizabeth, my dear."

Joy and excitement built within, but she kept her face void of any expression lest Papa suspect her feelings for Ben. He and his family had arrived late to church, so

Amelia had no opportunity to talk to him before the service began. All through the sermon she was very much aware of his presence a few rows behind her.

It was almost as if Papa had not wanted her talking to Ben, but now they were on their way to his grandparents' house. She'd never understand the workings of adult minds, but that didn't matter now since they were going to spend the next few hours with them. Somehow she had to find some time to be with Ben without her parents being around. Perhaps Mary Beth could find some activity for just the three of them.

"Amelia, your mother and I are concerned with the attention you paid to Benjamin Haynes last evening. Are you attracted to him as more than a friend?"

Her father's blunt question hit her square in the chest and knocked the breath right out of her lungs. She could not lie. Not only would he see right through it, but God would not honor such a misstatement. She caught a breath and faced him eye-to-eye.

"Yes, Papa, we are more than friends."

"I see. How far has this relationship gone without my approval?"

This time Amelia swallowed hard as though she could banish her fears to some remote place in her body. "We have been writing to each other, and he would like us to visit his home in Kansas." The truth of the statement made her heart race and her hands shake.

Her father's eyebrows shot up, and her mother gasped with her hand just below her neck. Papa's frown did not bode well, as storm clouds gathered in his eyes. His mouth worked in the way she recognized when he didn't like a situation. Her hands became blocks of ice in her lap that even her gloves could not melt.

Finally Papa spoke just before they drove up to the Haynes's home. "When he's returned to Kansas, you will forget him and concentrate on the young men who have a desire to call on you here in Boston. I have already given my permission for Mr. Philip Barlow to call on you."

Her worst fears had been realized, and she fought the tears threatening to rise to the surface. Papa would never tolerate her crying about such a thing and might turn the carriage around and head home, and she so desperately wanted these last hours with Ben.

Although her heart ached, she said, "Yes, Papa. I understand. I'm sure Mary Beth has something planned for us that will include her brother. I can't be rude and decline."

"No, you can't. You may be friendly while he is here in his grandparents' home, but once they leave on Tuesday, I want to hear nothing more about Benjamin Haynes."

Amelia could only nod. No words would pass the lump that sat in her throat like a piece of hard coal. An afternoon she had anticipated only minutes earlier now loomed as one that would break her heart and dash all hopes Ben may have had about speaking to her father. The time she had with Ben now became more important than ever if only she could get through it without breaking down in tears.

Papa had his say and remained quiet, but Mama sat staring out the carriage window holding her handker-chief to her mouth. Whether in sadness or sympathy for Amelia, she didn't know, but if Mama understood, then perhaps she could be an ally in the days ahead. Amelia sighed and resigned herself to the fact that was not likely to happen. Mama never went against Papa's wishes.

Ben followed Mary Beth into the parlor. "You have to come up with some ideas on how Amelia and I can spend some time together this afternoon. There's no telling when we'll see each other again."

"I've been thinking about that. It's rather cool for a carriage ride, so we'll need to stay indoors this time. Grandpapa has some new pictures for the stereopticon, so we could look at those. I'm sure Ma, Grandmama, and Mrs. Carlyle will want to visit, as perhaps will Mr. Carlyle and Grandpapa."

He hugged her. "I knew I could count on you to come up with something, and I do hope our mother has a lot to say to Mrs. Carlyle." Even an hour would be better than no time at all, but he prayed it would be longer than that.

The doorbell sounded, and the butler greeted the Carlyle family. Ben and Mary Beth entered the foyer, and their mother descended the steps. Amelia removed her cloak and hat and handed them to the butler. She turned and a smile lit her face when her gaze met with Ben's.

"Good afternoon, Ben, Mary Beth. I didn't have a chance to speak with either of you at church, so I'm glad we'll have time to visit this afternoon."

Mary Beth hugged Amelia. "So am I, and I'm still full of excitement from last night's ball."

Amelia laughed. "I know. It was wonderful. Several girls didn't make it to church this morning, but Papa's rule is that if we can play on Saturday night, then we must worship on Sunday morning."

Ben stepped forward. "And a good rule that is. Your father is a wise man."

Before she could respond, his grandparents appeared, and the greetings began all over again. Ben took the opportunity to observe Amelia and her ease with people of all ages. Even now she smiled at something his grandfather said and hugged the elderly man. Grandpapa did have a way about him that brought smiles from everyone.

Grandpapa extended his hand toward Ben. "Come, my boy, and escort Miss Haynes in to dinner." The twinkle in his eye gave evidence he wasn't simply making a polite gesture.

Ben moved to Amelia's side. "If I may have the pleasure."

Amelia grasped his elbow, and Grandpapa beamed with pleasure as he and Grandmama led the way. Ben glanced at Mr. Carlyle. The expression on his face and the narrowness of his eyes didn't escape Ben. His heart sank like a lead weight. No permission to call on Amelia would be coming from this man today, or for a long time. Clouds of doubt shadowed his joy at being with Amelia, but not even a rainstorm of disappointment would mar this day and the few hours he may have left with the girl he loved.

After dinner, Mr. Carlyle and Grandpapa retreated to his study, more than likely to enjoy a pipe and coffee. Ben followed with his heart in his throat. He needed to know exactly how he stood with Mr. Carlyle. Ma, Grandmama, and Mrs. Carlyle disappeared into the parlor, and Mary Beth led Amelia to the library.

"Mr. Carlyle, may I have a word with you?" Ben grabbed the back of a chair to support his wobbly legs.

"Does it concern my daughter?"

The pinched expression on his face didn't bode well, but Ben plunged ahead. "Yes, sir, I would like your permission to call on her next time I am in Boston." Ben's chest tightened and his breathing halted.

"Because you live in Kansas, I don't believe that is a good idea. Therefore I must say no."

Ben's breath escaped in a puff of disappointment, but the set of Mr. Carlyle's jaw warned Ben not to argue. He blinked, gulped once, and nodded. "Yes, sir, I understand." He didn't really, but he turned and left the room. In the hallway he slumped against the door until stubbornness washed over him. He pulled himself up to his full height. Somehow he'd find a way to change Mr. Carlyle's mind. In the meantime, he had this last afternoon with Amelia, and he didn't intend for it to go to waste.

He strolled into the library, his emotions now under control. Amelia and Mary Beth sat on the sofa, chatting. He rubbed his hands together. "I hate to interrupt, but what shall we do this fine afternoon?"

"I was just telling Amelia that Grandpapa informed me at dinner that he has given permission for Andrew Farnsworth to call on me this afternoon. I'm sure he'll be here momentarily, and then we can enjoy the stereopticon in the library."

Amelia's eyes sparkled with delight. "Isn't that wonderful, Ben? Andrew is a lucky young man."

Ben's eyes opened wide. If Mary Beth had a young man here, that may mean she wouldn't be coming back to Kansas. Pa would never allow her to stay here permanently, would he? She'd be too far away from her family. Then a painful jolt of realization struck his heart. He wanted Amelia to do that same thing to her own family! How could he ask her to leave behind everyone she loved?

The butler appeared with Andrew behind him. "Mr. Farnsworth is here to see you, Miss Haynes."

"Do come in, Andrew," Mary Beth said. "You remember my brother, and of course you know Miss Carlyle."

Ben shook Andrew's hand, taking note of his perfect grooming. Not a hair of his blond hair was out of place, and his blue eyes lit up when he spoke to Mary Beth. Ben smiled in greeting. This young man was indeed smitten.

Andrew returned the greeting then turned to Mary Beth. "I consider it a great honor to spend time with you this afternoon."

Mary Beth grasped his arm and led him to the library where they settled into two chairs by the fireplace to look at the stereopticon. Amelia sat on the sofa and glanced his way. What could he possibly say to her?

He stood by the window and stared out at his grandparents' garden, now in full bloom with the colors of fall. Yellow, gold, and bronze chrysanthemums filled the flower beds, and the roses burst forth in a last blaze of color. So alive now, but soon frost would come, and the garden would go dormant for the season. Would his love for Amelia have to do the same?

Movement caught his eye. He turned his head to find Amelia standing next to him.

"The worry lines in your face trouble me. What has

happened to cause such woe? We have so little time left that we must put aside our worries and savor the minutes."

His throat tightened. "Amelia, I have been hasty in stating my feelings for you. I should have waited to discuss them with your father. I see now that asking you to come to Kansas is more than I should have done. It wasn't fair to bare my soul to you knowing that your father wouldn't approve, and now that he has officially said no, I don't want to come between you and your parents."

Tears glistened in her eyes, and he wanted to reach out to hug her close and wipe them away, but he must stand firm.

She blinked her eyes and moistened her lips before speaking. Her brown eyes became deep pools in which he could very well drown. He turned away, but she grasped his arm.

"Ben, I know Papa doesn't really approve our seeing each other as anything but friends, but did he say you could not write to me? Could we not at least write and get to know each other better?"

Her words gave him hope, and he reached for her hand. "I think we can do that. For now, let's not think about my leaving, but enjoy the time we have. Whatever happens in the coming year will be in God's hands."

"Yes, and we must hold on to that." Amelia squeezed his hand and grinned up at him. "Now, let's confiscate that magic lantern from Mary Beth and Andrew and look at the pictures." She pulled him toward the couple now sitting and staring at each other.

Ben gulped and jerked his head. The way Andrew

now gazed at Mary Beth reflected Ben's own feelings for Amelia. God sure had a strange way of doing things. If He could take one girl out of Kansas and plant her in Boston, would He then turn around and replace her by transplanting a flower of Boston into Kansas? He could only hope it would be so.

Chapter 10

*T*wo weeks since the cotillion, and still no letter from Ben. He had warned her that this was a busy time on the ranch, so she'd have to be patient and wait for him to write. Mary Beth had received a note from her mother just this week letting the family know she and Ben had arrived safely back in Kansas.

At least Papa had said nothing about Ben since the Sunday they'd been at the Haynes's home for dinner. He expected her to be courted by Philip Barlow and to follow through with marriage, just as her sister had done before her.

This evening she would please her father by allowing Philip to escort her to a play at the Globe Theater. Some of the finest names in the theater played there, or so she had been told. Theater had never been one of her major interests, and she hadn't recognized the names even after Philip explained who they were. Perhaps she should have shown more interest in such things, but literature and music were more to her liking.

A knock on the door announced Maeleen's arrival. "Mr. Barlow has arrived. He is waiting in the parlor."

"Thank you, Maeleen. You may inform him that I'll be down momentarily."

The young woman left, and Amelia checked her appearance one last time. She must not let thoughts of Ben interfere with tonight, but that would take much effort and a great deal of attention paid to one Philip Barlow. This may be only the second time he'd called on her, but even so, leading him on to believe he may have a chance at winning her hand seemed rather cruel to her. Papa insisted that she give Philip a chance, and she would, but after a few more weeks, the relationship must be ended. Any one of the other young ladies would welcome his attention.

Once again after dinner Ben retreated to the stables. Blackie snuffled and snorted when Ben drew near the stall. He reached out his hand and stroked the horse's forelock. "Hey, boy, it's just me come to visit for a while."

A pitchfork hung on a nail near the stall, so Ben picked it up and began redistributing the hay around Blackie's feet. "Don't know why I can talk to you and say all the things I want to say to Amelia, but I have a blank mind when I try to write anything down."

He paused and leaned on the handle. "I love her so much, and I know she'd love it here in Kansas. We could ride across the range with the wind in our faces and see God's beauty all around us. She'd make our home a wonderful place to live and bring up a family."

For the past five days he'd tried to put on paper his

thoughts and feelings, but nothing came. Yet, here in the stables, he could talk to Blackie like an old friend. He ground his teeth and attacked the hay with his pitchfork. His anger at himself and frustration with the situation shortened the time it usually took to muck a stall.

He hung the tool back on its hook and decided to ride Blackie out to the north range and check with the boys standing guard tonight. The cows were at a good winter weight, and all of the new calves had been weaned and moved with the others to winter grass fields where they'd have water and feed to last through the cold season. He'd be on duty tomorrow rounding up a few strays, checking on the cows expecting calves in early spring, and generally keeping an eye out for any problems.

After he saddled Blackie, Ben shoved his arms into his heavier jacket. The nights had grown colder, and a hint of frost filled the air with a bite that cut through his usual apparel. He mounted his horse and headed out. The cloudless sky meant colder temperatures for the night, but it also meant the stars sprinkled the sky like the sugar coating on Ma's cinnamon cookies.

He drew near to the old mill on the stream running through the ranch. The weathered boards gleamed like silver in the moonlight. This was his favorite spot on the ranch. As a young boy he'd ridden out here several times a week during the summer to read, think, and contemplate his future.

That future had always included the ranch, but not until his trip back to Boston had it involved a girl. All that had changed in one brief visit to his grandparents' home.

The land he wanted for a ranch house was just up the

hill from the mill. It'd be a great spot that looked out over the range lands and plains of Kansas. Amelia would love it as much as he did. He pictured her now standing in the yard waiting for him to come home. Flowers filled beds around the porch with vivid color, and a vegetable garden added to the scene with its produce ready to be harvested.

A dream maybe, but one he hoped would become a reality by this time next year. The murmuring of the water as it passed the paddle wheel filled the night air with a peaceful sound that calmed and quieted Ben's soul. This place always had that effect on him, and he welcomed the peace it brought. Some day he'd have that wheel turning again just for the beauty of it.

Doubt replaced the peace and shrouded his heart. He loved Kansas and couldn't think of living anywhere else. Boston was Amelia's home, and now he expected her to leave and journey west. What if it was the other way around? Could he leave Kansas? Confusion once again filled his heart. How could he ask her to do something he wasn't willing to do himself? With no answer to that forthcoming, he headed for the range.

Ten minutes later he arrived at the cattle site. Steve Harris, one of the ranch hands, rode up to greet him. "Evening, Ben. What brings you out on this cold night? Don't you have watch tomorrow?"

"I do, but I need to clear my head and figured a ride in the cold would do it. How are things here?" He glanced over to where a fire had been built. Several other men sat around the flames warming their hands and drinking coffee.

"Quiet so far. Hope it stays that way."

Ben followed him a little ways, his breath frosty in the chill of the air. Thankful for his sheepskin coat, he pulled the collar higher on his neck. "How soon do you think we'll have snow?"

"Hard to tell. It's only mid October, but I've seen frost in the early mornings, so the temperature's getting lower every day. Don't think it'll be here before Thanksgiving. That should give us time to birth a few more calves. That extra feed your Pa bought will help fatten them up for winter."

Ben only nodded and remained quiet, listening to the night sounds of the herd. A coyote's mournful howl sounded in the distance, and the wind rustled the grasses. "Steve, what do you think about that piece of land by the old grist mill for a house?"

"That's good land there, but if you want a house, build it high so the flash floods along that creek don't wash it away." He paused a moment and peered at Ben. "What do you want to build a house for anyways?"

"Pa's making me a partner next year, and I'm thinking it's time for me to find a wife and settle down as a rancher. With all the talk about how the Kansas Centennial exhibit in Philadelphia is gonna bring in more settlers, I want to get my piece and get it ready. Pa bought that land when the Grahams moved away after the grasshopper plague killed all their crops."

"You planning any crops for yourself?"

"Don't know about that. I like ranching and working with the cattle." With the new barbed wire now being used for fences, he could probably set aside a piece to grow crops for provisions like Ma and Aunt Clara had done.

"Who's the little filly you have in mind for a bride?" Steve turned his horse back toward the campfire. "Is it that pretty little dressmaker's daughter in town?"

Ben rode beside Steve and waited a minute before answering. "No, it's nobody here. I met up again with a girl I knew as a kid back in Boston. Her parents and mine grew up together. She was almost thirteen when I last saw her until this past August. She's turned into a mighty pretty young woman."

Steve's long, low whistle echoed in the night air. He pushed his hat back on his head and turned to stare at Ben. "You planning on getting a Boston girl to come out here and live on a ranch where she won't have servants and others at her beck and call?"

"Amelia's not like that. She's free-spirited and does what she feels like doing." Steve's words did give him something else to consider. Life out here wouldn't be all horseback rides and flower gardens. Could Amelia do all the work that came with running a household?

Steve regarded him seriously. "You'd better think long and hard about bringing a girl all the way out here if she doesn't know anything about life on a ranch."

Steve had a point, and that was why getting her family to visit the ranch had become so important. If, after she visited, Amelia decided this life wasn't for her, he'd have to accept the fact and move on. However, in his heart he believed she'd love it and would be the best wife a man could hope for.

Steve shook his head. "I think it's time for some of that coffee. Seems the cold air has muddled your brain, but maybe some of Cook's coffee will clear it."

Ben didn't know about clearing his head, but it would sure warm his insides. He swung down from Blackie and accepted a tin cup. He wrapped his hands around it and raised it to his lips. The hot liquid slid down his throat. He'd ridden out in the night to seek answers but only wound up with more doubts. God knew the answer, but He wasn't revealing His plans this night.

After the evening performance Philip assisted Amelia up into the carriage and followed her. Once they were settled, he folded his arms across his chest and peered at her. "Well, what did you think of the play?"

"Interesting, and well acted."

Before she could add anything further, Philip launched into another long dissertation about his family, one of several during the course of the evening. "You know my parents are patrons of the arts. They are on the boards of several organizations looking to bring the best in culture to our city. They long for us to have a symphony orchestra, but Mother says that is still some years in the future. Seems that people in Boston are quite conservative when it comes to entertainment at the present. If you ask me, the old guard of Boston would ban everything that brings any pleasure if they could have their way."

Amelia would have to agree with him on that point, but then some conservatism never hurt anyone, and it kept some out of trouble for sure. He didn't give her an opportunity to respond and continued on with his ideas and feelings. He'd already told Amelia how much his father enjoyed working with her father on certain projects, and his mother was quite fond of Mrs. Carlyle as a friend.

Amelia tuned out the words. For such a handsome young man, Philip was certainly a bore. All he talked about was himself and his family and their wealth and prestige. The only time he'd asked about her had been that brief question as to how she liked the play. He never asked about her ideas or what she liked. Like most men, he assumed she would marry and carry on the traditions of one of Boston's elite.

The carriage came to a stop, and Amelia breathed a sigh of thanksgiving to be home at last. Philip alighted first then assisted her down from the carriage. He escorted her to the front door. "This has been a most delightful evening, Miss Carlyle. May I have the pleasure of calling on you tomorrow afternoon?"

A negative response almost slipped out, but she remembered her promise to her father in time and nodded. "Yes, that will be acceptable."

He grinned and bowed. "Then I shall look forward to seeing you again. Thank you, Miss Carlyle."

Amelia said goodnight to Philip and closed the door behind him. She sighed and leaned against the leaded glass panel. Tonight had been enjoyable to a degree, but not the most exciting one she'd experienced.

How different was Ben from this stiff, egotistic young man who had just left. Ben asked her opinion and how she felt about life. He cared about her. If only Papa would look at the good qualities in Ben and not at the distance he lived from Boston, he would find a level-headed young man who knew what he wanted out of life.

Amelia raced up the stairway to the landing but paused to walk sedately past her parents' closed door. No need to make noise and disturb them. Besides, she didn't want to discuss with them her evening with Philip.

In her room she flopped on the bed, giving no mind to the formal dress she wore. She slipped off her shoes and wiggled her toes in their white stockings. She grinned at the memory of the wedding and Ben's finding her shoeless at her table. He hadn't minded at all. Ben's easy manner had made the years disappear and renewed their friendship.

No matter what Papa and Mama wanted from her for the future, she'd never forget Ben. Her feelings for him made her feel good, but at the same time they hurt and left her with many unanswered questions. Were her feelings for Ben strong enough to endure the opposition of those she held most dear, her own parents? As yet, she did not know.

Chapter 11

en reined his horse in and turned back toward the ranch. The herd was in good shape, and he wanted to get home for a hot meal and warm fire. The long, heavy wool coat he wore shielded the wind from his body, and thick wool socks protected his feet inside the leather boots, but the cold still penetrated to the very core of his being. Although no snow had fallen as yet, the November wind bit into his flesh like pellets of ice. Soon the land would be covered in the white powder, and that made taking care of the stock even more difficult.

Four other ranch hands rode ahead of him, heads and shoulders hunched against the biting wind. All were anxious to get to the bunkhouse and warm up. This had been a hard year with the drought following the grasshoppers of last year, but the major portion of the herd survived and would be ready for market come spring.

Three weeks had passed since he'd written his first letter to Amelia. After that night on the prairie, he'd come home and bared his heart to her. Her reply was folded and in the shirt pocket over his heart. He had read it to memorize the lines until the creases began to wear through.

She had not changed her mind at all about wanting to come to Kansas. Amelia mentioned very little of her activities, but his sister Mary Beth kept him informed along those lines. In addition, stories and anecdotes about her relationship with Andrew Farnsworth filled her letters. Ma worried that life in Boston would cause his sister to desire to remain there, and from what Ben had observed, Ma had every right to worry.

As long as Amelia didn't harbor any feelings toward the young men who called on her, the fact that she obeyed her father pleased him. She respected her father, and that spoke to her strong adherence to the foundations of her faith, even if it kept them apart until he could convince Mr. Carlyle he was worthy of Amelia.

When they approached the ranch house, he waved good-bye to the men and headed up to the house while they turned to the bunkhouse. He opened the door to the warmth spread by both the fireplace and the kitchen wood stove. Something smelled good too. If his nose didn't deceive him, Ma had used some of her dried apples to make a pie. His stomach rumbled in anticipation of the meal ahead.

Aunt Clara and Ma sat at the table cutting up potatoes for supper. Ma laid down her knife. "There's hot coffee on the stove. That should help take some of that chill off. Supper will be ready in a bit."

He removed his long coat and hung it on a peg by the back door. "Thanks, Ma. I think we may have a hard freeze tonight."

Grace Ann ran to hug him. "I didn't think you'd ever get back. Gideon, Billy, and I were so cold coming home from school. Gideon put extra blankets on the horses, and I'm sure glad he did."

Ben hugged her and picked her up off the floor. "Well, aren't we the little magpie tonight. What has you so excited?" He set her down and tweaked one of her pigtails, the same dark color as Mary Beth's.

She giggled and ran to the dish cupboard. "Aunt Clara went into town after school and picked up the mail. You have one from Boston. Wonder who it's from?" She giggled again and handed him the envelope.

Amelia's name was written in the upper left corner, and his blood rushed warmth through his body. "Hmm, think I'll take this to my room and read it."

Ma grinned and winked at Clara. "I'll call you when supper's ready."

Pa greeted him in the hallway. "Glad you're back. How did things look?"

"Fine, Pa. There's plenty of feed, and they're all huddled together in the south section. That new barbed wire fence you used will keep them close together for the night. Think it might freeze hard."

"I think so too. I'll go out with the men tomorrow, so you can stay here and take care of the livestock in the barn." He glanced down at Ben's hands.

"That another letter from Amelia? You two have been writing a bit often, haven't you?"

"Yes, sir, we have, but we have a lot to say to each other since we can't be together in person."

His father paused then nodded toward his office. "Come and let's talk."

Ben noted the expression his father's face. He'd seen that look before, and following his father now would be the wise choice. One time he hadn't and wound up in the barn with a willow branch across his legs.

Ben joined his father in the office. Pa waved his hand toward a chair. "Have a seat, son; it's time to discuss Amelia Carlyle."

Ben sat and then waited for Pa to speak his mind. It didn't matter what he had to say, Ben would not change his mind or his feelings for Amelia. Pa paced the floor, and Ben's hands itched to reach out and stop him. Why didn't he just say what was on his mind? Deciding to cut to the chase, Ben cleared his throat and spoke. "Pa, I love Amelia and want to marry her."

"How can you be so sure? You were only together for such a short time." Pa finally stopped and swerved around to face Ben in the eye. "There's more to love than just seeing a pretty girl and thinking you want to spend the rest of your life with her."

"I know that, Pa. I've been thinking about Amelia a lot. We may not have much in common right now except how we feel about each other, but we come from the same stock, we enjoy being with each other, and we love each other." Surely Pa could see that this wasn't infatuation or fascination but deep feelings for each other.

Pa sat down behind his desk, and a frown furrowed his brow. "Your ma has asked me to consider inviting the Carlyle family to Kansas in the spring. Perhaps that is the wise thing to do. You've only seen Amelia in her own environment. Seeing her here, on the ranch, may give you more insight into how she'd really make it living this far from her parents." He rose and came around to Ben. "I'll invite them, but not until after the first of the year."

Ben nodded. That's all he could ask for now, and it would be his one chance to show Amelia that living on a ranch wouldn't be so bad, especially if he could get that piece of land down by the mill. He'd wait and approach his father about that as soon as plans could be made for a house to go on it.

Ma wouldn't make any more trips east with snow and ice covering the states between here and Boston. The six months until spring now loomed as an eternity. He could only write to Amelia and continue to pray that her feelings for him would not change.

Maeleen had come with a message that Mama and Papa wished to see Amelia downstairs. Now she stood in front of the parlor doors, her hands icy cold and her heart skittering in its beats. All types of scenarios danced through her mind. Pa had learned of the many letters with Ben and would forbid their writing one another. Philip Barlow had spoken to father about more than courtship even after her turning down his last request to see her. That scenario shot slivers of fear into her soul. She bit her lip, and her hand hesitated over the door knob.

Better to get it over with and know the cause of the summons than stand here trying to guess. Amelia inhaled deeply then exhaled before opening the door and stepping into the parlor. "Papa, Mama, you wanted to see me?"

Papa glanced up from the newspaper in his hands, and Mama's crochet needle stilled. Papa beckoned her to come to his side.

"Yes, dear, we have a few things to discuss."

Sternness set his face in stone, and no sparkle filled his eyes. Mama's eyes too spoke of her disapproval. Amelia squared her shoulders and stood before her parents.

"I understand you have been corresponding with Benjamin Haynes."

"Yes, Papa, I have." She made no secret about their correspondence. Her letters to Ben had been set on the hall table with all the other family mail, and his had arrived in like manner.

"I see. I also understand that Philip Barlow will no longer be calling on you."

Amelia swallowed hard. So Philip had understood her last answer, but had he spoken with her father about it, or had the Barlows mentioned it to Papa? Either way, Mama and Papa knew the truth. "That's right. We have no true interest in each other." At least that was true for her, and she hoped it was the same for Philip.

Papa glanced over at Mama then cleared his throat. "Exactly why have you turned him down as a suitor?"

Amelia's stomach roiled and bile filled her throat. She had to tell the truth, or Papa would surely be angry, if he wasn't now. She had no choice but to speak her heart and pray her parents would understand the deep waves of emotion that overtook her being whenever her thoughts settled on Ben and the future.

"I have no interest in Philip as a suitor. We did enjoy

our times together, but we could see that our relationship wasn't developing."

"And why was that?" The ice in her father's voice cut into her heart.

"I do not love Philip, and I do not wish to marry anyone if it is not for true love. I do not want a marriage based on only social position and convenience."

Her mother gasped and covered her mouth with her hand. Her eyes opened wide with disbelief. Papa's face turned red, and the veins in his neck thickened. Amelia pressed her hands together behind her back to quiet their shaking. Her world was about to be turned upside down, but telling the truth now and knowing exactly what she had to face with her parents may give her time to win them over by spring.

Mama's voice came out in a squeak. "Amelia, you can't be serious. Philip is a fine young man."

Papa nodded, and his voice held the sternness she hadn't heard since she'd misbehaved so badly at a family affair years ago. "I agree. What can a young girl of your age know about marriage of convenience? Your mother and I merely want what is best for you."

"I do understand, Papa. You and Mama, and Amanda and Charles married because you truly love each other, not just because it was a good blending of families. I care a great deal about Benjamin Haynes, and I believe we could have the same love as you and Mama."

Storm clouds gathered in Papa's eyes. "You have nothing in common with that boy. He may be the son of our friends, but he's lived away from Boston too long and does not understand our way of life. I told him he couldn't call on you, so leave it at that. You are to concentrate on the young men around here and plan to take your place in society just as Amanda has."

Amelia bit her lip. If it meant marrying a man she didn't love, she couldn't do it. Scriptures about honoring one's parents and following their rules swam through her mind in a jumble of words and phrases, but all stated a very clear meaning. She must be obedient.

"Yes, Papa, I will do as you wish." For now, but she would continue to write to Ben, and she'd never stop trying to help them see how suitable Ben was as a suitor. How she didn't know, but she'd find a way, or her name wasn't Amelia Rebecca Carlyle.

After Amelia left the room and closed the door, Lenora turned to Isaac. "Are we doing the right thing by forbidding her to be with Benjamin?"

Isaac picked up the newspaper and snapped it open. "Of course we are. You don't want her living clear out in Kansas, do you?"

"No, of course not, but I do want her to be happy. I've never seen such unhappiness in her eyes as I did when you made your proclamation." Lenora bit her lip. She couldn't bear the thought of her daughter being so far away. Still, what would the future hold for Amelia if she refused the attentions of all the local young men?

"I'd say defiance was more like it. I want her to be happy too, but her happiness lies here in Boston and not in Kansas on a cow ranch. Life around cowboys is no life for a daughter of ours, and the sooner she realizes it, the better off she'll be."

"Elizabeth seems to have adjusted very well, and she fit right back into things here when they came for the wedding and then again for the cotillion." If it hadn't been for a few subtle differences in Elizabeth's demeanor, Lenora would never believe her friend had been living on a ranch in Kansas for so many years.

"Are you saying we should let her go on writing and building a relationship with Benjamin Haynes?"

"I don't know, Isaac. My mind is just as confused as our daughter's seems to be. We must do what is best for her and for Benjamin. I don't want her so far away from us, but I don't want her to be an unhappy, unmarried young woman here either."

"Set your mind at ease, dear. Amelia will be happy with one of the young men she has met recently."

Ben's invitation to visit Kansas came to her mind. She'd love to see the family again, and in their own element. "Perhaps we should plan for a visit to the ranch."

Isaac stroked his chin. "You may be right. If Amelia sees how hard life can be on a ranch in the middle of nowhere, she will think twice about wanting to move there. If Amelia hasn't given up on Ben by spring, I'll write to Matthew about a visit." With that, he sat back to read the newspaper, clearly dismissing Lenora.

She sat for a few minutes, thoughts whirling through her mind like a windmill. Her precious girl had inherited her father's stubborn will. Lenora sighed. Having children grow and seek their own way was one of the most difficult aspects of parenthood. She and God would need a number of conversations in the days ahead. She must keep her heart and mind open to hear His voice and accept His will for her child, no matter how difficult it may be. The future happiness of her daughter lay at stake.

Chapter 12

*A*melia sat at her writing desk, the end of her pen tapping her lips. In the two weeks since Father had said she must forget about Ben, two letters had arrived from him. She had not responded, but his last letter made it now necessary to tell him what had happened. No words would come to mind that truly expressed the mixture of emotions swirling through her heart.

She tried so hard to be obedient to her father's wishes, but her longings for Ben refused to budge from her thoughts. Maeleen had intercepted the letters from Ben and brought them to Amelia. She hated being deceptive, but Papa would be most unhappy to know he still wrote to her. Even this letter would not be with the family mail. She planned to take it to Mary Beth and have her post it, that is if the words to write ever came.

Ben's second letter arrived yesterday, and Maeleen had whisked it up to Amelia immediately. She picked up the paper now and reread the words that gripped her heart in a vise and swept all words of response from her heart. He declared his love for her and said how much he wanted to see her again and wanted to know if his last post had reached her.

She choked back tears and tried to swallow the sadness permeating every part of her body. Her feelings for him had grown stronger since Papa's declaration, but what could she tell Ben as to the reasons she hadn't answered his letters? If it were only possible for them to see each other again in person, then she could express her heart more freely.

Finally she put pen to paper and attempted to explain the scene with her parents. As she wrote, words began to flow from the pen and across the page until she had two pages of words that described her thoughts, her feelings, and her hope that things would change.

She closed with a plea. *Please pray daily for God's will to be done. Only He can change Papa's mind and heart. I believe with all my heart that God will find a way for us to be together.*

There, it was done, and it had to be sent right away. She blotted the ink then folded the paper. She picked up an envelope and stamps from her stationery box. After addressing the letter, Amelia placed it in her purse and headed downstairs. She hadn't visited Mary Beth this past week, and today would be a good one to visit and deliver her letter.

At the foot of the stairs she paused and inclined her head toward the parlor. Although the doors were closed, voices still made their way through the walls. Her parents discussed some topic, and Amelia decided not to disturb them. Then Ben's name hit her ears.

Amelia throat constricted, and she stepped closer to the door. She didn't really intend to eavesdrop, but her curiosity as to why Ben's name had been mentioned overruled her convictions, and she listened.

Mama spoke first. "I'm sorry Mr. Haynes has been taken ill. I had no idea it was so serious until Mrs. Farnsworth told me after church yesterday."

"It looks like the Haynes family will be arriving on Wednesday just in time for the Thanksgiving holiday. Matthew's wire said they'd be in town until his father is better. I'm not sure having the whole group here is what is best for the old man, but if it were my father, I'd want to be by his side."

Amelia grasped her throat and swallowed hard. Ben was coming back to Boston because of his grandfather's ill health. This was not the way she wanted her prayer answered, but God always had a plan and worked things out in strange ways.

She glanced at the letter in her hand. No need to post it now. Ben would be here before the letter could be delivered in Kansas. She turned and dashed back up the stairs without waiting to learn more. All she needed to know was that Ben was coming.

Lenora twisted her handkerchief through her fingers. Isaac placed his hand on her shoulder. "It will be all right, my dear. Matthew must come to be with his parents during this difficult time. Since the holiday is so near, he had no choice but to bring the entire family with him. It may be the last time they'll see their grandfather."

She turned tear-filled eyes to his. "It's Amelia I'm worried about. With Benjamin here in Boston, she'll want to see him."

That had preyed on Isaac's mind, but one could not alter the course of events as God ordained them. He could, however, control the actions of his daughter. "I see no reason for our families not to be together during this time. Elizabeth will need your comfort and support in helping Mrs. Haynes to cope with her husband's illness. We simply will make sure those two young people have no opportunity to be alone together for any length of time."

"Thank you, Isaac." She brushed the tip of her nose with her handkerchief. "I've even contemplated having Grace Ann and Billy come stay here to help reduce the burden on the Haynes's household."

His wife's generosity had always pleased him, and his heart swelled with pride that she would be willing to take in two children to help relieve their mother and Clara of that responsibility. "Perhaps you could ask if that would be a help to them. Clara also will want to stay near her father, so she won't have the time to see to the needs of the children either."

The Haynes had servants just like his own household, but with the master so gravely ill, seeing to young children would take away from their responsibilities to keep things running smoothly. His concern for the growing relationship between Amelia and Ben would not keep Isaac from offering to help the family of his friend.

Lenora declared, "As soon as they arrive, I will visit Elizabeth and offer our help in any way that it may be needed."

"That's a good idea, my dear." He bent and kissed the top of her head. "I admire your desire to be of help, and I will instruct our staff to be ready for the young guests if they should happen to come. They will help you with the burden."

He strode to the door. "Now I must gather my belongings and return to the office. I shall not be home for the noon meal as I must catch up on some business." He retrieved his hat and coat from the hall tree. The next few weeks would be most difficult for Matthew, Elizabeth, and Clara, but the Carlyle family would be ready to offer friendship and companionship whenever and wherever it was needed.

This was not the time to impose strict prohibitions on his daughter. He'd make sure Ben and Amelia had no opportunity to do more than share friendship in the presence of their families. If Ben wanted more, he would not get it on this trip.

Once again Ben gazed through a train window at the landscape as the train clicked along the rails heading for Boston. Ever since the telegraph message that his grandfather lay close to dying, life had been one hurried action after another. Pa had made sure his foreman would handle the responsibilities of the ranch and that the school understood the reason for his children to be absent. Clara arranged for someone to take her group of children at the school and promised to help Billy and Grace Ann keep up with their schoolwork.

Ma and Clara had cleaned clothes and packed bags for

the trip as well as made sure they would have snacks and food to eat on the journey.

Open fields had given way to forests and towns that grew larger the closer they came to Massachusetts. They crossed rivers and streams on sturdy bridges and climbed hills in the western mountains of Massachusetts. Each clack of the wheels brought him closer to seeing Amelia, who hadn't written for a number of weeks and hadn't answered his last letter. Mary Beth's correspondence had shed no light on the problem either.

Amelia may very well have fallen in love with one of the young men vying for her attention after the cotillion. If that be the case, all hopes of their marriage and a life in Kansas dashed against the rocks and shattered. No, Mary Beth or Amelia would have let him know about something like that. His sister spent most letters writing about Andrew Farnsworth and their time together. Maybe she didn't have time to think of anyone else, or had she purposely omitted any details about Amelia's activities?

He'd know the answer to his questions soon enough, but between now and then he must believe only the best of circumstances, or he'd ruin the time for others with the sullen attitude that crept into his conversations.

He glanced across the aisle to his parents. The stern set of Pa's jawline gave evidence of his concern for his father's life. He held Ma's hand, and she brushed her nose with her handkerchief.

She leaned forward and turned toward him. "Ben, will you ask Clara to give Billy a snack? He's probably hungry by now. Have one for yourself too." Then she sat back against the seat and let her head rest on Pa's shoulder.

So much love his parents held for each other. He'd seen it not only in the way Pa teased her on occasion but also in the way he caressed her cheek and whispered to her at times. Someday he hoped that he and Amelia would share that kind of intimate, committed love. He sighed and stood to head for the seats where Clara sat with Billy and Grace Ann.

He tapped his aunt's shoulder. "Clara, Ma said to see if Billy is hungry, and give him one of the snacks you brought."

Clara pointed to the seat across from her where Billy lay sleeping. "He'll be hungry for sure when he wakes up. Why don't you sit here by me for a spell? I can see something is troubling you, and it wouldn't take three guesses to find out it is Amelia Carlyle."

Ben stepped around her legs and settled on the seat by the window. "You'd be right. She hasn't answered my last letter, and I'm worried. She should have my second one by now. Of course if she sends an answer to it, I won't be there to receive it."

"Many things could be the reason for her not answering the first one. This is a busy time for all the young ladies who were presented last month. Young men are calling on them in hopes of choosing a spring or early summer bride from among them."

He furrowed his brow and shook his head. "That's just what I'm afraid is happening. Amelia would be a well sought after young woman. Her father has influence, is wealthy, and is well thought of in their social group. Add to that the fact that Amelia is pretty, and you have all the makings for a perfect society match." Now that he voiced his fear aloud, it grew even more difficult to bear.

Clara grasped her hand in his. "I know it's difficult to wait to hear from someone. I remember how I hated waiting to hear from Tom while he was at West Point and then after he left to join the army."

"You waited, and Tom never came home. I hope I'm not waiting just to find out that Amelia is taken by someone else. I'm not sure I could stand the—"

Clara blinked her eyes and turned her face away from his. How could he have been so stupid?

He reached for her shoulder. "Clara, I'm so sorry. I didn't mean that the way it sounded. Your loss was far greater than any I may suffer if Amelia finds someone else. Please forgive my quick, unthinking tongue."

She said nothing for a few minutes. Then she used her fingers to swipe away the moistness in her eyes. "I forgive you. I know you weren't thinking about what you said. If Amelia has found someone else, her love was not the kind on which to build a permanent relationship. However, I don't believe that to be the case. Amelia is not a person to throw her feelings around. She's steady, not flighty. As far as I can tell, her feelings for you are true."

"I pray you're right." Amelia could be impulsive, but she wasn't irresponsible. He had to believe she loved him.

"I am, dear nephew. Wait and see. She'll welcome you with open arms and open heart. This is a most unfortunate visit, but God always has a plan and purpose. My father's illness came at a bad time with winter setting in like it is, but then no time is a good time for a family member to be gravely ill. We make do with what God hands us with the assurance that He will see us through whatever it is."

Life had made his aunt wise beyond her years. She accepted what God handed her and made her way forward. How weak his faith appeared in the shadow of hers! But she also gave him the strength he needed to rely on God and wait patiently as the plans God had for him unfolded.

He reached over and hugged his aunt. "You are so wise, and you help me every time we talk. Thank you."

Billy picked that moment to awaken and demand attention. He rubbed his eyes. "Aunt Clara, where are you? I'm hungry."

"I'm right here, Billy, and I have something good for you to eat." She reached down for the bag she and Mama had packed.

Grace Ann also sat up and took notice of the bag. "I'm hungry too, Aunt Clara."

"All right, my dear. You can have some cookies too." She rummaged through the bag until she came upon the bundle of cookies. She turned to Ben. "I have to feed them, but we can talk later if you like."

"Thanks, I might take you up on that." He tweaked his brother's hair. "Don't eat too many cookies, or you'll spoil your supper."

Billy shook his head. "No, I won't." He grabbed a cookie from Clara and stuffed it into his mouth.

A smile crossed Ben's face. Billy and Gideon were on their way to being even bigger eaters than Ben himself. Ma and Aunt Clara had their work cut out to keep those two filled up at mealtime.

He stretched and headed back to his seat with Gideon.

With seven of them, his family filled one third of the railway car, but the other passengers didn't seem to mind. Ben settled beside Gideon, who had his nose buried in a book as usual.

Just as well. Ben didn't care to talk with anyone right now. He'd rather sit and plan what he had to say to Amelia when they next saw each other. He regretted his grandfather's illness, but he welcomed the chance to see the girl he loved once again.

Chapter 13

hanksgiving Day dawned clear and cold, but
Amelia awakened to a toasty warm room. Maeleen
had been up early to make sure the coal stove in the room
was lit and ready for Amelia when she awakened. Amelia
yawned and stretched, once again thankful for the stoves
Papa had installed in each bedroom.

She shoved her feet into warm slippers and grabbed
up her robe. If the Haynes children were still asleep, she'd
have the bathroom to herself for a few moments of privacy.
She peeked into the hall, and nothing but quiet greeted
her. She scurried across the way to the bathroom and
closed the door.

A few minutes later a tapping sounded on the door.
Amelia finished her business and opened the door to find
Billy standing there. He hopped first on one foot and then
the other. His hair stood on end like a bristle brush. "I
gotta go, Miss Amelia."

She grinned and shoved him into the room with a pat
on the bottom. "You best hurry and get dressed. You'll

catch cold without a robe or shoes." She closed the door behind him and hurried back to her own room and its warmth.

Having Billy and Grace Ann arrive yesterday had created quite a stir in the household. Mama had placed Grace Ann in Amanda's now vacant room, and Billy occupied the room that had once been the nursery but now served as an extra bedroom. Amelia had wished Mary Beth would come and stay too, but she remained at the Haynes's home to help her mother and aunt take care of the elderly Mr. and Mrs. Haynes.

She had been quiet and not voiced her disappointment when Ben had not come with his father to deliver the children. Any outward show might have caused her father concern, and that may have led to not seeing Ben at all.

Instead, all but Clara and her mother were coming here for Thanksgiving dinner. Yesterday when Mr. Haynes brought Billy and Grace Ann, Mama had insisted that Mr. and Mrs. Haynes dine with the Carlyles. When Mr. Carlyle finally accepted, Amelia's heart leaped within her chest in anticipation of the holiday.

In just a few hours the house would fill with the delicious aroma of roasting turkey, yams, fresh yeast bread, and pumpkin pie. Even better, Ben would be here, and they would have a chance to visit so she could explain the reasons for not writing to him. Surely Father would allow her to have time with her two friends.

Amelia stopped at Grace Ann's room and peeked through the open door. Maeleen stood behind Grace Ann and brushed her hair. "Good morning, you two."

Grace Ann beamed a smile bright as sunshine. "Oh,

Amelia, Maeleen is going to put my hair up in long curls instead of pigtails. I'm so excited." She bounced on the dressing stool.

Maeleen tapped the girl's shoulder. "And ye best sit still or we'll not get it done."

"She's right, Grace Ann. She makes me sit still when she's doing mine. You'll be glad you did." Amelia turned back to the door. "I'll leave you two and go check on Billy. He'll be hungry as a little bear for breakfast."

She had marveled at the boy's appetite last night at dinner. She hadn't been around boys that young to know how much they ate. If only she could have had a little brother.

Billy opened the door to his room and dashed out. Amelia caught him by the shoulders. "Whoa there, not so fast. You wouldn't want to fall down the stairs, would you?"

He shook his head, and his eyes opened wide. "I wouldn't fall, Miss Amelia. I'm good at running down stairs, and I smell bacon frying." He hopped about under her grip and tried to squirm loose.

"If you'll walk quietly beside me, we can go down to breakfast now. I'm sure Lettie has plenty for you to eat." She grasped his hand before he could break free. "My mother doesn't like for us to run in the house, so let's be nice and quiet going down the stairs." Too many times in her younger days she'd been caught running or sliding on the banister. Mama probably wouldn't scold Billy, but she'd be much happier to see him walking into the dining room than running.

Grace Ann joined them, and when they entered, Mama

and Papa greeted them, and Amelia seated Billy next to her chair with Grace Ann by Mama. She planted her usual morning kiss on Papa's cheek. "I'll fill Billy's plate for him." She headed for the sideboard and the buffet meal spread there, followed by Grace Ann.

Mama smiled at Billy. "How did you sleep last night, young man?"

"OK, but I miss my ma."

"I'm sure you do, but for now, it's best that you stay here with us. Perhaps we can find some toys or games for you to play with."

Amelia plopped a spoonful of eggs onto Billy's plate. "I know where some are stored. Amanda and I played with them when we were your age."

Billy stuck out his bottom lip and frowned. "I don't want no girl toys."

Amelia laughed and finished piling food onto his plate. She walked around to set it in front of him. "They're not all girl toys, and we can look for them after you eat."

"That sounds like fun. Do you have any books?" Grace Ann's curls bounced on her shoulders.

Amelia laughed. "Oh, yes. The shelves in the playroom are filled. We'll look at them after breakfast."

Amelia went back for her own meal, and Lettie appeared from the kitchen with a glass of milk in hand. She set it in front of Billy and patted his head before stopping by Papa's chair. "Anything I can get you, Mr. Carlyle?"

Papa assured her that everything was fine, and Amelia spooned jam onto her plate. "This is a great meal, Lettie, thank you." She sat down and whispered her own prayer of thanksgiving since she'd missed Papa's. Part of it included a prayer for her time with Ben that afternoon. No matter whether it was twenty minutes or two hours, she had to tell him what Papa had said. She prayed Ben would not speak to Papa before she could.

Andrew Farnsworth courted Mary Beth, and Papa had pointed out what a well-made match they would be and he hoped that Amelia would do as well. To her mind the fact that Andrew and Mary Beth actually loved each other made it a good match, not Andrew's family's position. Amelia wanted the same kind of love in her own life, and she would have it with Ben.

After breakfast was finished, Amelia accompanied Grace Ann and Billy up to Billy's room. "This was once our playroom. Mama had all our toys stored away when Amanda and I got older, but I know where she put them."

Grace Ann knit her brows and surveyed the room. "This was just a playroom? You and Amanda didn't sleep here?"

"Not after we were older. When we were babies, this was the nursery. We had two cribs in here for us and then smaller beds for later. When we started school, we were given our own bedroom, and this became a playroom."

Amazement filled the girl's face. "It's so big. I share a room with Mary Beth at home, and we keep everything there, including all my toys."

"And I have to sleep with Gideon and Ben, but I think Ben's going to move out to the bunkhouse so Gideon and I'll have more room."

Amelia gulped. It never occurred to her that the children would be impressed with a playroom. Then she remembered their grandparents' house no longer had a playroom, and when Billy and Grace Ann came for a visit, they still had to share a room with their siblings. "I'm sure you would rather have them with you instead of sleeping alone at the ranch."

"Nope, not me. I'm a big boy, and I like having my own room here even if I do miss Ma and Pa."

"Then let's see what we can find to play with this morning." She went to the storage closet and pulled out several boxes. One toy box was filled with things to keep the two young ones occupied until their parents arrived.

"Here's a set of building blocks for you, Billy. I bet you could build a house just like your ranch house with those." She opened a set of wooden blocks that had been sanded smooth and cut into different shapes and sizes.

Billy grabbed them up and headed for a corner. Amelia pulled out two dolls that were lying on top. "Do you still play with dolls, Grace Ann?" At twelve, Amelia had still loved them, but Grace Ann may feel too old for them.

"Sometimes, but I'd rather have books if you have some."

"I certainly do. Look on those shelves over there and see if you can find anything you like." All of Amelia's favorites were there, including Bronte, Alcott, and Dickens. Although she kept busy the rest of the morning reading with Grace Ann and exclaiming over the structures Billy built, the hours until the rest of the Haynes family arrived crept by.

When Maeleen stopped in to inform them that it was time to dress for dinner, Amelia clapped her hands. "Let's get these things put away. Those wonderful smells coming from the kitchen have given me a real appetite."

The children scrambled to get the books, blocks, and other toys put away, and Amelia counted the minutes now until she could again be with Ben.

The horses clip-clopped along much too slowly for Ben, and his patience wore thin. However, if he complained, Gideon or Mary Beth would make some comment about seeing Amelia. It was best to keep quiet rather than start a conversation about his love life. He envied his brother and sister who had the pleasure of staying at the Carlyle home.

Amelia would be good with them and keep the two occupied with things to do. He would thank Mrs. Carlyle for her generosity because it had given his mother and Clara much more time to tend to Grandpapa's needs.

Pa had voiced his concern over Grandpapa's illness and said the visit may take longer than they first expected. Pa's two brothers were with their wives' families today, but all of the Haynes would be together tomorrow. Ben looked forward to seeing his cousins, but he anticipated seeing Amelia today far more.

After only fifteen minutes that may have well have been fifteen hours to Ben, the carriage stopped in front of the Carlyle home. The driver jumped down and opened the door to assist Mary Beth in stepping down. Ben followed Gideon and hurried up the steps and through the door the Carlyle butler held open for them.

Warm air as well as tantalizing aromas of pumpkin spice and roasting turkey filled the room, welcoming them into the house. Billy and Grace Ann ran down the stairs and into Pa's arms. He lifted Billy in one arm and hugged Grace Ann with the other.

Ben's gaze went right to Amelia, who descended the steps much more sedately than his two siblings had. Her parents greeted them, but Ben didn't hear a word. His eyes locked with Amelia's and stayed there until she reached the foyer and greeted Mary Beth. He furrowed his brow and stepped back. She hadn't come to him first.

When she finally spoke to him, her lip trembled. "I must speak with you later...to explain why I didn't write in the last few weeks."

The lines on her forehead and around her mouth didn't bode well for him. He simply nodded then followed the family into the parlor where they all sat down. Billy and Grace Ann grabbed their mother's attention and went on about what they'd been doing. Ben kept his attention on Amelia.

Whenever she happened to glance his way, heat flushed her cheeks, and she smiled before ducking her head away from him. Scenarios and questions raced through his mind faster than cattle in a stampede. None of them fit what he'd hoped may happen, and acid climbed to his throat.

They finally went in to dinner, but he found himself across and down the table from Amelia, who sat next to her father, too far away for conversation. Had that been her request or her father's? Mr. Carlyle had not been cordial in greeting Ben. His hands now grew moist, and he clasped them together in his lap while Mr. Carlyle asked the blessing.

Mrs. Carlyle sat to his right at the opposite end of the table from her husband and next to his mother, who dined across from Ben. She smiled at him and placed a napkin in her lap. "I'm glad your family could join us today. I know your grandmama and Clara appreciate the time they have together without so much interruption."

She glanced down the table to where Amelia bent her head toward Grace Ann. "You will have time to speak with Amelia later today. She has much to tell you."

Before Ben could respond, Mrs. Carlyle turned and began a conversation with his mother. He placed food on his plate, but he paid no attention to what he ate. It all tasted the same.

Gideon leaned toward Ben. "Amelia sure looks pretty today. Too bad you're not sitting by her."

Ben said nothing but glared for a moment at his brother. Ben would rather be sitting by her too, but he didn't care to talk about it. He didn't want to talk to anyone but Amelia. Then he realized the selfishness in that desire and turned to talk to Gideon in a more pleasant fashion.

After dinner Pa and Mr. Carlyle went into his study, and Ma followed Mrs. Carlyle to the parlor. Amelia grabbed Ben and Mary Beth's hands. "Let's go into the library."

Maeleen took over Billy and Grace Ann and led them up the stairs to their rooms. He hoped the young woman would let them play because neither of them would want to take a nap, but at least they wouldn't be underfoot.

Amelia paced the floor by the window looking out over the snow-filled yard. So much Ben wanted to say to her, but he sensed her need to get her words in first. He sat on the sofa near the fireplace and waited. If Mary Beth hadn't been in the room, he would have stopped Amelia's pacing and held her in his arms.

Finally she stopped and sat beside him. Her nearness sent his heart galloping, and the fresh scent of lavender filled his nostrils. It must be her favorite because he remembered it from last time.

Amelia cleared her throat, but her first words still squeaked. "Ben, I have something…oh, dear." She cleared her throat again. "I must explain why I didn't answer your last two letters." She nodded toward Mary Beth. "She knows all about this but promised not to say anything until I could speak with you."

She twisted her hands in her lap, and fear rose like a wave of despair in Ben's chest. He braced himself against what may come next although he wanted to get up and run away from what she would say.

"Ben, Papa is against our relationship. He says we must only be friends."

Relief replaced despair, and he smiled. He'd expected that much from Mr. Carlyle. "That doesn't surprise me, Amelia. It will take time for him to see how we care about each other." He paused and peered at her. "You do still care about me, don't you?"

She grabbed his hands. "Oh, yes, Ben, I do care, even more than before."

He held her hand to his lips. "Then we must be very patient and not anger your father. If we respect his wishes for now, in time he will come to see that we love each other."

Tears moistened her eyes. "Oh, Ben, I pray that will happen, but Papa can be so stubborn."

"So can mine, but if God ordains us to be together, then He will work out the details and make it happen. You have to believe that." He must be strong for her and give her hope when his own faith weakened at the thought of winning Mr. Carlyle's favor.

"I want to believe it. I'll keep praying and being obedient to Papa."

"That's all you can do, and I'll keep praying too." No prayer he'd ever sent up before would be as fervent and full of plea as the ones in the next few months and beyond.

Lenora led Elizabeth into the parlor where they could talk without interruption. She searched her brain for the correct way to present her dilemma to her friend. Ben was Elizabeth's son, and certainly she had to be proud of what he had accomplished in life thus far. Lenora didn't want to hurt any feelings or make it sound like Amelia was too good for Benjamin.

Elizabeth placed her hand on Lenora's arm. "I can see something is troubling you. You still crinkle your forehead when you're worried about something."

Lenora let her breath out in a gasp, not even aware she'd been holding it until this moment. "I never could hide anything from you." She twisted her hands in her lap. "It's about our children, Amelia and Benjamin."

"I thought so. Ben claims to be in love with her, but I fear they don't really know each other."

"Amelia is the same. I get the impression she thinks she can just up and go to Kansas and start living on a ranch without any problems. She can be quite the stubborn one when she sets her mind on something."

"So can Ben, but he knows life can be hard on the

ranch. He's seen us deal with diseases in the herd, harsh winters, and lean years when we have to be careful about spending. He's thinking ahead to a piece of land and a house. But I'm afraid he's not considering the situation from every angle."

She gave Lenora a sympathetic look that opened the door for her to confide her feelings to her friend. "Oh, Elizabeth, it would grieve me so for Amelia to move away like you did. I missed you so much those first months, and I'd miss her even more. She and Amanda are all we have. After we lost our son in his infancy, I knew those two girls would be all we ever had. Am I being selfish in wanting her to stay here where Isaac and I both believe she belongs?"

"No, Lenora. We want our children to be happy, and that's why Matthew and I agreed to let Mary Beth remain here. Now that she's here, I can see how this life fits her so well. It hurts my heart for her to be away. These past few years we've been more than mother and daughter; we've been friends. However, when I see how happy she is with Andrew Farnsworth, I can't help but be happy for her and let her go."

A stab of pain twisted itself into Lenora's heart. Elizabeth had four other children left at home and could keep her hands and heart busy with them. No one would be left at home for Isaac and her if Amelia were to leave.

Elizabeth reached over and covered Lenora's hands. "Caring for our adult children may prove to be even more difficult than when they were young. We can't live their lives for them, but we can guide them and help them make the wisest choices." She paused a moment then continued. "A trip to the ranch would give all three of you a real glimpse into our life. Sometimes the fear of the unknown can influence us to the point of not seeing the truth."

"I...I think you may be right. If Amelia can see what goes on and what will be expected of her, maybe she will have second thoughts. Mercy, the girl can't cook or sew and knows nothing about running a household."

Elizabeth laughed. "Neither did I, but Clara and I learned very fast. We had to or starve to death. Of course I did get a few pointers from our cook before we left, but mostly Clara and I taught ourselves, and it wasn't always fun."

Lenora settled back against the sofa. She would not express her opinion too openly until after their visit in the spring. Everything would work out as God willed it, but someone would be hurt after all was said and done, and right now she couldn't decide whether that should be Amelia—or Isaac and herself.

Chapter 14

$\mathcal{O}$n Sunday before church, Amelia waited with Billy and Grace Ann in the foyer of the church for the Haynes family to arrive so the children could sit with their parents. Friday Mr. Haynes had picked them up to spend the day with his brothers and their families. The house had been much too quiet after they left, and she had welcomed their return that night.

When Mrs. Haynes stepped through the door, the children ran and hugged her. Ben skirted around them and headed for Amelia. "It's so good to see you this morning. I wanted so badly to come to your house yesterday, but Ma suggested it wasn't a good idea. I'm not sure I'm going to be able to stand not seeing you every day while we're here." He grasped her hands in his.

"Neither do I. This is so hard. Papa wants me to continue to consider other young men, but my future is with you." She had to cling to that hope, or she'd never make it through the months ahead.

"Ma wants us all together at Grandmama's house

today. I offered to bring Billy and Grace Ann back to your house this evening, but I don't know if that will happen or not."

"I will pray that it does and that Papa will invite you in for a hot drink before going back into the cold. Even if we can't be alone, we can be in the same room. Just having you near makes me happy."

She glanced behind Ben and spotted her mother frowning and shaking her head. Papa stood next to her with his back toward Amelia as he conversed with a fellow church member.

Her gaze returned to Ben. "I have to go now. Mama is beckoning me. Papa hasn't seen us together as yet, and she's afraid he'll be angry." She pulled her hands from his grasp. "I'll look for you to bring Billy and Grace Ann tonight."

She hurried to stand beside her mother just before Papa turned and escorted them into the sanctuary. They filed into their pew box at the same time the Haynes family entered theirs a few rows back. Even as she settled onto the cushioned pew, Amelia sensed Ben's presence and his eyes gazing at the back of her head.

All through the singing and the message, her thoughts rolled through her mind like a kaleidoscope with each turn coloring her emotions. She glanced up at the stained glass windows and focused on the one of Jesus praying in the Garden of Gethsemane. Her troubles diminished at the anguish shown in Christ's face.

Nothing she ever had to endure would be as hard as that of her Savior going through the anguish of Calvary. Tears misted her eyes, and she bowed her head. Whatever lay ahead, the Lord would walk before her and prepare the way. She had to trust Him and follow wherever He led her. If that happened to be into the arms of Ben, she would be most happy, but if not, she'd have to learn to live with the alternative, whatever that may be.

Mama slipped her hand over to cover Amelia's as though she understood the turmoil going through her daughter at the moment. Amelia prayed for Papa to understand how she and Ben loved each other. Until he did, she could do nothing but be obedient to Papa and perhaps thereby increase his trust in her.

After the service she hurried to the foyer, but Ben had already left. When she opened the door to the outside, she spotted him helping Mary Beth into their carriage. He turned, and when he saw her, a smile grew wide on his face. He touched his fingers to his forehead in a mock salute that said he'd see her later.

That must mean he'd be bringing his brother and sister back to her house tonight. Her spirits soared with the assurance she'd have even a few moments with him that day. The hours would drag by until his return.

She turned to look for her parents and bumped into Philip Barlow. "Oh, excuse me. I didn't realize you were behind me."

He grinned and steadied her with his hands on her forearms. "I saw you step out here and wanted to speak with you before you left. The Farnsworths are giving a Christmas party in two weeks, and I'd like to escort you to it."

That invitation had come in the mail on Friday, and Mama had insisted Amelia must attend. Now here Philip had asked to escort her, and she had no reasonable excuse for not accepting. Papa would be most pleased, but what if Ben and Mary Beth had been invited too? The expectant look in Philip's eyes unnerved her, but she managed to answer, "Yes, that will be an honor." Apparently her earlier rejection had no effect on his efforts to court her. Next time she'd have to be clearer, if there was to be a next time.

"Thank you, Miss Haynes. I'll be in touch as to the time." He tipped his hat and strode off toward his carriage.

Mama wrapped her arm around Amelia's shoulders. "I assume that was about the Farnsworth party, and from the look on Philip's face, you accepted his invitation to take you."

"Yes, Mama, I did."

"Well done, my daughter." Papa's voice sounded his approval. "You will have a grand time with Mr. Barlow." He grasped Mama's arm. "Now let's get home to the dinner Lettie has prepared for us."

Amelia followed them across the street and climbed up into the carriage to sit opposite her mother. "The house will be rather quiet this afternoon without the Haynes children there. I shall miss them."

"Yes, it has been rather nice having children about the house again. Of course the noise is a little more with a boy than it was with you and Amanda. Grace Ann is growing into a fine young lady as well."

Papa patted Mama's hand. "Don't get too used to having them around. Remember, they all will be returning to Kansas before very long." His gaze cut to Amelia as a reminder of his dictum about Ben.

The message didn't miss its mark, and Amelia wracked

her brain to come up with something or some way to change Papa's mind about Ben. One thing for sure, she'd never stop trying.

After dinner Isaac beckoned for Lenora to meet with him in his study. When she had taken her seat in the chair near his desk, he pulled the Farnsworth invitation from the drawer. "This could be the opportunity for young Philip to declare his intentions."

"Yes, it could, but will Amelia return his affections?"

"Of course she will. Our daughter knows what her duty is, and a good marriage is part of that duty." Even though he'd seen the exchange between Ben and Amelia that morning, he refused to believe there could be more than friendship between the two. He'd never allow Ben to seek Amelia's company for courtship, much less consent to marriage between the two.

"A good marriage is important, but what exactly is a good marriage? You and I are most fortunate that we loved each other before we became betrothed. I fear Amelia's heart lies elsewhere." Her hands twisted the handkerchief in her grasp.

"It may well indeed not be love for young Barlow that she feels now, but many a marriage has started out with far less than Amelia would have with Philip. He'll be good for her and to her. She'll be close by and will have the life to which she was born." He'd settle for no less for Amelia, just as he hadn't for Amanda, and that had turned out quite well. Amelia was a good Christian girl and had been taught to honor her parents, and she'd do just that.

"Isaac, you realize that none of this means to Amelia what it does to me or Amanda. Amelia is a free spirit who doesn't see the need for using our wealth and position to gain a place of recognition in life."

"As the wife of Philip Barlow, she will have all the recognition she needs. She'll be expected to hostess any number of functions along with his mother, and of course with you, my dear, just as Amanda will be." Women of Boston society knew their duties as the wives of prominent men and daughters of prominent families. Amelia would come around and be one of the best. With her love of people and charming personality, her dinners and parties would be the talk of Boston. His chest swelled with pride at how well his two daughters were doing in life.

"All I want is for our daughters to be happy. Amanda seems to be, but Amelia is a different matter. She's being obedient to you in her actions and doing as you ask, but her heart rebels. I see it every time she is around Benjamin Haynes."

He had seen it too, but he hesitated to actually forbid his daughter again to see or talk with Benjamin. Once should be enough, and her rebellious spirit might unleash itself if he used too harsh a treatment. "We do not need to worry about that relationship because Benjamin will be returning to Kansas soon, and he'll be too far away to be much of an influence on her." He had to cling to that hope, or else find himself inflicting harsher guidelines for Amelia to follow.

Lenora gripped her handkerchief with white-knuckled fingers. "If there's nothing else you wish to speak to me about, I will retire upstairs. I feel a headache coming on."

He hastened around the desk to her side. "I'm sorry. I didn't mean to trouble you. Go and take a rest. You've had a hard week with the Haynes children here. I should have been more aware." He kissed the top of her head then lifted her with gentle hands from the chair. "I'll be in to check on you later."

After she left, he returned to his desk and sat down. He formed an arch with his fingertips and considered his position. *Lord, help me to do what is right for Amelia. If she left Boston and went far away to live, it would hurt Lenora and cause her much grief. Help me to decide what is best for these two women I love very much.*

Why couldn't Amelia be more like Amanda? All through their growing years, Amanda had been the neat, well-organized young lady, but Amelia had been messy, soiling her aprons with dirt from play, running up and down the stairs, as well as taking a ride or two on the banister. In the past year she had grown into a beautiful young woman, but she still had a bit of rebel streak in her, and he prayed it wouldn't become full blown in the days ahead.

Ma straightened Billy's coat and buttoned it. "Now you be good for Mrs. Carlyle. She's helping me and Grandmama, so we can take care of Grandpapa while he's sick."

Billy shook his head, the dark brown curls bouncing on his forehead. "I remember, Ma. Miss Amelia and Maeleen play with us. They have lots of toys and games for us to play with."

"That's nice of them, but don't forget, Maeleen has other responsibilities too."

Grace Ann tied on her bonnet. "When she's busy, Miss Amelia spends time with us. I love reading her books."

Ma stood and turned to Ben. "I appreciate your willingness to take them back tonight, but my guess it has nothing to do with love for your siblings."

Grace Ann giggled. "He's sweet on Miss Amelia, and I think she likes him too."

Ben's cheeks grew warm. "Yes, I am, little Miss Know-It-All, but you best mind your manners and not say anything around her family."

Ma placed her hands on Ben's shoulders and gazed up at him. "I know you have feelings for her, but be careful. I know Isaac Carlyle, and he can be quite stern. I don't want to see either of you hurt."

He kissed her forehead. "Thank you, but I already know how Mr. Carlyle feels, so Amelia and I are going to be patient and wait for him to change his mind." He wrapped a woolen scarf about his neck and nodded at his brother and sister, who hurried out the door and to the carriage.

"I hope to stay a few minutes and talk with Amelia. I'll let you know how that works out." He couldn't help but note the worried frown on his mother.

A few minutes later the carriage made its way through the streets of Boston. With fresh snow on the ground, the scene reminded him of the times he'd played in the snow with his brothers and sisters back in Kansas. The snow stayed prettier longer in the country than it did here in the city. Even now the streets had turned to slush from the constant wheels of carriages, and instead of pristine white, muddy black ruts ruined the streets.

In a short time they arrived at the Carlyle home. Ben helped the children down from the carriage. Billy ran up to the door, but Grace Ann walked. He shook his head in wonder. His youngest sister behaved more like a young lady than a child every day. With her thirteenth birthday coming in February, she had blossomed into a very pretty young girl. If Mary Beth stayed in Boston, Grace Ann would become the center of Ma's and Clara's attention. The girl didn't have a chance. She'd learn all things a woman needed to know about a home and family.

He followed them to the door where the butler stood holding it for their entrance. Ben hurried his steps to keep from letting too much cold air enter the house. He handed over his hat and coat as Mrs. Carlyle appeared.

She smiled at them and held out her hands toward Ben. "It's sweet of you to bring them here this evening. I trust they had a good visit with their mother." She hooked her hand onto his arm. "Let's go into the parlor. Lettie will bring hot tea to warm you."

Maeleen headed upstairs with Billy and Grace Ann, the three of them chattering like old friends. At least they didn't mind coming here, and it sure helped Ma and Clara with all they had to do.

When he entered the parlor, Amelia sat near the fireplace. The sparkle in her eyes revealed her pleasure that Ben had come. Most likely she hadn't greeted him in the hallway in order to please her father, who stepped through the door of his study and joined them.

"Good evening, Benjamin. I trust you had a good day with your family."

"Yes, sir, we did. Grandpapa's condition has not changed. The doctor would rather he be in a hospital, but Grandmama insists that she can take better care of him at home." Why she didn't trust the hospital remained a mystery, but then Grandmama was used to the old ways.

"That's what your father told me. Well, have a seat. I believe Lettie will be in momentarily with a bit of refreshment."

Ben sat in the chair opposite Amelia. As long as her parents remained in the room, he'd have no opportunity to speak with her directly, but he'd settle for just her presence.

Mr. Carlyle asked him about the ranch and who was taking care of it in his father's absence. As Ben explained, he noted how Amelia leaned slightly forward and listened to every word. She really did care about his life in Kansas.

After only fifteen minutes, Mr. Carlyle stood. "We won't keep you from your family any longer. Thank you for bringing the children here."

Ben could do nothing else but stand and follow Mr. Carlyle. Amelia did come with them, and she stood close to Ben.

Her whisper barely reached his ears. "Mary Beth has a plan. She'll tell you about it."

Ben blinked his eyes. A plan? That sounded like his sister. He nodded and grasped his hat and coat from the butler. She stood behind her father as he said good-bye. Ben smiled and nodded to Mr. Carlyle, but the smile came because of the silent words formed by Amelia. "I'll see you soon."

He bounded down the few steps and out to the carriage, his heart filled with the joy of seeing Amelia again. He couldn't wait to get home and see what scheme his sister had cooked up.

Chapter 15

The message from Mary Beth crackled in Amelia's pocket as she descended the stairs and headed for the dining room and breakfast. Billy and Grace Ann preceded her into the room and took their places at the table.

Both said good morning in unison then giggled. Mama smiled and said, "Good morning to you too." She gestured toward the sideboard. "We have oatmeal this morning if you'd like."

After her daily kiss for her father and a hug for her mother, Amelia headed for the food. Billy and Grace Ann both wanted the cereal, so she filled two bowls with oatmeal, added sugar and milk, then set them before the children. She filled her plate with scrambled eggs, a slice of ham, and two slices of toast, then sat down.

Papa bowed his head and asked the Lord's blessing over the meal. Amelia sensed Billy squirming beside her and reached her hand over to still him. Papa's prayer ended, and Billy dug into his oatmeal.

Amelia lifted her fork, breathing in the pleasant

aroma of toast and fried ham. Her appetite had increased immensely after receiving the note. The last two days she'd barely eaten at all in anticipation of hearing from Mary Beth. The invitation to lunch today had arrived late yesterday afternoon.

Mama sipped her hot tea and peered across at Amelia. "I understand Mary Beth invited you for lunch today. Do you think it wise to create an extra burden for her mother?"

How did Mama know? Amelia had shared Mary Beth's note with no one. Mama must have talked with Mrs. Haynes. "Actually, we're going to the Parker House for lunch. Mary Beth has heard about the wonderful breads they serve there and wants to try it. Since the weather is sunny and not so cold, we're also going to Faneuil Hall and Quincy Market. We'll probably do a little Christmas shopping."

"That sounds nice, dear. Be sure you have enough money with you for your purchases."

"Yes, Mama, I will." If Andrew and Ben happened to arrive at the same destinations as she and Mary Beth, that would be a nice coincidence, but she didn't dare share that with Mama.

Billy tugged on her sleeve. "Is Santa Claus going to find us here in Boston?"

"Of course he will. Santa Claus knows where everyone is. I'm sure you'll have some nice presents under your tree. Papa and I always put ours up on Christmas Eve."

Grace Ann's eyes clouded, and she frowned. "Ma says we may not have a tree and decorations this year because Grandpapa is so sick."

That hadn't occurred to Amelia, and she wished to

take back her excitement about the holiday. Surely they wouldn't completely dismiss the day for the children. "Perhaps you will be allowed to share ours. I know it won't be the same, but we can make candy and cookies and drink warm, spiced apple cider."

She glanced at her mother to seek her approval for such an occasion. Her smile and nod gave Amelia the answer she wanted. "We'll talk with your mother about it when she comes tomorrow to visit."

Both children returned to their eating, but without the smiles of joy that the holiday should bring. Maybe if she played some carols on the piano and told them the story of baby Jesus, they might feel better about the holiday. She made a mental note to discuss the matter with Mary Beth and Ben today. They would have a better understanding of what was happening with their grandfather.

After breakfast the children scampered back upstairs to play. Amelia found a book she'd been wanting to read and retired to her room to wait the interminable hours until the time for Mary Beth's arrival.

After reading a chapter and realizing she didn't remember a word of it, Amelia shucked aside the novel. Maybe deciding what she should wear would help the time pass more quickly. She stood in front of her wardrobe and fingered the shoulders of several garments. She'd have to wear her cape even over the heavier fabrics, but she still wanted to wear something attractive as well as fashionable.

She decided against a lot of ruffles and trimming that really didn't suit her tastes, but Mama said they were fashionable and so should be in her wardrobe. Finally she settled on a three-piece royal blue woolen garment. The skirt had a panel of black in the front and gathered to a mid-sized bustle in the back that was secured with a large black bow. The only embellishment on the skirt and jacket top was black embroidery along the edges of the sleeves and the skirt.

The clock in the upstairs hall chimed eleven times. Mary Beth would be here a little past noon, and it would take that long to get dressed, even with Maeleen's help. As if in answer to her thoughts, Maeleen appeared in the doorway. "Best be time for ye to dress for luncheon with Miss Mary Beth."

"Thank you, Maeleen. I appreciate your help." Petticoats, corsets, and camisoles were too much for one person to handle, and she enjoyed the servant girl's help with dressing.

After getting all the pieces together and then on her body, Amelia sat at her dressing table with Maeleen behind her. Maeleen picked up the brush and began running it through Amelia's hair. "Ye wouldn't happen to be seeing Mr. Benjamin this afternoon too now, would ye?"

Heat flushed Amelia's cheeks. "He might be there. I know Mr. Farnsworth will be meeting us, so we might run into Mr. Haynes as well."

"Best not be letting your papa know. Most unhappy 'twould he be to hear it."

How true that was, but she couldn't lie to Papa. "I cannot help it if Mr. Haynes happens to show up at the same time as Mr. Farnsworth. I will tell Mama and Papa that we met them by coincidence at Faneuil Hall."

Maeleen shook her head. "And ye think he'll be believing that story."

"He has to, he just has to. This is the only way I can have time with Ben...I mean, Mr. Haynes."

"I know what ye mean, and I've seen the way ye gaze at him when he's around. He does the same with ye. My thoughts are that ye be in love with the lad."

Amelia turned around and grabbed Maeleen's hands. "Oh, we are, we are in love." If Maeleen was so aware of their feelings, Mama must be as well as Papa. That was the reason for his saying she couldn't see Ben. Papa may be able to control her behavior, but he'd never have control over heart.

Ben followed Mary Beth down the stairs as she pulled on leather gloves. "Do you really think this will work? What if her father catches on that it was all planned and not by chance?"

"You leave that to me and Amelia, big brother. Being with Andrew will give a perfectly good reason for meeting us accidentally."

"I hope you're right. Andrew didn't seem bothered by this ruse?"

"Some. He knows that Philip Barlow is interested in Amelia, but he also has a mischievous streak, and this goes right along with that. He promised not to say anything to either Philip or Mr. Carlyle."

If anything spoiled this afternoon, he'd never forgive himself. Better to see Amelia on family visits than to be banished and not see her at all, and that's exactly what Mr. Carlyle would do.

Mary Beth left and he retrieved his own coat and hat.

Andrew would be here soon, and so would begin his sister's plan. Although Mary Beth really did want to eat at the Parker House to taste their breads, her real motive lay in getting time for Ben and Amelia to be alone with each other. His sister's generous gesture made him love her even more.

Come to think of it, this would be a good time to learn more about how Andrew felt toward Mary Beth. Pa probably already knew, but being her big brother gave Ben the right to question Andrew himself. It wouldn't surprise him any to learn Andrew sought marriage to Mary Beth. The two looked very nice together, and Mary Beth had all but come right out and said that she loved Andrew. He'd make a fine brother, but they'd be too far away from each other to be friends.

Ben spotted Andrew's carriage, donned his coat and hat, and hastened out to meet him. Ben pulled on his gloves and stepped into the vehicle. "Right on time, I see."

Andrew chuckled. "Of course. We can't be late for our little rendezvous."

In no time the carriage arrived at the Parker House. Inside they met the maitre d', who guided them to the table where the two ladies waited for them. Andrew grasped Mary Beth's hands. "I thought I'd be ahead of you, so you wouldn't have to sit alone." He grinned at Amelia. "And look who I've brought along."

Amelia's cheeks burned bright red. "Why, hello, Mr. Haynes. What a pleasure to see you."

Ben's gaze locked with Amelia's, and he sat next to her. "I can't believe my good fortune in finding you dining here today." They had to keep up the front in case any friends of the Carlyles happened to be nearby. Everything about this meeting must look like an accident or happy coincidence instead of a well-planned scheme.

They exchanged pleasantries during the meal, but Ben's heart raced. He so wanted to be alone with Amelia so they could talk about their situation.

Mary Beth loved the breads and even went so far as to ask the waiter for a third round of their plump dinner rolls. Finally the meal ended. As they gathered their belongings to head outside, Amelia said, "I have a bit of Christmas shopping I'd like to do. Would you care to walk along with us?"

"I'd be delighted, Miss Haynes." Andrew winked at him and grasped Mary Beth's arm to steer her out to the street.

They sauntered along for a few minutes before Amelia spotted a book shop. "Oh, I must stop in there. There's a book I want to get Papa for Christmas, and this shop should have it."

Mary Beth turned to Andrew. "The dress shop Grandmama uses is right near Faneuil Hall. I need to pick up some things she ordered, so we'll meet you over there."

They ambled across the street. Ben bowed to Amelia and opened the book shop door for her. "After you, Miss Haynes." At least he was close to her though not alone. He had to find a place where they could talk.

She grabbed up a children's book. "Oh, look, it's a book about Santa Claus, *The Night Before Christmas*. I'm getting this for Billy and will read it to him tonight. He was worried at breakfast that Santa Claus wouldn't find him here in Boston."

"He'll love the story. Thank you for thinking of him. I

trust you told him that Santa would find him here?" Just like Billy to worry about something like that. He was on the verge of not believing anymore, but he needed this Christmas.

"Oh, I did." She hurried to another display. "Here's the book I want for Papa." She headed for the store clerk. "I won't be but a minute."

He stood back and observed as she paid for her purchases. She wore a jaunty black hat trimmed in blue feathers and bows. Now where did they find a bird that color of blue? It sat atop her golden brown hair and dipped to one side. Two perfect curls lay against her neck, dangling from the rest of her upswept hair. Her smile for the clerk warmed his heart. He could tell she enjoyed talking with people of all backgrounds.

She completed her transaction and headed for him. "Now I have almost all my Christmas gifts purchased. Let's find a place to sit and chat."

That's exactly what he had in mind. They walked a few blocks until they came upon a place where they could sit and enjoy something warm to drink. As they settled into place with cups of cocoa in front of them, all the things he wanted to say became a jumbled puzzle in his mind. He tried to sort the pieces, but none would fit together the way he wanted.

Amelia clasped her hands in her lap and chewed the corner of her lip. "I've waited since last Thursday to have time with you, and now that we're here, everything I wanted to talk about has vanished from my brain. All I can think about is that you'll be leaving to go back to Kansas soon and I have no idea when I'll see you again."

He extended his hands across the table. "Here, put your hands in mine. I'm the same way. The words I'd worked out are all out of place now. All I know is that I want to be with you."

She reached out and let him grasp her hands. "This is so hard. My heart aches when we're apart, and my brain turns to mush when we're together."

"I feel the same. Your father wants you to marry well and stay here close to him and your mother. I can understand that. I don't particularly want Mary Beth to marry Andrew and stay here in Boston, but if that's what she wants to do, she will. It will hurt Ma and Pa to have her so far away, but they know they can't stand in the way of her happiness." If only Mr. Carlyle could realize the same for Amelia.

The noise of the other patrons rose around them with laughter and joy filling the air. Glasses clinked as people toasted each other and enjoyed the afternoon. They sat in silence for a few minutes letting the sounds envelop them in a cocoon of frustration and despair.

Amelia's eyes glistened with moisture. "I don't see any hope for us, Ben. Philip invited me to a Christmas party, and I had to accept. Mary Beth will be there because it's at Andrew's home."

"Yes, I know about it as I was invited too, but unfortunately I need to leave before then. Gideon and I will return to the ranch, where we're needed for the time being. We will be back for Christmas, but of course with Grandpapa's health, we have no way of knowing what will happen between now and then." His grandfather lay dying, and here he was talking of going to a party. Most likely he wouldn't live until Christmas, and how hard that would be on Grandmama, who loved the holiday season. No one had even discussed decorating the house or getting a tree as yet.

"I'm worried about Billy and Grace Ann," he said. "Christmas has always been special to them, and now things are in such disarray, I'm not sure Ma or Pa have had time to think about what to do for them."

"I got that impression this morning at breakfast. We invited them to stay with us for Christmas Eve, but I know they want to be with your mother and father."

He squeezed her hands. "Let's take what happens one day at a time. I love you, and that will not change, but circumstances will, especially if Grandpapa dies. As long as I know your love for me holds true and strong, I can handle your father's objections. I firmly believe the Lord is going to work things out for us just as He did for my parents."

"It will, Ben, oh, it will."

No matter what happened in the days and weeks ahead, if they fully relied on God and were obedient to His will, their problems would take care of themselves. When he returned to Kansas, he would make plans hoping for the best, and God would take care of the results.

Chapter 16

*A*melia loved the church services on the Sunday before Christmas. The words from the prophet Isaiah brought comfort to her soul, especially this Christmas Eve Sunday. Jesus was indeed her Wonderful Counselor, and she would need all the guidance He could give in the weeks ahead.

The glow from all the candles situated around the church added to the beauty of the Scriptures, and the red bows and greenery that decked the railings around the choir loft and pulpit added to the gaiety of the season. Peace and joy filled the faces of those around her, and Amelia sent up a prayer of thanks for the blessings she'd received the past year, especially in meeting Ben. The voices of the congregation had risen to sing the carols of Christmas, and Amelia had joined in with gusto as they sang "Joy to the World."

The Haynes family sat in their customary pew without Ben and Gideon, who would arrive by train later this afternoon to spend the holiday. Mary Beth had slipped her another note from Ben, and it all but burned a hole in Amelia's pocket.

He'd already sent one in which he described the land he'd chosen for a house. She pictured the stream and old mill in her mind and prayed she would sometime soon see it in person. She had no idea what the country looked like really and had seen it only through Ben's and Mary Beth's eyes. What if Mama was right, and it wasn't really a place she would want to live, even with Ben there? More often in the past week, those doubts had crept into her head and tried to settle in, but so far she'd been able to sweep them out.

Once again his message came to mind. Not only did she have his letter to savor in the quiet of the afternoon after dinner, but she also had his arrival to anticipate. Mr. Haynes had rallied enough that he wanted to spend Christmas with his family. All the aunts, uncles, and cousins would join Ben's family for the celebration this night. She would miss having Billy and Grace Ann at her house, but Christmas meant families being together, and that's where those two belonged.

Amanda and Charles, along with Grandma and Grandpa Carlyle, would be at the house later today and Christmas Day, but Amelia still longed to be with Ben. If the Lord was willing, they'd have the next Christmas and all the Christmases after together.

The service ended, and Amelia joined her parents as they greeted Clara and Mr. and Mrs. Haynes. Mary Beth pulled her aside. "Andrew is planning to ask Ma and Pa for my hand in marriage tonight!"

Amelia stifled a squeal of delight and grasped Mary

Beth's hands. "That's wonderful! I knew it would happen soon. I'm so happy for you."

"Don't say a word to anyone yet. He has his grandmother's ring he will give to me on Christmas Day. This is where you come in. We're going to take a carriage ride to celebrate our betrothal on Tuesday. Andrew is going to ask your father to allow you to come with us. Ben will be along too. That way you can be with him."

Her short, clipped sentences spoke of her haste to impart the message before their parents called them away. Amelia hugged her. "I'll be ready. Surely Papa can't refuse such a request from Andrew. He wouldn't do anything to offend a Farnsworth."

Mama called for her to come, and she squeezed Mary Beth's hand before joining her parents. Her heart now rang with as much joy as the carols they'd sung earlier. What a blessed Christmas this would be.

When they arrived home, the most delicious aromas filled the house. Lettie must have been cooking all night to have this ready for the family after church. Amelia's nose detected ham with a honey glaze, sweet potatoes, and the cinnamon aroma of apple pie. Her stomach rumbled in anticipation, and she rushed upstairs to freshen up before the meal.

Dinner didn't disappoint any of them. Grandma and Grandpa complimented Lettie, and Grandpa asked for seconds. After dinner Amanda joined Amelia upstairs in her bedroom while the men retired to Papa's study and Mama entertained Grandma. Amelia hugged her sister. "We've had so little opportunity to visit since your wedding."

"Yes, Mama and Mother Bishop keep me busy with

social obligations, and you've been involved with all the social events of coming out." Amanda arranged her bustle and sat on one of the purple velvet boudoir chairs in the room.

Amelia sat in the matching chair on the other side of a cherry side table. "You look so happy. I can tell Charles dotes on you. Every time we're around you two, he jumps at your beck and call."

"Married life has been wonderful, although some parts of it would be hard to bear if I did not love him so immensely." She leaned toward Amelia. "I do hope you find a love like Charles and I have. It makes a world of difference despite what others may tell you."

"I think I have."

"Oh, is it Philip Barlow? What a catch he would be."

Amelia's cheeks burned, and she lowered her head to escape detection. "I know he would be, but Benjamin Haynes has captured my heart."

Her sister gasped. "Benjamin Haynes?"

"Yes, and he feels the same about me." Amelia grasped her hands and twisted her fingers together.

Amanda knelt beside her. "Oh, my, what does Papa think? With Benjamin living in Kansas now, I'm sure he's opposed."

"He is, and I don't want to be disobedient, but I love Ben with all my heart. We renewed our friendship at your wedding, and our love has grown since then." She blinked back tears. "Oh, Amanda, I don't know what to do. Papa and Mama expect me to marry Philip or some other suitable man from Boston, but I just can't."

"You do have a problem. Have you told Mama of your feelings?"

"Yes, but she feels the same as Papa. When I'm with Philip, I feel nothing but friendship, but with Ben, I want to spend every moment with him and share my thoughts with him. He talks of building us a house in Kansas where we would live on land he will own a share of next year. We've been writing to each other."

"I see, and I suppose Papa knows nothing about the letters."

"No, because they come through Mary Beth." So far no one had asked her about Ben or hearing from him, and she had volunteered nothing. "I think Papa believes I'm interested in Philip now and have forgotten Ben, but Mama knows differently, and I'm afraid she'll tell Papa."

So far neither Maeleen nor Mama had said anything, or Papa would surely have issued an ultimatum now that Ben was back in Boston. She bit her lip as Amanda began to pace across the room and back.

"This is a dilemma. I'm sorry Papa disapproves. If I didn't love Charles so much, I'd tell you to forget Benjamin and concentrate on Philip. If you and Ben are meant to be, somehow it will work out." She narrowed her eyes and furrowed her brow in the way she did as a child when thinking or developing a plan.

Hope rose in Amelia's heart. That look was quite familiar. Many times Amanda had come up with a solution to get Amelia out of trouble. Surely this time would be no different.

She stopped her pacing in front of Amelia. "I can't think of anything yet, but I'll discuss it with Charles. We'll come up with something we can say to Papa or find a way for you and Ben to see each other while he's here."

Amelia stood and hugged her sister. "I knew you would help me. Between you and Mary Beth, a solution will be found." Amanda had not let her down. Her love and loyalty still held despite her marriage and being away from the family.

Amanda laughed. "Oh, so Mary Beth is in on this too. I understand that Andrew Farnsworth may be asking for her hand in marriage."

Boston might be a large city, but their social circle was like a small town and everyone knew everyone else's business. Amelia shook her head. "I suppose everyone knows about it. Andrew is speaking to Mr. Haynes today, and Mary Beth truly loves him."

Amanda clapped her hands. "That is wonderful. Mrs. Farnsworth and Mother Bishop serve on many of the same committees, so Mary Beth and I will have great fun together. I am surprised, however, that her parents are willing to let her stay in Boston."

"I'm not. I think they understand her situation and Ben's even more because they left home so many years ago to travel to Kansas and become ranchers."

Amanda tapped her lips with her forefinger. "I'm going to speak with Grandma. Being Papa's mother, I imagine she still has some influence over him, and from what I've gathered in conversations I had with her when Charles courted me, she is quite the romanticist herself. I'll speak with her tonight after our family gathering."

"Oh, I hadn't thought of that. She'd be perfect to help Papa and Mama to understand." Once again Amanda had come through with a solution. Although it wouldn't completely resolve the problem, it might be enough of an influence to orchestrate some changes in attitude and opinion.

Ben gazed at his grandfather seated in the wingback chair by the fireplace. Although pale and somewhat thinner, he looked much better than he had before Ben had left a few weeks ago. Still, one could tell by the man's eyes and shaky hands that he was not well. Thankful that Grandpapa could enjoy Christmas with them, Ben bent on one knee to give the man a hug.

"I'm so glad you feel well enough to be downstairs to enjoy Christmas Eve with us. We've all been so worried about you."

A wrinkled, blue-veined hand grasped Ben's. "I wouldn't think of missing Christmas with my youngest son and his family here. It's so rare that you're home for the holiday, so this is a treat."

His voice, though low, still had a strong resonance to it that reminded Ben of his younger days when Grandpapa laughed and played with Ben and his cousins. He'd showed them how to whistle through their fingers, much to the chagrin of their mothers, and he'd taught them all to play chess.

Ben stood when his father and Andrew entered the room. They'd been in Grandpapa's study, and from the smile of joy on Andrew's face, the meeting had been successful. Pa clapped his hands for attention.

"Everyone, Mary Beth and Andrew have an

151

announcement to make." He grinned broadly and nodded for Mary Beth to join Andrew.

Andrew grasped her hand in his and swallowed. "I would like to announce that Mary Beth and I plan to marry. Mr. Haynes has given us his blessings, and we pray the rest of you will also."

Aunt Clara squealed, and Grandmama muttered something about it being time he declared himself. Ben chuckled. Nothing escaped Grandmama's attention. As busy as she'd been taking care of Grandpapa, she'd still been aware of what was going on in her family. She'd already told him what a wonderful girl she thought Amelia was and wished him success in winning her father's approval. With Ma, Clara, and Grandmama all praying for him and Amelia, God had to hear and answer with a positive response.

Ma gathered everyone except Grandpapa around the piano. He had a place of honor in a chair nearby. She began playing Christmas songs, and they all joined in the singing. Twice Ben had to retrieve Billy from beneath the tree. The eight-year-old's enthusiasm for Christmas was difficult to curb, but he'd have to wait like everyone else.

Ben noticed Mary Beth and Andrew slip away. A few minutes later they returned, and his sister wore the happiest expression on her face he'd ever seen on her. When the carol ended, she leaned over and whispered to Ma.

Ma's eyes lit up bright as the Christmas tree, and her hands flew to her mouth. Mary Beth turned around and held out her hand. "Andrew has given me his grandmother's ring for Christmas to make our betrothal official."

Grandmama, Clara, and Grace Ann all gathered around to admire the ring. Ben leaned over his youngest sister and gulped when he saw the dark blue star sapphire. He'd never be able to afford anything like that for Amelia. Grandpapa may be wealthy, but Ben was not, and he wouldn't dare ask for money to buy jewelry, even for Amelia. Whatever he gave her would be with his own money.

A few minutes later Mary Beth beckoned to him to join her and Andrew in the foyer. Andrew said his good-byes to the rest of the family and thanked them for their hospitality. Whatever his sister had to say, he hoped it would involve Amelia somehow.

Andrew and Mary Beth stood hand in hand, and Mary Beth's smile looked like a kitten lapping up cream. "Andrew and I are taking a carriage ride the day after Christmas. We want you and Amelia to go with us. Andrew will ask Mr. Carlyle's permission for her to go. We believe he'll say yes because of his respect for Andrew and Andrew's father. Ma and Aunt Clara know what we're doing, but we haven't said anything to Pa. We don't think he'd object, but he might not be highly supportive. So what do you think?"

What did he think? Anything to be with Amelia would be fine with him, especially if her father knew and consented. "It's fine...no, more than fine. It's wonderful, and I can't thank you enough for both of you being so willing to give up time together to help Amelia and me."

Mary Beth beamed up at Andrew. "We have the rest of our lives together, and anything we can do to help you and Amelia be as happy as we are is a blessing for us."

Andrew extended his hand toward Ben and grinned. "Besides, since we're going to be brothers, I thought it prudent to be on your good side."

Ben laughed and shook the offered hand. "Fine with me, and I look forward to having you as a member of our family."

He then left them to say their good-byes and returned to the parlor where Ma continued singing carols, her clear alto voice filling the room with words telling of the Savior's birth. Ben glanced around the room. With his family gathered together and a roaring fire to keep them warm, Ben experienced a peace and contentment he hadn't felt since Grandpapa's illness. No one could know what tomorrow might bring, so this night he savored the moments in this room with loved ones. God had blessed him in wonderful ways this past year, and if all went as planned, more blessings would come in the year ahead.

Chapter 17

*A*melia waited for Ben to come with Mary Beth and Andrew, her fingers tapping lightly on the lamp table. The fire on the hearth danced and swirled, its red, yellow, and gold flames matching the leaping and twirling of her heart.

Father had consented to her going out with Ben this afternoon, but the stern lines of his face told of his reluctance to grant the request. He had hesitated then nodded and gave his approval.

With Grandma and Grandpa present as well as Amanda and Charles, Papa had no choice but to say yes. Amanda had grinned and nodded her approval behind Papa. She and Charles had returned to their own home last night, and now Amelia missed her.

Grandma came into the parlor with her knitting basket. They were staying another night, and Amelia welcomed her company.

"I understand from Amanda that you care deeply for Benjamin Haynes." Grandma sat on the burgundy brocaded sofa and pulled out her knitting needles. Her glasses sat on the tip of her nose, and she peered over them at Amelia.

"Oh, I do, I do, but Papa is very much against it." She moved closer to her grandmother. As a child she had loved snuggling in Grandma's lap and listening to her stories.

"Yes, and I can understand why. Kansas is a long way from Boston, and he fears the distance will be too hard for your mother to accept." Grandma twisted yarn around the needles to make the first stitch then began forming the first row.

"I know, but she should want me to be happy with the man I love. She loves Papa like I love Ben, but I don't think either one of them is concerned with that. They only want to see me marry one of the young men here, preferably Philip Barlow, and settle down like Amanda and Charles." Only part of that rang true. Mama and Papa did want her to be happy, but they just believed that happiness could be found right here at home.

"Yes, your parents love each other and have from the beginning, as have Charles and Amanda, but often love can come later when the couple is evenly matched." She stopped the clicking needles and once again peered over her glasses at Amelia.

"My dear, if you have prayed about this, and you still feel Ben is God's plan for you, nothing will stand in the way of your happiness." Then she frowned and shook her head. "Unless that son of mine is too stubborn to see what is before his very eyes and insists on having his way."

Such an ultimatum from Papa cast a shadow over every meeting she had with Ben. It always lurked in the background and jumped to the forefront when they talked about the future. With so many people understanding her love for Ben, Papa had to come around to seeing it himself. *God, please open Papa's eyes to the love I have for Ben.*

"My dear, I believe I'll have a little talk with your mother. If she can be persuaded to see how much you care about each other, perhaps she will be able to show your father that your moving away will not be that difficult for her. Of course, I don't have much time, but I'll do what I can."

Amelia reached over and wrapped her arms around her grandmother's shoulders. "I'm so glad you're my grandma. I love you and knew you'd do something to help me."

Grandma laughed and picked up her needles. "Between you and Amanda, I don't have a chance. You girls are so dear to me. Your uncles have given me only grandsons, so you two girls have a special place in my heart."

All but the two youngest cousins had married, and one would soon add a great-grandchild to the mix. The boys had been the bane of her existence growing up, and she had longed for just one girl cousin, but now she relished the idea of being one of two girls. With Mama being an only child, the boys were the only cousins she had.

If she married Ben, she'd be in a larger family with two new sisters and two brothers, as well as all of Ben's cousins and aunts and uncles. What fun it would to be part of such a family. Then she jumped to the future and the children she and Ben would have. She loved children and wanted at least four or five of her own. The boys would all look like Ben, and the girls would look like her or Mama. The perfect family.

The butler's voice broke her daydreaming. "Miss Amelia, Mr. Haynes is here." He stepped back, and Ben stood in the doorway holding his hat in his hands.

Amelia jumped up and hurried to him. "I'm so glad you came." Grandma cleared her throat, and Amelia pulled Ben into the parlor. "Ben, you remember my grandma, Mrs. Carlyle."

"It's been awhile, but yes, I do remember meeting you." He extended his hand in greeting.

Grandma grasped his hand in hers. "Yes, it was awhile ago. I'm so sorry that you are here because your grandfather is ill. How is he this day?"

A grin spread across Ben's face. "He was with us around the tree yesterday to exchange gifts and is feeling better."

"That's good to hear. Please give my regards to your mother and father and especially to your grandmother. We haven't had time to visit like we once did." She gathered up her knitting and stood. "I know you two must be getting along. I'm going upstairs for a bit of a nap before supper." She kissed Amelia's cheek. "Have a wonderful afternoon, my dear."

When she was gone, Ben offered his arm to Amelia. "Are you ready? Andrew and Mary Beth are already in the carriage."

"Oh, my, they must be getting cold. Let me get my coat." She stepped into the hallway where Murphy held her coat ready. She glanced back to the study and then toward the library, but she found no sign of her parents. That was strange, but perhaps they didn't know Ben had arrived and that she was leaving with him. Best not to call them in.

She pushed her arms into the sleeves of the coat Ben now held. "Murphy, will you tell Mama and Papa that I'll be home before evening?"

He nodded and handed Amelia her scarf and glove. "I will see that they know, Miss Amelia."

"Thank you." She reached for the hat she'd brought downstairs earlier and set it atop her upswept hair. After securing it with pins, she grinned up at Ben. "I'm all set now." What a glorious afternoon this would be. Joy over-flowed in her heart and down to her feet, and she longed to hop and skip out to the carriage.

Ben liked seeing Amelia happy, and he wished to see her in the same spirits more often. He helped her into the carriage where she settled into the seat opposite his sister and Andrew.

Mary Beth leaned forward. "I'm so glad your father allowed you to come with us. We're going to Andrew's home for a while, but you and Ben can use the carriage for a ride. The driver knows when to be back for us."

Amelia's mouth dropped open at the revelation, and she turned to face Ben. "Did you know about this?"

"Not until we were on the way to pick you up. My sister and Andrew wish everyone to be happy like they are." He'd scolded Mary Beth because of what Mr. Carlyle might say if he learned Amelia had been alone with Ben for the afternoon.

"We explained to my mother, and she's such a romantic that she suggested the carriage ride for the two of you, and if your father objects, she's ready to tell him it was her fault." Andrew held Mary Beth's hand tight in his, and his eyes held hers with a gaze that spoke of their love.

Amelia relaxed against the back of the seat. "That's amazing. I can't believe so many people know about Ben and me."

Mary Beth grinned and held out her hand. "Well, they do, and someday you'll have a ring like this to declare that love."

Amelia squealed, grasped Mary Beth's hand, and admired the deep blue sapphire. "It's gorgeous."

Ben sucked in his breath. If Amelia expected something like that from him, he'd have to disappoint her, and that he didn't want to do. Somehow he'd have to raise the money to buy her something when they could share their love openly without any secrets.

The carriage stopped, and Andrew stepped down to assist Mary Beth. "Have fun, you two, and we'll see you back here when it's time." He closed the carriage door and tipped his hat to the driver. A few seconds later the carriage once again moved down the road.

At first neither one spoke, and the clip-clop of the horse's hooves kept time with the beating of his heart. He moistened his lips and reached for Amelia's hand. "Why is it that when we're finally alone, I can never remember the words I want to say? I'm as tongue-tied as a schoolboy caught in mischief in the classroom."

"I'm the same way, and there's so much I want to know about you and the ranch. You know about my life here, but I know very little about yours."

That would be a boring subject for her, but he loved to talk about the ranch. "We have quite a few acres of land that are flat prairie, but we also have stands of trees that are actually small forests. We have a creek on the west side and the stream with the mill on the northeast section where most of the trees are."

"Oh, yes. You told me about the mill in one of your letters, and that it's where you want to put a house. I've thought about that so often."

"I have the plans all set in my mind." He described what he wanted to build and how. She listened with such interest that he wished the place was ready for them now. If they came for a visit in the spring, he would have part of it built and ready to show her.

He grasped her hands. "I'll draw out the plans and send them to you, so you can get an idea of how the house will look. Ma and Pa have promised to invite your parents to come to Kansas next spring, but with Grandpapa's health so uncertain, they haven't done anything about it yet."

"I can't wait to get there. Springtime is a lovely time here in Boston with the trees budding out and flowers blooming. What is it like in Kansas?"

How could he adequately describe the beauty of springtime on the prairie? "It's a beautiful season with all the wildflowers bursting forth in an expanse of color you have to see to believe. The water in the creek and the stream stay icy cold until late in the season when the sun grows warmer, and then the water is warm and wonderful for wading."

"Hmm, I can't wait to see them, but what about the cattle and the horses?"

Ben laughed. "Oh, we have plenty of those. We have a lot of horses for our trail drives to cattle market. Extra horses, a remuda, are taken along, so we rest them and alternate which ones we ride and work. Of course, Blackie is my favorite and the one I ride most of the time, but even he needs a rest from the work of riding herd on a drive."

The blank expression on her face revealed her lack of knowledge and understanding of what he talked about. "You'll see and understand once you have an opportunity to visit and ride around with me."

"That I look forward to with all my heart. Is your house large enough for us to stay with you, or will we have to stay in a hotel in Sweetwater Springs?"

"We have room at the house. Gideon, Billy, and I will most likely move out to the bunkhouse so your parents can have our room, and you will occupy Mary Beth's room. Grace Ann will go in with Clara." He'd already planned to move to the bunkhouse in the spring anyway, and Gideon and Billy would leap at the chance to be out with the cowboys.

"Sounds like you have it all planned out."

Heat rose in Ben's cheeks. "As a matter of fact, I happened to overhear Ma and Clara discussing the room arrangements one afternoon. They're looking forward to your visit too."

"If Papa says no at first, I have Grandma and Amanda on my side. Maybe by then Mama will be more in favor of the trip too."

Two more allies to plead their case meant a better chance for Amelia and him in the future. Desire to wrap her in his arms and kiss her rose with a warmth that flooded his heart. He released her hands and clenched his hands into fists to fight off the waves of emotion. She furrowed her brow and squinted at him.

"Did I say something wrong?"

"No, but what I would like to do now would not be proper or in our best interests."

She grinned. "Benjamin Haynes, if you want to kiss me, please do. I can't stand it another minute." Amelia placed her hands at the back of his neck.

He couldn't resist that temptation, and after all, she'd given her permission. He bent his head toward hers and settled his lips on hers. They tasted as sweet and were as soft as he'd imagined, and her response awakened all his senses. He pressed harder.

Suddenly the carriage stopped, and Ben jerked back. He moved away from Amelia and glanced out the window. They had returned to the Farnsworths' home, and Mary Beth stood with Andrew on the porch waiting for them. The couple waved and hurried down the steps.

Amelia fussed with her skirt, and Ben tugged at his collar. That was close. Mary Beth and Andrew would probably be horrified if they knew, and for certain Mr. Carlyle would string him up like a side of beef. One thing for sure, he'd have to be mighty careful being alone with Amelia in the future.

Chapter 18

$\mathcal{A}$melia sat in her room, her heart breaking for Ben and all the Haynes family. Only a short while ago a messenger had delivered a note saying that the elder Mr. Haynes had passed away peacefully during the night, only three days after Christmas. Ben loved his grandpapa, as had Mary Beth. Both had expressed their gratitude that he had lived to see and enjoy Christmas with all his family present.

Moisture trickled down the windows like tears matching the ones on Amelia's cheeks. She stared out at the bleak winter day and shivered. New snow had fallen during the night and now covered the gardens below with a blanket of white. Low-hanging clouds promised more of the same later today. The bitter cold of winter made the death even more difficult to bear.

Plans made with Mary Beth and Ben for an outing today would not take place, and most likely she wouldn't see either of them until the funeral unless Mama and Papa decided to pay the family a visit and offer condolences.

Since Mama and Mrs. Haynes were such good friends, that would probably happen, and they would take her along because of Mary Beth.

She strode over to the armoire and searched through her dresses for something suitable to wear. Certainly the red silk dress she now wore would not be appropriate. Amelia pulled out a dark blue wool garment she'd worn when she and Ben went to the bookstore. This would a good choice, especially since it had little adornment. She laid it across the bed in anticipation of Mama coming to tell her they were going to visit the Haynes's home.

The noon meal had been solemn with Mama and Papa discussing the merits of the late Mr. Haynes. Papa admired his business acumen and his strong Christian faith. He'd been an elder at their church for many years and had served on various committees. The church would miss him, but they would find someone to replace him. Not so with the family. Grandpapa Haynes had been a powerful influence, and the success of his three sons proved his faithful attention to their needs.

She plopped back in her chair and gazed about her room. When she and Mama had redone it two years ago, the yellow and lavender floral wallpaper had been her first choice, and she still loved it. It gave her room the feel of sunshine and flowers all year round. The white painted furniture had been a little too feminine for her taste, but after it had been put in place, she had grown to love it.

What would it be like to live in Kansas? What kind of home would Ben have for them? Questions swayed and tossed like tree limbs in a summer storm. She'd miss this room and the luxuries she had, but her spirit of adventure called to her and told her she'd love the Midwest. For that matter, she'd love anywhere Ben took her to live.

As a rancher's wife she'd have many different things to do that she didn't do now. She sat up straight in her chair. One of those would be cooking, and what she knew about cooking wouldn't fill the head of a dressmaker's pin. Amelia chewed her lip. One thing she'd never considered until this minute was what she'd be expected to do as Ben's wife. She'd been so caught up in romance, she had lost sight of reality.

Ben had an appetite and talked about what a great cook his ma was. How could she live up to that? Only one thing to do—she had to learn to cook now so she wouldn't disappoint him later. Lettie would help her, and Mary Beth could tell her other things she needed to learn.

She scampered down the stairway, being careful not to make noise and arouse her parents, who had retired to their own room after the noon meal. Papa always took off from his work the week of Christmas, so having him home on a weekday was unusual but rather nice. Would Ben be home during the day or out on the range all the time? No matter, he still had to eat when he came home, and she wanted to feed him good, hearty meals.

Amelia followed the wonderful aromas emanating from the kitchen and found Lettie stirring something that smelled delicious. She glanced up at Amelia. "Mercy, child, what are you doing down here at this time of day? Supper won't be ready for several hours."

"It just occurred to me that I don't know a thing about cooking, and I've decided I want to learn." Lettie would think that curious since there was no need for Amelia to know anything about cooking. She'd have to come up with a good excuse. Why hadn't she thought of that before approaching Lettie?

"Now that's an odd request if ever I heard one. What makes ye want to cook, child? Isn't my cooking good enough for you?"

"Oh, yes, Lettie. It's wonderful, and that's why I wanted to learn from you."

Lettie stopped stirring the pot on the stove and planted one hand on her hip. The other hand held the ladle aloft, its contents dripping back into the pot. "And what do ye want to learn to cook? Cakes and pastries?"

"No, I mean yes, but that's not all." Amelia moved to the stove and sniffed. "What is this you're making? Can I make it?"

Lettie laughed. "'Tis an easy dish to make. It's stew for Toby, Maeleen, and Mr. Murphy's supper."

"Well, it smells delicious. Why haven't you ever served it to us?" She couldn't remember ever having anything like this before. Soup they ate numerous times, but not stew. She peeked over the rim of the pot and found carrots, potatoes, celery, and chunks of meat floating in a mass of thick, dark red liquid.

Lettie placed the lid back on the pot and laid down the spoon. "Come over here and tell me what's really on your mind."

Amelia winced. She had to come up with an excuse fast. Lettie motioned for Amelia to sit down and then sat across the table. "Would I be right to assume this notion of cooking has something to do with a young man from Kansas?"

Heat burned in Amelia's cheeks. Had Lettie overheard her conversations with Papa or Mama? Had Maeleen told her mother about Amelia's interest in Ben? Whatever the reason, she now must tell the truth.

"Yes, but how did you know?"

"Oh, I hear more than ye think I might." Lettie smiled and leaned on the table. "Ye know there's more to being a wife than cooking, don't ye? There's laundry to do, beds to make, furniture and floors to keep clean, and mending."

Amelia's mouth dropped open. "I...I hadn't thought about all that." Those chores were always done where she didn't see what was going on. How would she ever learn to be a rancher's wife? After she completed breakfast, her bed was always made and her clothes appeared clean and fresh in her wardrobe. A few times she'd seen Maeleen dusting or sweeping, but it hadn't occurred to Amelia that she might have to do that someday.

Lettie sat back in her chair and pursed her mouth. "Your grandmother and I had a little chat about the situation. He's a fine young man, but I can understand your parents' objections."

"That doesn't matter...well, yes, it does, but I plan on marrying Ben someday even if Papa never comes around to liking it." When had she made that decision? At this precise moment, and it was true. Someday they would be married, no matter how long it took to work it out.

"Brave words, lassie; if ye have prayed about it and ye feel the Lord leading ye, then that's what will be done. Just be sure 'tis His bidding and not ye own leading ye be following."

Amelia chewed her lip. She had prayed, but had she

truly listened to what God told her to do? She always prayed about things, especially big decisions, but this one time she wanted a specific answer.

"I'll teach ye the things ye need to know, but what will your mum be thinking about ye learning such things?"

"I don't know, but I must learn. I'll come up with some excuse." What that would be certainly wasn't clear now, but surely a reason to give her mother would come. So much to learn and so much to do in the days ahead. She prayed she'd be up to it.

Ben grabbed Billy before he headed out their bedroom door. "Stay and play quietly here for the afternoon. Grandmama is resting." He'd heard her in the night taking care of Grandpapa and her keening wail when he died. Ma and Pa and he and Mary Beth joined her along with Aunt Clara. He'd never forget the sight of his grandfather lying on the bed. He wore the most peaceful expression ever seen. Grandpapa had gone home to Jesus.

That reassurance helped keep his tears at bay. He had taken charge of Billy and Gideon, and Mary Beth claimed Grace Ann. His parents, Grandmama, and Clara had many decisions to make in the next few days. Even now Pa was with his brothers and Clara in the study as they planned what to do for the funeral.

Ma and her sisters-in-law had taken over the running of the household during this time, but thankfully his younger cousins had stayed at home under the charge of their older siblings. This was no time for a lot of running and playing in the house.

Perhaps he could take Billy and Grace Ann to Aunt Helen's house where they could play and not worry about trying to keep quiet. After making sure Billy was engaged in play that would keep him busy for a while, Ben made his way downstairs to find his mother. She sat at the dining table with his two aunts. Talk of refreshments, meals, and condolences reached his ears. They must be planning what to serve when people came to pay their respects. He'd wait and speak with Ma later. Their black dresses were a somber reminder of what had happened during the night.

Two servants were sent about the house with black ribbon to adorn the mirrors, newel posts, and doors as a sign of mourning for the household. One would be placed outside on the front door to inform neighbors of a death in the family.

He left the ladies to their task without disturbing them and strolled into the library to peruse the books on the shelves. Reading was one of his favorite pastimes, but he had very little time at the ranch to enjoy books. He found a copy of *Oliver Twist* and removed it to take upstairs and read while he watched Billy. The story of the orphan boy and the gang of little thieves had fascinated him the first time he'd read it.

Billy played with some blocks by the fireplace. Grace Ann must be with Mary Beth elsewhere in the house. Billy's eyes drooped as he fought sleep. His lids closed then opened wide, then closed again. Ben swooped him up from the floor and carried him to his bed.

Billy opened his eyes, but his head lolled on Ben's shoulder. "I'm not sleepy. Want to play."

"Let's just rest a bit. I'm tired from being up so much

last night, so you must be too." Ben blinked his own eyes. A little sleep wouldn't hurt either one of them. Billy didn't complain again and curled up on the bed with one hand resting under his cheek. His dark brown curls, so like Ben's, tumbled about his forehead. Ben pulled the cover up over the boy's shoulder and tip-toed from the room.

A noise and voices in the foyer below caught his attention. He leaned over the stair railing, and his heart jumped to his throat. Amelia stood below with her parents and his ma. He bounded down the stairs, his steps light as a feather.

"Good afternoon, Mr. and Mrs. Carlyle. Amelia." He stopped a few feet from her, but noticed the pink in her cheeks as she smiled and ducked her head.

Ma looped her arm through his. "Come into the parlor. Matthew and Clara will be in shortly. They're finishing up business with his brothers. Mother Haynes is resting. The long night was quite difficult for her."

Ben followed them into the parlor, staying as close to Amelia as he could without calling attention to himself. His two aunts rose to greet the guests, and they all settled down to visit.

Mrs. Carlyle clasped her hands in her lap. "We're so sorry to learn of Mr. Haynes's passing. If there's anything we can do to help, you must let us know."

Ma responded, but the words were lost on Ben. He had eyes only for Amelia. She glanced at him twice, but her cheeks again turned red as she jerked her gaze away from him. One of the servant girls brought in a tea tray, and Ma served her guests. Ben took one of the raisin scones and munched on it, his eyes still focused on Amelia.

When the men and Clara came in to join them, Ma stood then turned to Ben. "Son, why don't you take Amelia and find Mary Beth? I'm sure she will want to visit with her friend."

Ben gulped. "Yes, ma'am. I believe she's upstairs. I'll go get her." He offered his arm to Amelia. "We can go into the music room. Pa lit the logs there, and it will be nice and warm."

She smiled up at him. "I'd be delighted."

Once out of earshot of the others, Ben stopped and grasped both her hands in his. "I know we don't have much time alone, but I'm so glad to see you."

"Oh, Ben, I'm sorry about your grandfather. I know this must be a difficult time for you as you loved him so much."

"Yes, it is, and I will miss him. The comforting part is that he possessed a strong Christian faith and is in heaven today. Someday I'll get to see him again, and that's a blessing." His grandfather's death had brought home to him the fact of life's uncertainty and the inevitability of death.

"We'll be leaving on the train for home on Tuesday. Pa and Aunt Clara are staying here to finish taking care of Grandpapa's estate." He squeezed her hands. "I so wish you were coming with me, but Kansas is not the place you need to be right now. Once we work things out with your father, then we can plan for it."

"I so look forward to that time. We have so many who are willing to speak up for us and support us that I know God is working it all out."

She gazed up at him with so much love in her eyes that

all he wanted to do was kiss her and reassure her that he believed that too. Not here though, where at any moment someone could come in and see them. No, he'd wait until they were truly alone.

"I must go and find Mary Beth now. I won't be but a minute." He raised her hands to his lips and kissed them. "Until we can have more privacy." He grinned at her blushing cheeks and turned to head upstairs and find Mary Beth. In just a few days he'd be a thousand miles away from her. What would they do if she couldn't come to Kansas in the spring?

Chapter 19

*A*fter church on Sunday, Mama stopped to talk with Mrs. Haynes for a few moments. Amelia searched the area and found Ben picking Billy up from the floor. The boy squirmed and tried to get loose, but Ben held firm. When he set his square jaw and scowled at his brother, the boy quieted immediately. Ben would make a wonderful father.

He grinned when he saw her and headed her way. His usually well-groomed hair curled about his forehead, and his brown eyes sparkled. Even in his suit, his tanned face and broad shoulders spoke of his time in the sun roping and herding cattle.

He stopped by her side and set Billy back to the floor, but issued a warning to stay close by and not run in the church. Billy shrugged and went to stand by Mary Beth. Ben shook his head. "That little boy can find more to get into than I ever did."

"He was quite well behaved at our house." Not

completely the truth, but he hadn't really been disobedient or rude, just a little rambunctious.

"I'm glad to hear that. But enough about my brother, I have something to give you." He extracted a folded piece of paper from his jacket pocket and pressed it into her palm. "This is the house plan I told you about. Please take it and tell me what you think. It's really rough, but I think you'll get the idea."

She started to open it, but his hand stopped her. "No, wait until you're alone. I don't want your pa to get suspicious of our talking right now."

"All right, but I'm really curious to see what you've drawn." She moistened her lips and swallowed her fear. "Um, I have asked Lettie to teach me how to cook and to do other household chores. I don't want you to find I have no skills at all and not want to marry me."

Ben laughed. "That's something I'd like to see. Your domestic skills hadn't really entered my mind, but I know you'll do well at whatever you attempt to learn." He glanced over her shoulder. "Your mother is looking this way, and her expression is very strange."

"What do you mean?" She so wanted to turn around and see, but Mama might call her away. Besides, she didn't want to be rude.

"I don't know for sure. It's not a frown of disapproval, but she's not smiling either. It's more of contemplative look, as though she's studying us."

"Oh, dear, then I better go to her now. If she studies too closely, she'll see more than she needs to right now." Amelia stepped back and spoke loud enough for Mama to hear. "Thank you for the good time last Tuesday. I look forward to seeing you the next time you're in Boston." She'd be thinking of the kiss of that afternoon and hoping for one if and when she saw him again.

He nodded and grasped Billy's shoulder to lead him to their mother, who talked with Mary Beth and Andrew. The wedding. Amelia hadn't considered what this might do to their plans. She'd have to wait beyond June now and possibly into the fall. That also meant she and Ben would also have to wait at least that long, but then again, maybe the mourning time wasn't as long for men.

The funeral yesterday had not been the sad and somber affair she'd expected. The preacher had extolled Mr. Haynes's contributions to the church and his generosity throughout the city. He told the family that grief was a natural part of human emotion, but they could rejoice in their grief that their loved one was in heaven.

A soloist had sung an arrangement of "Amazing Grace," and the congregation sang "Praise to the Lord, the Almighty." The older Mrs. Haynes had such a peaceful look on her face. A shiver ran up and down her back. Someday her grandpa and grandma would have a service like that. She shook off that thought and looked for her parents.

Papa finished speaking with the reverend, and Mother grasped his arm. They headed for the doors, and Amelia scurried to follow them. Once in the carriage Papa said, "Your mother and I are going to the Farnsworth home for dinner tonight. It will be just adults, no young people. We don't like leaving you alone on New Year's Eve, but I'm sure you will find something to occupy your time. Too bad the Barlows are out of the city for the holidays, or you could enjoy the evening with him."

Just as well Philip wasn't here. Their last time together hadn't gone well. "Yes, sir, I will." She would, but if she'd known sooner, she could have made arrangements with Mary Beth to be at her house tonight. No, that would be intruding on precious family time since Mrs. Haynes and the children were leaving so soon. She had no real reason for going there except for the fact she desperately wanted to see Ben one last time.

Mama and Papa talked quietly to each other and left Amelia to her own thoughts. Ben filled her mind with his smiling face and dancing eyes. The paper he'd given her crackled in her velvet handbag. She'd forgotten it was there. That would be something to look forward to seeing.

Mama spoke again. "Amelia, dear, we said our good-byes to Elizabeth Haynes this morning. We don't plan to be at the station to see them off this time around. They need the time together. Mr. Haynes and his sister will remain here until the estate is settled. They're hoping it will take only a few weeks so they can get back to Kansas."

"I understand." Her hopes dashed against rocks of disappointment. She had so hoped to see Ben that one last time before he left. Now she feared they had seen each other for the last time for a very long time.

Then her hopes rose again. Tomorrow was New Year's Day. There had to be a way for her to see Ben again. Perhaps Mary Beth and Andrew would come through for them once again, but with Mary Beth staying here, would they have a good reason to visit?

After Sunday dinner, Papa dismissed the servants for the rest of the day. As soon as their chores were completed, they were off to celebrate the ringing in of the New Year with their friends. That meant Amelia would be all alone this evening. Now it loomed even longer and lonelier than it had before.

Amelia hurried up to her room and closed the door. She flung herself across her bed and wept. How long would it be before she saw Ben again? After a good cry, she sat up and spotted her handbag on her dressing table. She leaped across the floor and grabbed it. She had forgotten the paper Ben had given her.

She retrieved the paper and sat by the window. She spread the paper on the table by her chair and perused it. A bunch of squares and rectangles stared back at her. What did they mean? She looked more closely and found writing in the designs. One rectangle had "FRONT PARLOR" written on it and another square had "BEDROOM" on it. Her heart fluttered and her hands shook.

Upon closer inspection, she found the plan to have two bedrooms and a storeroom in the back with a parlor, a dining area, and a kitchen across the front. He had drawn a porch that ran the length of the front of the house with plenty of room for chairs and a swing for afternoon or evening sitting.

She twirled about the room holding the plans to her chest. This was the house where she would live with Ben. She stopped in front of the armoire and unbuttoned the thick wool top she'd worn to church. Time to slip into something much more comfortable if she were to be alone all evening.

After shedding the skirt with its cumbersome bustle, she donned a simple shirtwaist and plain plaid skirt. This was attire for wearing around the house and not out in public.

Amelia much preferred this style of dress for her wardrobe, but Mama insisted on the latest fashions when in public. She removed the pins from her hair and let it fall about her shoulders. A good brushing brought out the shine, and she tied it back with a green ribbon. Now, that was much more comfortable. She then lit the lamp to shed more light in the room and sat by its glow to study the floor plan.

It was a perfect house. Soon as she learned the basics of housekeeping, she'd have no trouble at all taking care of it. Meals would be ready and waiting for Ben when he returned home from a day with the cattle. Then a cradle appeared on the scene, and she rocked it with her toe as she did the mending.

A loud knocking sounded from below. She bolted upright from the chair, but relaxed. Lettie or Murphy would answer. The knocking came again, louder this time. Then she remembered all the servants were gone. Goosebumps raised on her arms, and she tip-toed out to the landing and looked down into the foyer.

A voice accompanied the knocking this time. "Somebody, please open the door. It's Charles."

Amelia raced down and unlocked the door. When Charles burst through, his eyes opened wide in his pale face and his hair stood on end as though he'd been raking his fingers through it.

"What in the world is going on?" Amelia asked. "You scared me half to death."

He grabbed Amelia's shoulder. "It's Amanda. She's bleeding something awful. She's in the carriage, but when we passed your house, she screamed for her mother. Where is she?"

Amanda was bleeding? Had there been an accident? "Mama and Papa are at the Farnsworths for dinner. Let me get my coat and I'll come with you."

She snatched her cloak from the hall tree and ran after Charles, who had returned to the carriage. Amelia climbed inside then clapped her hand over her mouth. Amanda's skirt was covered with blood, and the stench almost overpowered her.

The coach began moving, and Amelia lurched forward. She caught herself and knelt on the floor beside her sister. "Amanda, what happened? Why are you bleeding?"

Amanda reached out to grasp Amelia's hand with hers as Charles held tight to the other one. Her face grimaced in pain, and she bit her lip.

Charles moaned and buried his face on Amanda's arm. "I don't know what to do. Please help her."

Something was terribly wrong here. Amelia gagged once again, but reached up to smooth her sister's hair from her face. "What is it? Tell me what happened."

Amanda gasped for breath as the carriage swayed and bumped along the streets. "I'm pregnant, but I started cramping really bad a little while ago, and then I suddenly started bleeding all over the place." She moaned again and lolled her head back against the seat cushion.

Her sister was pregnant? But why was she bleeding? Amelia swallowed the fear clogging her throat. What was she supposed to do? She didn't know anything about babies or pregnant women.

Then the carriage stopped and the door flew open. The driver reached inside for Charles. "We're at the hospital, Mr. Bishop. Let me help you get her inside."

Amanda sobbed and grabbed Amelia's blouse. "Don't leave me, please."

"I won't. I promise." She released Amanda's hand and waited until Charles and the driver carried her inside. Then she scampered down from the carriage and followed them into the hospital. Nurses immediately took charge, telling Charles he had to wait outside the room while they tended to her.

Amelia stood in the doorway but back from the doctor and nurses. The odor of antiseptics, ether, and alcohol assaulted her nose. It wasn't much better, but at least it didn't gag her like the blood had. "I'm here, Amanda. I won't leave you. You'll be all right now." *Please, God, she had to be all right.*

"Amelia, where is she?"

To her surprise and relief Mama raced down the hallway toward her. Amelia opened her arms and fell against her mother. "She's bleeding something awful. She said something about being pregnant, but this isn't supposed to happen, is it?"

"No, it isn't. It's the Harrelson curse." She held Amelia for a minute or so then let her go to peer into the room. Satisfied the doctors were doing their job, she turned back to Amelia. "She'll be all right, sweetie. This happened to me twice."

Amelia shook her head. What did her mother mean by that? She bowed her head. *Thank You, Lord, and I'm sure glad You sent Mama along.* She jerked her head up. "Mama, how did you know, and how did you get here?"

"Charles's butler rushed over to the Farnsworth house to find Mr. and Mrs. Bishop. He didn't know we'd be there too. He told us Amanda was hurt and Charles was taking her to the hospital. We all came. His parents and Papa are with Charles now."

"But what is happening? I don't understand."

Mama reached up and stroked her cheek. "There's so much you don't know, and it's time you were told all the complications of marriage." She glanced into the room once again.

The doctor strode out. "We're taking her up to surgery. We have to make sure all tissue is gone. She's been sedated, so you'll have to wait to talk with her."

Mama nodded, but worry and fear lined her face. "I understand. I've been through it."

Amelia grasped her mother's hand, and they stepped back to let the nurses bring Amanda out and take her to surgery. Amanda's face was as white as the sheet covering her, and her eyes were closed and her face relaxed. Amelia's heart thumped wildly. Her sister looked barely alive. When she disappeared around the corner, Amelia turned to her mother. "Now, please tell me what is going on."

Mama moistened her lips. "Amanda told me Christmas Day that she believed she was pregnant. I was so worried, but I didn't say anything to her. Pregnancies have always been hard for the Harrelson women, but I thought maybe Amanda would escape the problem. She hasn't, and now she's miscarried the baby and has lost it."

Amelia sucked in her breath and leaned against the wall. Her legs threatened to fold on her, but she forced herself to stay upright. Her sister was...had been pregnant, and now the baby had died. Tears forced their way to the surface and trickled down her cheeks. Amanda loved children and would be a wonderful mother. How could this have happened? Would it happen to her?

Her mother grasped Amelia around the shoulders and led her back to the waiting room. She glanced up through the blur of tears, and a familiar figure loomed in front of her. Ben? How did he get here? When he wrapped his arms around her, she didn't care. All that mattered was the fact he was here and held her in his strong arms.

Chapter 20

$\mathcal{A}$melia stepped back from Ben and swiped at her cheeks with her fingers. "I'm so glad you came, but how did you know?"

"Mary Beth and Andrew arrived at his home just as your parents were leaving. Mrs. Farnsworth told us that Charles was taking Amanda to the hospital. They stopped at our house and picked me up. Mary Beth knew I'd want to be here with you."

Relief flooded through Amelia like a wave of fresh spring water. Amanda had Charles and Mama, Mama had Papa to comfort her, and Ben had come for her. "I'm so thankful you did. I needed someone to cry on."

He wrapped his arms around her again. "I wouldn't want to be anywhere else."

She didn't care if Papa did see them. She needed Ben's presence and his arms more than she needed anything else. Papa could scold her later, but right now contentment and peace filled her.

"Tell me what happened to Amanda. Did she have an accident?"

Amelia pressed her cheek against his chest, the beating of his heart almost in complete tune with hers. "She was expecting a baby and something went wrong. They took her to surgery. Oh, Ben, she lost the baby." Fresh tears flowed for a tiny life now gone from this earth.

"I'm so sorry. Is Amanda going to be all right?" He rubbed the palms of his hands across her shoulders and back.

Amelia's sobs slowed, and she backed away, wiping her eyes. "Yes. The doctor says she'll be fine physically, but it's going to take a while for her to get over this emotionally." Here she stood talking with Ben about pregnancies and babies and miscarriages, all delicate female matters, but no embarrassment or timidity kept her from sharing. Instead, peace and comfort from the man she loved bolstered her hopes that everything would be all right.

They said nothing for a minute or two, and then he led her to the area where the rest of the family waited. No one spoke, but Mary Beth came over and hugged Amelia. Mama peered at her with a strange look in her eyes that didn't speak of anger but of puzzlement. However, Papa's scowl left no doubts as to his mood. She'd just have to deal with that later.

Ben sat beside Amelia holding her hand, and Mary Beth sat on the other with Andrew beside her. So much sorrow in the past week, but so much love seen as friends comforted one another. That was one thing Amelia loved about being a Christian. When bad things happened, Christian friends were immediately present to offer help.

She peered up at Ben. His love flowed from his heart to his eyes and then through the hands that held hers. "How do people who aren't Christians make it through times like this week? Without the assurance that your Grandpapa is now in heaven with his Lord, and that God had a reason for taking this baby too soon, I couldn't bear the loss."

"I don't know. So many things we don't understand about how God works in our lives, but we have to believe that His plans are best."

They sat without talking. The rustle of skirts and the footsteps of doctors and others going about hospital business were the only sounds to break the silence. Mama's head rested on Papa's shoulder, and her eyes were closed. Mary Beth and Andrew stayed lending their support. Charles paced up and down the hall raking his hands through his hair. His parents sat nearby holding hands.

Ben squeezed Amelia's hand, and his strength ran up her arm to her heart. They would get through this and Amanda would have other babies in the future.

Charles stopped his pacing and hurried down the hall. Mama jumped up, then Papa. The doctor appeared with Charles at his side. Amelia stood, and Ben was right beside her. The doctor then smiled. "She's going to be fine. She's still sleeping off the anesthetic, but everything went as planned. She was approximately eight weeks into the pregnancy, and if this had to happen, it's better to be now than weeks later."

The doctor gripped Charles's shoulder. "It's a good thing you brought her here instead of trying to get a doctor to your home. We couldn't have treated her as completely at home, and the blood loss would have been much more severe. She would have been brought here for the surgery anyway, so you used good judgment, young man." Then he smiled gently. "You may go sit with your wife now. The rest of you will have to wait. Come with me, Mr. Bishop." The two men disappeared down the hall.

Mama slumped against Papa, her pale face pressed into his chest. His cheek rested on her head as he wrapped his arms around her. "She'll be all right, Lenora. Our girl will be all right."

Amelia leaned against Ben for support. For the first time she noticed the blood on her skirt. The enormity of the situation now hit her full force, and her legs threatened to crumple beneath her. Ben held her steady, and once again his strength sustained her.

Mary Beth pulled her cloak about her. "Andrew and I will be leaving. I know Ma and Clara will want to know what has happened." She looked up at her brother. "Do you want to go with us, or stay?"

Ben's hand tightened on Amelia's arm. "I want to stay if it's all right with Mr. and Mrs. Carlyle."

Amelia smiled up at Ben. He had been her tower of strength tonight. "It will be. We can drop you off at your grandmother's house on the way home. I just don't know how much longer they will want to stay."

"However long it takes, I'll be right here by your side." To Mary Beth he said, "Tell Ma I'll be home when the Carlyles bring me."

The couple bade them good-bye and left the waiting area along with Charles's parents. Amelia and Ben returned to their chairs where she collapsed and breathed deeply. Mama sat down beside her. "I'm so glad you were able to come with them. I know Amanda appreciated your being there. I'm so sorry you had to see all that, but you need to know about things like this."

Tears threatened again, and Amelia swallowed hard before responding. "Mama, it was terrible. There was so much blood everywhere." She glanced down at her skirt and grimaced. "I'll never get that picture out of my mind."

Mama patted her hand. "You will in time, you will." She tilted her head toward Ben. "I'm glad you are here for Amelia. She needed a strong shoulder to lean on, and I couldn't provide it tonight. To be honest, before I got to know you, I thought you might be a mule-headed, cow-loving dust buster, but I've seen that you are a sensitive, caring young man, and I appreciate your presence here tonight."

Amelia's heart swelled with pride in Ben. To have her mother speak as she did gave hope that the problems with her father could somehow be worked out. God was putting it all in motion, and it would be exciting to see where He planned to lead them.

A nurse appeared and spoke to Mama and Papa. "She's awake now and wants to see you. I'll take you to her room."

Mama grabbed Amelia's hand and started down the hall with Papa following close behind. When she glanced back at Ben, he waved and returned to his seat.

Ben slumped down into the chair. He pulled out his pocket watch and checked the time. The hands pointed to a little after midnight. A new year had begun, and none of them had even noticed, but then their minds had been elsewhere the past four hours or so. He wondered for a moment what the year 1877 would bring.

Amelia hadn't mentioned the house plans, but when had she had time? She may not have even looked at them yet, but in the hours since church this morning, she must have had some opportunity to do so.

Although he had wanted to stay for Amelia, he now questioned that decision. He did want to be with her, but the frowns and scowls from her father didn't indicate any acceptance of Ben on Mr. Carlyle's part. What could he say to the man to help him understand how much he loved Amelia?

His head nodded, and his eyes wanted to close. In that state he saw Amelia in the house he would build. She hung clothes on the line, and a child ran through the sheets flapping in the wind. A basket beside her held a baby sitting up and clapping its hands at the antics of the other child. His chin flopped to his chest, and Bed sat up with a jerk. He blinked his eyes rapidly to ward off sleepiness.

He stood up and shook his head and shoulders. A noise from down the hall caused him to turn around. Amelia and her parents hurried toward him. From the joy in their faces, they must have good news.

Amelia reached him first. "Amanda's sleeping peacefully now. The doctor said Charles could stay with her tonight, and she can go home Tuesday. Isn't that wonderful?"

"Yes, it is. Are you going to stay?"

Mr. Carlyle shook his head. "No, it's time for us to go home and get some sleep. It's well after one, and we will want to come back in the morning."

Mrs. Carlyle's eyes opened wide as though she'd just thought of something. Amelia gasped. "Oh my, it's New Year's Day, and we missed the coming of the new year."

Her mother patted Amelia's arm. "That we did, but it doesn't matter now. Amanda is all right, so we can go home." She glanced at Ben. "I take it you're going with us?"

"Yes, ma'am, if it's not too inconvenient." Ben swallowed hard. What if Mr. Carlyle objected? It was a long walk in the cold to his grandmother's house, and he didn't relish the idea of doing it in the middle of the night.

Mr. Carlyle retrieved his coat and handed his wife's coat to her. "I think it's the least we can do for your coming and staying so long. We've been up this long, so another fifteen minutes or so won't hurt us." He pushed his arms into the sleeves of his coat then picked up his hat. "I'll go find Toby and the carriage. Meet me out front."

With that he hurried down the hall toward the main entrance. Ben helped Mrs. Carlyle with her coat while Amelia tied her cloak around her neck. He escorted the two ladies out to the street just as Toby drove up with the carriage. Mr. Carlyle assisted his wife and Ben lifted Amelia up.

Once they were settled, the carriage began to move, its wheels rattling on the cobblestone streets, disturbing the quiet of the early morning hour. No one said anything, and Ben's mouth became dry as a parched prairie in a drought. He tried to moisten his lips but couldn't even raise enough spit for that. Only his hands were damp as if he'd just washed them.

Mr. Carlyle leaned forward in his seat a bit as the carriage swayed and turned a corner. "Your father tells me that he's making you a partner in the ranch when you turn twenty this year."

Ben's heart jumped, but his muddled brain righted itself in order to answer. "That's right, sir. I'll get my share just like Gideon and Billy will when their time comes." Ben rubbed his palms against his thighs and wished for a sip of water.

"I see, and how do you like ranching?"

Mr. Carlyle studied Ben as though he was a specimen in a science lab. He sent a prayer asking for guidance as to what to answer. "I thoroughly enjoy working with my father. Being out on the wide open range gives me the opportunity to see all of God's work in nature."

"Isn't that dangerous work? I mean, being around so many cows and the danger of a stampede."

"We don't have many stampedes. In fact, I don't recall but one since I started working with the herds." The one he did remember was one of the worst things he'd seen in his life. The thundering hooves and the dust that blinded him so he couldn't see anything created a lasting memory. Thankfully his horse had known just what to do and kept Ben from being injured.

"I still say it's dangerous work. How far are you from the town...Sweetwater Springs, isn't it?"

"Yes, sir. It takes us about half an hour to reach church on Sunday mornings. We live on the side of the ranch closest to town." Why was he asking so many questions? Surely he and Pa had discussed the ranch more than once in their time together. If he was trying to catch Ben unawares and saying something wrong, he'd sure picked a strange time to do it.

"Have you considered coming back here and working with your uncles in carrying on your grandfather's business?"

Ben gulped. Come back to Boston? That had never entered his mind. "No, sir, I have a number of responsibilities on the ranch, and I want to help Pa."

"I see." He said nothing for a moment then narrowed his eyes as though he'd made a decision. "Your parents have told us a great deal about the ranch and, as a matter of fact, have invited us to come for a visit in April."

Amelia stiffened beside him, and her arm brushed against his. Both of them had hoped this would happen but had heard no discussion of it. Pa had been busier than he thought, or maybe it had been Ma. Whoever had done the asking didn't matter, but what Mr. Carlyle planned to do did.

"That's a wonderful idea, Papa. May we go?" Amelia tried to keep the excitement from her voice, but it didn't fool her father.

"Well, your mother and I will have to discuss it. We don't know how Amanda will fare in the coming weeks, so we'll wait and see."

Not very encouraging, but at least he hadn't dismissed the idea completely. That gave Ben hope that a visit would be forthcoming.

The carriage stopped, and Ben stepped down. "I appreciate the ride home, Mr. and Mrs. Carlyle. I pray Amanda will be better soon and able to go home."

Mr. Carlyle nodded his head. "Thank you, son. Give our regards to your parents. Tell your father I will let him know about our decision to visit in a month or so." With that he signaled the driver, and the carriage took off into the night.

Ben shivered despite his heavy coat. Such a strange way to begin a new year, but if it had softened Mr. Carlyle's attitude, every minute had been worth the time. He turned and trudged up the steps, his body weary and cold. Funny, with Amelia beside him, he'd been quite warm, but now alone, he felt the icy air bite into the bare skin of his face as he fumbled with the key in the lock.

One thing for sure, if the Carlyles did come for a visit, he'd have to get busy with those plans for the house so he'd have it ready to show Amelia in the spring.

Chapter 21

On Tuesday, Mama and Papa planned to go back to the hospital before noon to help Charles take Amanda home. Monday had passed in a blur after the frantic efforts with Amanda and the long hours at the hospital Sunday night. After wrestling with the bedsheets and quilts to get warm and settle down, Amelia had finally slept as streaks of gray lightened the sky and brought in the first day of the year.

Amelia had then slept most of the day, exhausted from the emotions and turmoil of her sister's ordeal as well as the sleepless night. Even now, a full day later, she eyed the bed with a notion to crawl back beneath the covers.

The only bright spots had been Amanda's prognosis for full recovery and Ben's presence at the hospital. Her cheeks grew warm when she remembered their conversation and her appearance. What must he think of her in her plain skirt and shirtwaist? And her talk about babies and pregnancies was no topic for an unmarried woman to be speaking of to a man.

Still, her insides warmed because he had cared enough to rush to the hospital to be there with her and to stay until the end. Papa had not said anything else about the carriage ride home or the fact that she and Ben had been close all during the hours at the hospital. Her hopes that he would be less critical of her relationship with Ben dimmed the longer Papa kept silent. However, that also might be a good thing. If Papa's objections were still strong, he would have let that be known either at dinner last evening or today at breakfast.

Amelia sat at her dressing table now brushing her hair and wishing she could say good-bye to Ben today. The train for St. Louis would leave at two this afternoon, and Ben would be on it with his mother and his brothers and sister. She'd miss him dreadfully.

Someone knocked on her bedroom door. Mama's voice followed. "Amelia, may I come in?"

Amelia dropped her brush on the table and hurried to open the door. "Of course, Mama, you're always welcome."

Mama hugged her and kissed her cheek. "You've been such a blessing these past few days. But there are some things I need to discuss with you." She grasped Amelia's hand. "Come, let's sit over here by the window."

Amelia knit her brow. Had Amanda relapsed? Curiosity burned a hole in her soul. Mama looked so serious. She sat down and nodded toward the other chair for Amelia to sit. The sun sent its golden rays through the window but did little for the chill surrounding Amelia's heart.

"What is it, Mama? Did something happen to Amanda?" She sat on the edge of her chair, her hands clasped together to still their shaking.

Mama reached over and covered Amelia's hands with hers. "No, dear, Amanda is fine and still going home today. What I have to discuss concerns what happened to her."

Amelia's body stiffened. Not quite ready to hear about such things, she caught her breath and said nothing. Couldn't this wait until some other time?

"I know this is a delicate topic, but in light of the fact that you are now of marrying age, you need to be told. Haven't you ever wondered why you have only Amanda for a sister and not several others?"

Her statement brought a smile to Amelia's face. "Yes, I have. I would have enjoyed a larger family."

Mama bit her lip, and her eyes grew moist. "I would have too. Before Amanda, I lost two babies, just like she did. And you and Amanda were too young to remember, but a baby boy also died at birth when you were two."

Amelia's heart lurched. Three babies had died, and Mama never said anything about it. How that must have hurt her all these years when her close friends had more children. Her heart ached for her mother and the pain she must have suffered. "I'm so sorry, Mama. I had no idea. Why didn't you ever tell us?"

A cloud formed over her mother's eyes. "I didn't want to talk about it, but of course I did explain it to Amanda before she married Charles, and after what has happened with her, I knew I must tell you too.

"You see, the Harrelson women have always had difficulty in childbirth. Something in our bodies doesn't want us to have babies, and something goes wrong either in the early stages like Amanda, or at birth like your brother."

A lump formed in Amelia's throat, and no amount of

swallowing made it disappear. How hard that must have been for Mama, who was an only child, and now Amelia understood why. "Will Amanda be able to have another baby?"

"The doctor said they could try again, but it would be risky. She'd have to be under the doctor's care as soon as she suspects a baby is on the way."

Amelia leaned back against the chair. What did this mean for her? Would she have the same trouble as Mama and Amanda? The visions she'd had of children filling her home melted away like the icicles now dripping outside her window. She turned her face toward the warm sun and let the tears now forming spill over and slide down her cheeks.

Mama's hand squeezed hers. "I know this is difficult for you to hear, but since you're so attracted to Benjamin, I had to let you know what to expect. I imagine you will have children, but just not as many as you might have hoped for."

Amelia and Amanda had learned about the relationship between a husband and wife when they had their sixteenth birthdays, but this information had been withheld. When had Mama planned to tell her? After she became engaged to a young man who expected a large family? Ben. She had to tell him. He had four brothers and sisters. Wouldn't he expect to have a large family himself?

Mama patted her hand then stood. "It's a lot to take in, so I'll leave you alone." She headed for the door, but paused before she closed it behind her. "Change into something nice, dear. We have a surprise for you after we eat. Lettie said dinner will be ready in half an hour." With that she was gone.

A surprise? Half an hour to get dressed? She grabbed a handkerchief from her dressing table and dabbed it at the dampness on her cheeks. Surely it couldn't be Philip Barlow coming to call on her. She had half a mind not to change into a nicer dress or put up her hair. If he saw her like this, he might lose interest.

With a sigh, she pushed up from the chair and headed for the wardrobe to select something to wear. After she donned a two-piece green wool garment with a smaller bustle, she decided not to pile all her hair on top of her head. Instead, she brushed it back, leaving just a fringe across the forehead, and secured it with a tortoise shell clasp at the back of her neck. Mama may not approve, but there was no time for anything more elaborate.

All through the meal, curiosity ate at her like a mouse nibbling cheese, but neither Mama nor Papa would answer her questions. Lettie brought in the dessert, and when she set the bowl of custard on the table, she grinned and winked at Amelia. Now what in the world did that mean?

Voices sounded in the hall. Amelia's heart jumped, and she almost choked on a bite of custard. That was Mary Beth's voice. What was she doing here? She pushed back from the table and noticed the smile on Mama's face. What was going on?

She rushed to greet Mary Beth but stopped short when Ben's smiling face greeted her. "What…how…oh, my!"

Mary Beth hugged her. "This is your surprise. I'm taking you with us to say good-bye to the family."

Amelia whirled around to face her parents. Mama

smiled and nodded. "Yes, it's your surprise. Now get your cloak; you don't want to make them late."

Maeleen handed her the cloak, but Ben grasped it and placed across Amelia's shoulders. He leaned close and said, "If you could have seen the look on your face just now; it was wonderful."

The scent of spice on his skin tickled her to her toes. One more hour with Ben was more than she could have dreamed for today. She kissed her mother's cheek. "Thank you."

A few minutes later they were seated in the carriage on the way to the train station. Ben grasped Amelia's hand in his. "When Ma sent the request to your mother, we didn't know what to expect as an answer. When I told her about what happened at the hospital and on the ride home, she decided it was worth a try. I'm so glad your father agreed."

"I haven't been that shocked since my tenth birthday when they gave me a surprise party and I got to ride a pony."

As much as she wanted to be with Ben and his family today, the revelation her mother had made this morning niggled in the back of her mind. She needed to tell Ben what really happened with Amanda and what it meant for their relationship. Ben deserved to know because he wanted a large family, just as she had before learning about the problem faced by the women of her mother's family. Should she tell him now, or wait and do it in a letter? Either way, the idea of such a conversation sent a shiver of dread up her spine.

Isaac waited as Lenora pulled on her gloves in preparation for their trip to the hospital. If things had gone well today, they would be helping Charles get Amanda home and into bed. Not that Charles needed the help, but Amanda understandably wanted her mother by her side.

Another problem was of more concern to Isaac than Amanda. He couldn't help but see the feelings that flowed between Amelia and Benjamin. If only the young man lived in Boston and not out in the wild lands of Kansas. Of course he'd heard those lands were fairly tame now, but it was still too far away from home.

He assisted Lenora with her coat. "Do you think we may have made a mistake granting Elizabeth's request to let Amelia go to the train station with them today?"

Her sweet smile spoke of her approval of what he'd done. She raised a gloved hand to his cheek. "I think it was the nicest thing you could have done for her today. He obviously cares a great deal about her, as she does him. It will be awhile before they see each other again, so there's no harm in giving them a little time today."

"I hope you're right. Benjamin's a fine young man, and I've always admired his father, but they don't live here, and they can't give Amelia the life she deserves and would have here in Boston."

"That's true, but for some reason, this life we want for her has little appeal for our spirited daughter."

He grasped her arm, and they headed downstairs and outside where Toby waited with the carriage. Lenora's words rang true, but he had hoped the social events of the past months would distract and amuse her. Instead she seemed even more determined to go her own way.

Once they were seated and rolling toward the hospital, Isaac cleared his throat. "I suppose a trip to Kansas will be in order. Perhaps if we visit and Amelia sees the kind of life Elizabeth and Clara have on the ranch, she won't be so hasty in wanting to leave home and live there."

"Perhaps so, dear, but she also might like it enough to want to marry Ben and move there. Apparently Amelia has no interest in the young men she's met these past months. We really can't force her into marrying someone she doesn't love or want to be with."

Isaac recognized the truth of her words. He'd never force Amelia into anything like that, but he'd had hopes that Philip Barlow would meet with her approval. After the happiness of his marriage to Lenora, he wouldn't think of asking his daughter to marry without love. However, he'd almost rather she remain single than marry and move out to Kansas.

He grasped Lenora's hand in his. "She deserves to have love like ours, and perhaps she will still find it at home. We'll see if what she feels now can survive the many months of separation between today and April."

Lenora glanced up at him then lowered her eyes. "I told Amelia about the women in my family and the problems with having children."

Isaac's eyes opened wide. "How did she react?"

"I am sure she thought of Benjamin and their future. I wish I had told her sooner because she's always talked about having a houseful of children after she married."

"Yes, I noticed how well she did with Grace Ann and

little Billy." He wrapped an arm around her and pulled her close. "All we can do is pray for both her and Amanda. The Lord will take care of how many children they may have." He'd have to do more praying about both his daughters. One needed solace and peace after the experience she'd just had, and the other needed guidance in finding what the future held in store for her.

The carriage rolled to a stop in front of the hospital, and Toby hopped down to assist Lenora from the carriage. Amanda was one daughter they could help right now. Amelia would come later, and he prayed for God's wisdom in guiding her the next few months.

Chapter 22

*W*hen they arrived at the station, Amelia and Ben joined his family in the waiting area. Mrs. Haynes hugged Amelia. "I'm so sorry about Amanda, but I'm happy she's all right and will be going home today."

"Thank you, Mrs. Haynes. It was quite an ordeal for all of us."

Ben grasped her hand. "I'm just glad I could be there with you." He nodded to a bench across the way. "We have half an hour before we have to board; let's sit over there and talk."

Amelia nodded to his parents and followed Ben to the corner and the bench there. So many things she needed and wanted to say rushed through her thoughts, but where should she begin? They sat facing each other, and love filled every ounce of her being for this wonderfully sensitive, caring, and strong man before her.

He cleared his throat before speaking. "First of all, I'm so very thankful your parents consented for you to come with us today. We took a chance, and it worked."

"Only this morning I prayed that there was some way we could say good-bye, and now God answered that prayer. I have so much to tell you." How much she should reveal still wasn't clear, but she must tell him something of what she had learned this morning from her mother.

Before she could speak, he did. "Did you look at the plans I gave you Sunday? What did you think?"

"Oh, yes, I did. I love the house arrangement! I like having a dining area separate from the kitchen as well as a kitchen large enough for a table and chairs."

"Good. I want to start on the construction right away, so you'll have something to see when you come in April."

"But that's not certain as yet. Papa hasn't said a word more about it since Sunday night." She'd wanted to ask him this morning but had decided not to press her luck.

"I think you'll be there. In fact, I'm almost certain of it. I want to take you out there to the land I picked and have at least the framing if not the walls ready for you to inspect. That way you can have a better idea of what you want to put into it."

"I pray you are right, because it sounds so wonderful. I can't wait to see it." She bit her lip. Better tell him now before he became too wrapped up in his plans for her and the future. His feelings might change when she told him the truth, but if they did, their love didn't have a chance to begin with.

She glanced up at the big clock. Only twenty minutes left. Time went too fast when she wanted it to slow down and much too slow when she was in a hurry for something to happen. She chewed the corner of her lip, trying to find the words to tell him her plight.

Ben grasped her hands. "What is it? You have a troubled look in your eyes. Are you worried about Amanda?"

"No...not Amanda exactly." Amelia took a deep breath and blew it out. Might as well plunge ahead. "What happened to Amanda will most likely happen to me when I want to have children."

Ben's head moved back, and his brow furrowed. "What do you mean?"

"The women in my mother's family always have problems in childbirth. That's why Mama and Papa have only the two of us. A baby brother died at birth, and Mama had two incidents just like Amanda's." Heat burned in her cheeks at the mention of such things with a man, but he must know. "That's why Mama didn't have any more babies and why she's an only child."

His hand reached up to caress her cheek. "That's a terrible thing to bear, but how does it concern you and me?"

"Don't you see? The same could be true with me. I want a houseful of children, but I may not be able to have more than one, if that many. I know how much you want a big family like your own, but that may not be possible with me as your wife."

"Shh, don't talk like that. Anything is possible with God. If we have ten children or only one or even none, then we will have each other. All I want is you by my side as my wife for the rest of my life."

He said the words now, but how would he feel five, ten years into the future? As much as she loved him, she couldn't marry him without his knowing the truth and knowing for sure he would be happy with the possibility of no children.

"Ben, don't be hasty. Think about it over the next few months. Really think about it and what our lives would be like without children. If you feel the same when I come to Kansas, we can discuss more of our future then." Her feelings would never change, but she had to give him the opportunity to change his and find a woman who could give him what she couldn't.

A voice announced the time for St. Louis passengers to start boarding. Their time was over for today, but would it be over for good the next time she saw him?

Ben groaned at the call for boarding the train. How could he ever convince Amelia he loved her no matter what might happen in their future? He wanted to grab her and kiss her with all the emotions sweeping over him, but he refrained. It would show his love, but it would also be an embarrassment if someone else should happen to see and have the wrong impression. Amelia's reputation came first.

"I think that means we have to go now. Mama and the others are waiting." He held her hand, and they walked back toward the gate leading to the trains. When they met the tracks, Ben stopped and gazed down at Amelia.

"I'll remember this week and all that has happened for the next few months until we meet again." He placed his hands on her cheeks. "I want you to remember this. I love you very much, and nothing will change that. You'll see when you come to Sweetwater Springs in the spring." He bent and kissed her forehead then dropped his hands, picked up his satchel, and stepped up onto the train platform.

A whistle blew and smoke gushed into the air. The wheels turned, and Ben jerked at the movement. He waved at Amelia, who waved back with one hand covering her mouth. Mary Beth stood beside her, waving her good-byes as well. The two women he cared about very much grew smaller as the train picked up speed and increased the distance between them. Then the train curved and they were gone.

He dropped his hand to his side and entered the Pullman car where they would reside until they reached St. Louis. Even though the train had a dining car, Ma and Clara had packed a basket of snacks to while away the time and fill the hungry stomachs of Gideon and Billy.

Billy now snuck a peek under the checkered cloth, only to be scolded by Ma. He sat back on his seat with his bottom lip stuck out so far he'd trip over it if he stood up. Ben snickered, and that brought a glare from his little brother. What a little pest he could be, but Ben wouldn't trade him for anything else

That led his mind to Amelia and her revelation. Not having children would be difficult and a little less fulfilling than having a large family, but Amelia was what was important—not how many children she could have. Orphan trains came regularly, and if he and Amelia couldn't have their own, many children needed parents, so they could adopt. Then again, maybe Amelia wouldn't want to have children who didn't belong to her. He sobered at that idea.

Lord, give me wisdom as to what to say in my letters in the months ahead. She needs to know that my love for her will never change no matter how many children we

can or cannot have. The very thought of not having her in my life is more than I can bear.

Billy reached over and pulled Grace Ann's hair. She hit at him, and her scream split the air. "Mama, make him stop. He's hurting me."

"Billy, leave your sister alone and sit still. It's a long way to St. Louis, and I don't want to listen to squabbling all the way."

The boy again stuck out his bottom lip and folded his arms across his chest. His little pink tongue shot out between his lips in the direction of his sister, and Ma grabbed his thigh. Ben stifled a chuckle. He glanced up, and Gideon was doing the same.

"Those two are going to be little pests all the way home. Looks like it's up to you and me to handle 'em. I'll take Billy, and you can have him later." Gideon rose from his seat and headed for Billy. He picked the boy up and said, "Let's you and me play a few games."

Ben breathed a sigh of relief. Between the two of them, they ought to be able to keep Billy busy for the trip and give Ma some rest. She'd need it now without Clara around to help her once they reached home.

Grace Ann buried her nose in a book, so Ben moved over to sit beside Ma. This would be a good time to talk with her and seek her advice.

Ma reached out and squeezed his hand. "I'd hug you, but you're so tall and broad shouldered now that I can barely get my arms around you. You're taller than your father."

"Well, I can always hug you." He slipped his arm around her shoulders to prove it.

She grinned up at him with a sparkle in her eyes. "How was it with Amelia? I'm so glad her father gave his permission for her to come to the station."

Ben removed his arm from her shoulders and clasped his hands between his knees. "It was fine, but I need your help. You know how much I love her."

"Yes, son, I do. I couldn't help but see it every time you were together, but I sense there may be a problem. Has her father objected again?"

"No, it's not that. You know what happened with Amanda." At his mother's nod, he continued. "It seems that it happens with the women in her mother's family. Mrs. Carlyle is an only child because of the difficulties her mother had, and Amelia has only the one sister for the same reasons. Amelia is afraid that she won't be able to have any children at all. I got the feeling she didn't want to burden me with that because she knows how much I love children."

"And what did you tell her?"

"I said I'd love her no matter what, but I sensed she didn't believe me. She told me to think about it and what it meant for our future. What can I do to make her believe it doesn't make a difference in how I feel about her?"

"What were you planning to do before she told you?"

"To get that piece of land down by the old mill and start building a house on it for us."

"Then you should keep right on with the house. Since your father invited them to come later in the spring, you can prove your love by going ahead with your plans as though nothing had changed."

"Then that's what I'll do." It's the same conclusion

he had drawn, but hearing it from his mother made his choice more than right. "Ma, how long will Pa and Clara stay in Boston?"

"Not more than a few weeks. As soon as the estate is settled, they will return home. Until then, you and Steve can run the ranch." She hesitated a moment then tilted her head to one side. "We were going to wait to tell you this, but I believe I should tell you now. Your grandfather left a nice sum for each of his grandchildren in his will. It will be enough for you to build your house and buy a few head of stock to start your own ranch."

He gulped. Grandpapa left him enough money to do that? His mind raced with all that he could do in the future to help Mr. Carlyle see that he could provide for Amelia. "I had no idea." He knit his brows together. "Pa planned to make me a partner this year and share in the profits of the ranch. Will this make a difference?"

"Yes, but the plans aren't fully developed yet. We discussed it at length last night, and what I think will happen is that he's going to sell you enough land for your own ranch. You can pick out your brand, buy a few head, and get started this spring. He even talked about giving you a few of the new calves that will be coming soon."

His own ranch with his own house on it. That was more than he'd ever dreamed of having. He'd have to go it alone until he could hire hands to help, but with Pa's assistance and what Ben already knew about ranching, he could make it a success.

Ma laughed and shook her head. "I know your pa wanted to tell you himself, and I spoiled his little surprise, but I thought maybe it would help you in deciding what to say to Amelia in your letters in the days ahead."

If he'd had his hat in his hands instead of on the seat across the aisle, he'd have thrown it in the air in jubilation, but all he could do was sit and grin before throwing both arms about his ma and hugging her. "I think I must have the most wonderful parents in the world." He sat back then stood and moved back to his seat. The countryside raced by in a tapestry of white, pale greens, and browns. Each click-clack of the wheels took him closer to home and fulfillment of his dreams.

Thank You, Lord, for Your mighty love. You made provisions for my needs before I even realized I had them. You know my dreams for the future, and I pray Mr. Carlyle will see how much I need Amelia to be a part of that future.

God provided all along the journey so far, and He would continue to do so as long as he and Amelia sought Him and followed His will. Ben's pure conviction was that God intended for Amelia to be his bride and would pave the way for Mr. Carlyle's acceptance. How and when that would come about would be for the Lord to decide. Whatever happened, Ben looked forward to being a part of it.

Chapter 23

$\mathcal{A}$melia read Ben's last letter once again. He declared his love for her, but doubt still riddled her thoughts about him. Most men wanted a son to carry on the family name or a daughter who would grow up as the apple of his eye. In the six weeks since Ben had returned home to Kansas, all four of his letters had expressed the same love he'd declared for her before he left. He'd even told her that he had the land and the materials to start building the house he planned for them. So why couldn't she believe he really did love her?

At least Papa no longer objected or complained when she turned down suitors who had asked for permission to call on her, but he hadn't as yet said whether or not they would be going to Kansas either. The uncertainty ate at Amelia until she no longer enjoyed the social activities she did attend.

Amelia finished pinning up her hair and folded the letter before returning it to the box where she now kept all of Ben's letters. Mary Beth was due for afternoon tea in a few minutes, so she ventured downstairs to wait for her.

Maeleen met her at the bottom of the stairway. "My mum said to tell ye she has the tea ready for your guest. She has a plate of scones for ye too."

"Thank you. Please tell her to serve them when Mary Beth arrives." Maeleen turned to leave. "Wait, have you seen Mama?"

"No, miss, I haven't since she last went to her room after checking meals with Mum."

"All right. She'll probably come down when Mary Beth is here." Amelia wandered into the parlor where she stopped to run her hand across the brocade fabric on the sofa. The rich wine color complemented the cherry wood trim. What kind of furniture would she have in a home in Kansas? Mama's decorating tastes were somewhat more elaborate than what Amelia wanted for her house, but she wouldn't mind having a few pieces of the well-made furniture to be found in Boston. Oh, posh, why was she even thinking about such things? Having her own home was a ways off in the future, if it ever happened.

The door knocker sounded, and a few moments later Mary Beth rushed into the room and embraced Amelia. "Oh, I'm so glad we can have this time together. It seems every time we try, something else is going on that we must attend." She arranged her skirts as she sat down on the sofa.

"Have you heard from your father or Aunt Clara?" Amelia lifted her hand toward the door to signal Maeleen to bring in the tea set.

"Yes, they arrived safely home at the end of last week. I wanted to tell you in church Sunday, but I didn't see you."

"I'm sorry, but I had a touch of a cold with a scratchy throat, so Mama made me stay home. I'm much better today." She paused while Maeleen set the tea tray on the table in front of the sofa. "Thank you, Maeleen; I'll ring if we need anything else."

She turned back to Mary Beth and reached for the teapot. "I had another post from Ben yesterday, and he's working on the house he's building down by the mill."

"Yes, he showed me the plans. There's something else you should know. I just learned of it myself last week." She reached for the offered cup of tea and picked up a scone.

Amelia's thoughts flitted like a pesky gnat in her mind. Ben had changed his mind and didn't want to tell her. Something had happened to somebody in the family. She forced herself to wait until Mary Beth was ready to talk again and picked up her own teacup. It took both hands to keep it from rattling on the saucer.

Mary Beth swallowed a bit of scone. "These are quite delicious. I must make sure to get the recipe from Lettie." Then she grinned. "You're so curious about what I learned that I can see it coming out your ears."

Heat rushed to Amelia's cheeks. She hadn't been as discreet as she hoped.

"The most wonderful thing has happened. Grandpapa left all of his grandchildren an inheritance in his will. Ben and I will receive ours now, but the others will have to wait until they're eighteen. Isn't that wonderful? That's how Ben was able to get started on your house so soon."

Ben had an inheritance and spent it to buy land and

build a house for her. That should prove his love for her. "Yes, it is, but how can Ben still want me for a wife when I may not be able to give him children?"

Mary Beth laughed. "Because, my dear friend, he loves you as much as I love Andrew. When we Haynes fall in love, we do it forever despite the circumstances, and I know you love him the same way."

Her voice held such confidence that Amelia's doubts began to fade. Still, she'd have to wait until she saw him again to fully believe he still wanted her as his wife. The days until they could go to Kansas loomed longer and longer.

Amelia remembered her friend's betrothal. "Have you and Andrew been able to set a date for your wedding as yet? I know you had wanted it in June, but that would be too soon after your grandfather's death."

"Yes, but Grandmama has said we could have it by the end of summer, so we chose the first day of September as our wedding day. It will be at the church, and Grandmama has already secured the date for us."

"That's wonderful. I'm so happy for you both." Even though Mrs. Haynes may still be in mourning, she and Mrs. Farnsworth would plan the most fashionable and elaborate wedding one could have in Boston. It would even be grander than Amanda's had been. As far as Amelia was concerned, however, an elaborate wedding was a waste of money. If she had her way, her wedding would be a small affair and take place here in her own home.

Mary Beth set her cup down and leaned toward Amelia. Her blue eyes sparkled with enthusiasm and love. "I'm asking you and Isabella to stand with me. Grace Ann is too young to be able to do it, but we'll find something for her to do in the wedding. I would like for you to be my senior maid."

Amelia's throat tightened. She had come to love Mary Beth as a sister, and the invitation brought as much honor as standing with her sister had. "Of course I will. What an honor to be chosen, and how much fun we'll have."

Mama stepped into the room. "Did I hear you say you are making plans for your wedding?"

"Yes, ma'am. We've chosen the first Saturday in September for the ceremony."

Mama leaned over and hugged Mary Beth. "I'm very happy for you, dear, and I know how much your mother would like to be here to help with all the plans. You tell her I'll do everything I can to help Louise Farnsworth and your grandmother with anything they may need."

"Thank you, Mrs. Carlyle. I'm sure they will appreciate any help you can give them. Mama will arrive in June to spend the last few months with me. The rest of the family will come in mid-August."

"That's wonderful. Your mother is certainly proud of you. We talked a great deal about you and Amelia when she was here for Christmas." Then a secretive look and a smile like that of a conspirator swept across her features. She stepped back and gazed first at Mary Beth and then at Amelia. "It's good that you're here, Mary Beth, so you can hear the news too."

She paused for a moment, and Amelia swallowed the scream threatening to escape. This was the second time in a half hour that she had to wait for someone to make a statement.

"Your father has decided that we will all take the trip to Kansas in April. He's sending a wire to Sweetwater Springs today to inform Mr. Haynes and the rest that we'll be arriving the second week after Easter."

This time Amelia didn't squelch the yelp that burst forth. She leaped from her chair and hugged her mother's neck. "Oh, thank you, Mama. Thank you."

"It's your father you have to thank. Of course I may have planted a hint or two, but he's the one who said yes. Be sure you tell him so tonight, but do curb your enthusiasm for seeing Ben. Papa needs more time to absorb that situation."

Yes, she'd thank Papa tonight at dinner. Now that she knew for sure they would be going, Amelia's heart swelled to the bursting point in anticipation of seeing Ben. By then all her doubts and questions would be resolved, and she could enjoy the plans he'd made for their home. Now she and Mary Beth had even more reason to celebrate and plan in the next few months.

Despite the cold weather and patchy snow, Ben had been able to spend time on his new property almost every day and still get his chores and responsibilities with Pa done. Building supplies had arrived last week, and the first signs of building had begun. He and Gideon had stepped out the measurements and laid rope for the outside walls and walls between rooms. He rode out to the site tonight with even more joy in his heart for what he had accomplished so far.

This evening Pa shared a wire from Mr. Carlyle that

said he and his family would arrive the second week after Easter for a visit. Ben had shouted for joy then, much to the amusement of Gideon and Clara. He didn't care. Amelia was coming to Kansas, and he wanted everything to be ready. He'd spend every Saturday on his property working on the house until they arrived.

He pulled his jacket collar up closer around his neck. The temperature would remain in the forty-degree-range tonight, but the chill wind made it colder on his neck and face. No clouds in the sky allowed the stars to shine forth in all their glory. Riding in quiet solitude like tonight always brought peace to his heart and soul. After observing the laid-out rope once more, he headed toward home.

The jewel-filled sky, wide-open spaces, the moon shining bright, and the gentle lowing of the cattle revealed only a few of the wonders of God's great world. Snow still covered areas protected from the sun's rays in the daytime, but soon spring would arrive, and the fields would burst forth in glorious color. How could anyone ride out here, see all the beauty, and still not believe in a God who created it all? Why people couldn't accept that went beyond Ben's comprehension.

The cattle were in winter pasture now, and all appeared peaceful and quiet. As he rode back to the ranch house, the only sounds were of Blackie's shoes against the hard earth and the creaking of his saddle. He began singing, not worried about who would hear him out here. All he could think of to sing was a song that Clara played and sang just about every day. His voice didn't carry near the quality of hers, but the words of one verse had touched his heart and lodged there.

The words rang out in the cold night air. "All praise and thanks to God, the Father now be given, the Son, and him who reigns with them in highest heaven, the one eternal God, whom earth and heaven adore; for thus it was, is now, and shall be evermore."

When he stopped and stayed quiet and still, he could almost hear the stars rejoicing in the heavens God created. Never had his faith been so strong as it was out on the range under the moon and stars this night. And just ahead was spring with its promise of new life and new beginnings. God was in His heavens, and all was right with the world.

The howl of a coyote in the distance broke the silence, and the stronger wind whipped about him. He nudged Blackie homeward and picked up speed as they neared the stables. Time for the warmth of the fire and a cup of hot coffee.

The glow from the lamps inside the house welcomed him, but he took care of Blackie first. Only after he made sure his horse was warm and well fed for the evening did Ben go inside.

Grace Ann sat at the kitchen table finishing her math schoolwork with Clara's help. She glanced up as he came into the room and headed for the stove and the pot of coffee warming there.

"A bit cold to be riding, isn't it?"

He shrugged and poured a mug of coffee. "Not really. Are there any cookies left, or did Billy and Gideon get the rest of them?" Gideon was known for his constant hunger and raiding the cookie jar whenever he had the chance.

Clara laughed and shook her head. "You boys are

always looking for something to eat. Cookies are in the tin there by the sink." She closed the math book. "I think that's enough for tonight, Grace Ann. Time for you to be in bed."

Grace Ann gathered her supplies with a sigh. "I hate going to bed in that room all by myself. I still miss Mary Beth. It's lonely without her."

"I know, chickadee, but since she's in Boston and planning her wedding, you'll have to get used to it. I'll come in a little bit and sit with you if you want."

"Oh, please do, Aunt Clara." She hugged Clara's neck and headed for her room and bed.

"Where are Ma and Pa?" Ben sat down with his coffee and a handful of cinnamon sugar cookies.

"Your mother was tired and has already gone to bed. Your pa is in his office." She tilted her head and stared at him with a twinkle in her eye. "You were mighty happy when your pa made his announcement at supper."

"Guess it was kinda obvious. I know that Amelia will love the ranch and Sweetwater Springs. If we can just convince her father that living here isn't as bad as he thinks, perhaps he'll change his feelings toward me. He was much nicer to me that New Year's Eve, and he did allow Amelia to go to the train station to say good-bye."

"Perhaps, but you had also been a help at the hospital, and he wanted to show his appreciation." Clara ambled to the stove and poured herself a cup then returned to the table.

Her reasoning was probably right, but he'd rather believe the man's heart was softening a bit.

Clara stood behind him with her arms around his

shoulders. She laid her cheek against his head. "I pray every day that God will work things out for you and Amelia. She's a wonderful girl, and I too believe she'll love it here in Kansas." She pulled back, ruffled his hair, and returned to her chair.

Lots of people were praying for them. God couldn't ignore so many requests, but He could answer in ways that might not be exactly what Ben wanted. He must have faith because God always did what was best for His children, and Ben certainly counted himself one of them.

April loomed as the pivotal date. Whatever happened then would be up to God. *Lord, continue to give me the patience to wait on Your timing and Your plans.*

Chapter 24

*A*melia gazed out the window with her heart racing as fast as the scenery through the window of the train coach bound for Sweetwater Springs. Yellow and purple wildflowers clustered across the landscape, lending their vivid colors to the otherwise drab scene. The closer they come to the town, the more excitement built in her chest. They had left the Pullman cars behind in St. Louis and transferred to a smaller coach with bench seats. At least they wouldn't have to spend the night on this part of the trip.

Weeks of letters telling of the progress on the house Ben was building, his love for her, and his plans for her visit filled her with the anticipation of seeing him again and learning about the ranch and his home. Ben had also said April brought many days of rain, but he was praying for sunny days while she was there.

Mama had purchased new clothes for this trip, electing to leave her more stylish garments behind and opt for the comfortable ones suggested by Mrs. Haynes and Clara.

She had also suggested that they bring warm clothing too as the weather was unpredictable for this time of year. The outfits worn on the train were from Mama's usual wardrobe as were Amelia's, but their baggage contained much simpler skirts and shirtwaists.

Amelia looked forward to riding with Ben and wearing her new attire for horseback. It was certainly more appropriate than the riding habit she had worn in Boston. The picture of her on a Western-style saddle with the fancy skirt and jacket of her usual dress brought a grin to her face.

The conductor stopped beside Papa. "Sir, the train will be arriving in Sweetwater Springs in half an hour. Your bags will be unloaded to the platform as soon as we stop."

"Thank you." Papa folded his newspaper and peered across at Amelia. "Well, my dear, are you ready for this adventure? Things have been pretty barren since we left St. Louis."

Amelia folded her hands together to still their shaking. "Yes, and I truly look forward to seeing everything I can while we are here."

Mama pulled on her gloves and shook her head so that the feathers atop her hat danced with the motion. "I must say every station I've seen so far has been very primitive. I offered to stay in a hotel while we are here, but Elizabeth insisted that we stay with her because it would be more convenient for everyone. I do hope it's not an imposition on her to do this."

"Now, Lenora, she wouldn't have put out the invitation if that were the case. You know Elizabeth and how she loves a houseful of people. I remember her being quite the hostess back in the days she and Matthew lived in Boston."

"Yes, that's true."

Mama went on to make more comments to Papa, but Amelia tuned them out and once again worked on how she would greet Ben after all these weeks of separation. Would he truly feel the same as he had in January? She so wanted to feel his comforting arms about her once more, but they'd have to withhold any affections around Papa and Mama. No sense in giving Papa something to object about.

The swaying of the car lessened as the train slowed. The shrill whistle blasted through the air to alert the town that the train had arrived. Amelia stared out the window and searched the platform for the Haynes family. She spotted Ben first, and he waved then tapped his mother on the shoulder.

Amelia waved back and then scurried down the aisle to follow Mama and Papa off the train. Mr. and Mrs. Haynes welcomed them with hugs and handshakes. Ben stood to the side and waited to greet Amelia and her parents. She sneaked a look at him, and he smiled, which only added to the impatience growing within. Why was Papa being so slow in greeting everyone? Manners bade she wait until he had finished before acknowledging Ben.

Finally Papa turned to Ben and shook his hand. He nodded briefly, as did Mama, who also murmured something Amanda couldn't hear. At last it was her turn, and it took every ounce of willpower she had not to run into his arms. As it was, she simply said, "Hello, Ben. Thank you for meeting us."

He doffed his cowboy hat, and his grin became a full-blown smile that lit up his face. He grasped her hand and placed it on his arm. "You didn't think I'd do otherwise, did you?"

They stepped off the platform and walked over to the surrey and wagon waiting for them. "I'll help your father and Pa load up the bags, and then we'll be off. You can ride on the wagon with me." He assisted her up onto the bench and tipped his hat again.

Despite the cool air, warmth flooded every part of her being. Just being near him again brought on feelings she'd never had and didn't quite understand. If this was the next step in love, she liked it. Her body tingled in anticipation of all the new discoveries that would come from these days on the ranch.

In five minutes the men had placed all the bags and satchels in the wagon, and Ben climbed up beside her. "It's about thirty minutes or so out to the ranch, so I hope you don't get too uncomfortable."

The wagon seat was rather hard and narrow, but her numerous petticoats should help the ride be more comfortable. "I'll be fine." The warmth of his body next to hers on the seat warded off any chill that might come from the weather and replaced it with the glow that came with love.

Their wagon followed behind the surrey, and every few minutes or so Mama glanced back as though to make sure the wagon still trailed along behind. Or perhaps she was checking Ben to make sure he didn't act improperly. That thought caused a smile. He had already kissed her, and if Mama knew that, she might have apoplexy, and Papa would have broken off their relationship completely. Some things were best left hidden.

"You don't have many trees out here. It's all grass and bushes." She had to agree with Papa that the landscape did look rather forlorn and barren. If it hadn't been for the bright spots of flowers dotted about, she could almost believe the land had been left to its own devices.

"To the north and east of us is farmland. Fences separate it from our range, but all our grazing range is to the west and south of here. You'll find trees down by the mill where our house will be. They provide some good shade as well as timber."

"I can't wait to see it. You described it so well in your letters that I have a mental picture of what it looks like. Didn't you say the waterwheel still turns?"

"Yes, and I hope to repair and paint the mill itself so it'll be a pretty place once again."

"I'd like that." She breathed deeply then exhaled. "The air is so fresh and exhilarating out here. I love it already."

He grinned down at her. Curls lay against his forehead under his pushed-back hat. She fought the desire to reach up and push them back. Instead she tucked her hand under his arm and leaned against his shoulder. How good it was to be so near to him again. The two weeks ahead were going to be the best she'd ever had.

When Amelia leaned on his shoulder, he breathed in the familiar floral scent in her hair. Whatever it was, he'd think of her whenever he was near a bouquet of fresh spring flowers. The little feather poking up from her hat tickled his nose, and he sneezed.

Amelia jumped at his side. "Oh my, that was some sneeze. Are you catching a cold?"

He sniffed and grinned. "No, it was just that cute blue feather sticking out in your hat. I don't think I've ever seen a bird with that exact color of blue before." The only blue birds he'd seen were the lighter ones, not any with such a deep blue on their wings.

She poked his arm. "They're dyed, silly. So are the green ones on Mama's hat." She turned her head toward the fields. "What are those gorgeous yellow flowers out there?"

"Can't tell really from this distance, but I think they may be early buttercups or prairie dandelions. We'll have a chance to look closer at some of them when we're out riding." He'd have to find Clara's book on wildflowers and learn the names of some he didn't know and then hope he'd recognize them. He'd just never thought much about wildflowers before.

The sun warmed them as they rode. Its rays brightened the landscape and the nearly cloudless sky. Too often in April the clouds covered the blue and brought rain. They'd need a lot of rain this spring, but he hoped it would delay for the next two weeks so he and Amelia could spend more time on the range and out at the mill.

"I know you didn't see much of Sweetwater Springs when we were there, but it's a nice-sized town and is very friendly. You'll meet some of the people at church on Sunday." How proud he would be to escort Amelia to church. He'd be the envy of every single young man present.

"I'd like that." She squeezed his arm. "Oh, Ben, I'm just so happy to be here."

"I'm glad you are too. It's been a long three and a half months." It had been more like three years to him, but she was here now, and that's all that mattered.

They rode in silence for a the next few miles, the wind blowing its soft caress across their faces and the sun beaming down as though God gave His approval for their relationship. Ben had waited with patience for these days with Amelia, and he intended to make the best use of them. He snapped the reins to speed up the horses as the wagon lagged behind the surrey. Mr. Carlyle had turned to see where they were, and that look on his face didn't bode well if the wagon didn't move closer to them.

Beside him Amelia drank in all the wonders of nature around her and didn't seem to notice her father looking back. Ben would have to be more careful than he had first thought. Mr. Carlyle still didn't fully approve of the relationship with Amelia. But Ben would do everything in his power to change that opinion in the days ahead.

Isaac turned to check on the wagon behind the surrey. They were lagging behind. That wasn't good. He scowled and faced forward. Maybe this wasn't such a good idea. If Amelia liked Kansas and the ranch, his plan would be ruined.

Lenora placed a hand on his arm and whispered,

"Don't look so unhappy, dear. It'll be all right. They're just glad to see each other."

He shot a look at their hosts, who were in the front seat, then patted her hand and murmured, "That's what worries me. She's not some little gem he can pick up and put into his setting and expect her to sparkle like a jewel. Amelia belongs with her own kind." Being a snob was not his usual style, but this was his daughter, and he wanted only the best for her. Living in Kansas was not it.

"Let's just see how these two weeks turn out with them. I must admit, the countryside is quite pretty this time of year despite the fact that it's so far away from everything."

He glanced around since he hadn't even noticed the land they traveled. His mind had been too occupied with Amelia and Ben. Lenora was right. The clusters of wild-flowers nestled among the grasses did make a pretty picture, but it lacked the hustle and bustle he loved in the city.

Lenora grinned and shook her head as the surrey hit a bump in the road. "The cobblestone streets back home aren't quite as bad as this, but it hasn't been a bad ride," she commented in a louder voice.

Elizabeth turned her head and smiled. "This is one of our better roads since it's traveled so much into town. We have the surrey and two wagons to get us around on the ranch and into town for supplies and attending church. In the winter time we bundle up with coats and blankets to make the trip."

So they had no enclosed carriages to protect them from the elements. He'd have to pray it didn't rain on Sunday. That would make for a rather miserable ride to town. Isaac glanced back again at the wagon. It had pulled closer, and from the look on Amelia's face, she truly enjoyed the ride. He would let them be for now, but if things went further, he'd have to step in and put an end to it.

Saying something to Amelia now would let her know not to be so enthusiastic, but then that would most likely end up spoiling the trip for everyone, not just Amelia. Lenora had looked forward so much to this trip and her visit with Elizabeth, and he'd do nothing to hurt her.

They had passed through a gate with a metal arch above it a little ways back. The Haynes's brand, a Rocking H, topped the arch. Now a house came into view, and Isaac leaned forward to gain a better view.

His eyes opened wide. What lay before him far exceeded the expectations he had for a prairie ranch house. A wide porch wrapped around the corners of the house and halfway around the sides. A sloped shingled roof with three dormer windows topped the wood structure. Flower beds bordered with stones lined the front, flanking a stone path leading up to the porch. Two rockers and a swing completed the picture of the front of the house. To the left the barn and stables rose with an attached corral that contained several horses.

"Matthew, this is a very nice spread. The house is larger than I thought it would be." Then he chuckled. "But then with five children, I suppose it has to be."

"That's the reason for the second story. After Gideon was born, we decided that if we wanted more children, we'd better add on to the house. Then Clara came to live with us, and Grace Ann and Billy came along, so it's good that we did."

The surrey stopped and Isaac stepped down then

turned to assist Lenora. She smiled up at him as his hands lingered about her waist. "This is going to be a most wonderful two weeks. Wait and see."

Isaac glanced toward the wagon just as Ben set Amelia on the ground. His hands also stayed longer than necessary about Amelia's waist. Fear rose in Isaac's throat and threatened to choke him as the young couple gazed into each other's eyes. This was not what he had planned. What had he been thinking? Putting those two together anywhere was a big mistake, and Isaac had just made the biggest one of his life.

Chapter 25

$\mathcal{A}$melia shook out the split skirt the dressmaker made for this trip. Today she would see the site where Ben was working on their house. His parents and Clara knew about it, but no one else did; the three of them had been sworn to secrecy. Ben told Amelia that he'd been afraid his little brother or sister would let the news slip, and he wasn't ready for her parents to know yet.

She leaned on the sill of her second-floor window and filled her lungs with fresh country air. The weather cooperated in beautiful fashion today. Billowy white clouds raced across the sun that sent its bright rays to warm the temperatures into the high fifties. Her new jacket would be exactly right for their ride this morning.

Breakfast had been fun even if somewhat chaotic. She'd never been around a table at mealtime with that many people except at special dinners and parties. Billy and Grace Ann had kept a lively conversation going with questions about their trip and suggestions as to what they could do on the ranch.

Papa planned to ride out with Mr. Haynes to see the land and the herds, and Billy wanted to go along so he could see and pet the calves that had been born. He even boasted about helping deliver one of the calves and started to go into detail about the experience before his mother put a halt to it. "That's enough, Billy. You can't go this morning because you have school, remember?"

The little boy pouted, but Mrs. Haynes stood firm. A smile played about Amelia's mouth. That look brought back memories of some of her antics to get out of going to school at his age. She didn't have any success either.

Envy of Ben's large family set in, and once again she worried that he would change his mind about her the more he thought about not having a large family of children to call his own. He'd assured her over and over again that it wouldn't make a difference, but what if it did later when they were married and had no children?

Best not to think about such things on this beautiful morning, so she shoved them into the recesses of her mind and concentrated on dressing for their ride. She pulled a soft brown skirt up around her hips. Then she pulled on a pair of boots Mary Beth had left behind. She stood and tried walking in them. They were a good fit, and she had no trouble with them; in fact, they were quite comfortable. Mary Beth had also left a hat that Amelia now picked up and set on her head. Letting her hair stay loose and tied back only with a ribbon allowed the hat to fit firmly over her hair.

She moistened her lips and headed down to the parlor where Ben planned to meet her. Mama and Mrs. Haynes sat in the parlor drinking coffee. Clara, Billy, Grace Ann, and Gideon had gone to school, so the three women had time to chat and visit.

Ben came through the front door, and his face lit up with pleasure when he saw her. "You're all ready for our ride. That's good. I can't wait for you to see everything."

"Thanks to your sister I have everything I need to be comfortable on a horse." Amelia held up a pair of leather gloves. "She even had these to protect my hands."

"You'll need them." He removed his hat and entered the parlor. "Good morning again, Mrs. Carlyle. I'll take good care of Amelia. She'll be riding Mary Beth's horse, and the mare is a good one, gentle and easy to handle."

"Have a nice ride then." She peered at Amelia. "Will that hat be enough to protect you from the sun?"

Amelia laughed and hooked her hand on Ben's arm. "I'm sure it will. Mary Beth said she wears it all the time when she's riding."

Mama nodded as though satisfied and picked up her cup and saucer. Amelia said her good-byes to Mrs. Haynes then strolled outside with Ben. They crossed over to the stables where he had two horses saddled and ready to go. Up close the two animals were twice the size they appeared to be from the porch. Amelia gulped. She had ridden horses in Boston, but none loomed as large as the two before her. How would she ever be able to stay atop one so big?

Ben held the reins of the beautiful red mare she was to ride. "Her name is Victory, and she's really easy to handle. Just hold the reins loosely and then tug on them to tell her which direction you want her to go. Here, let me help you up."

He held the stirrup while she lifted her foot to slide it

into the leather. Then he put his hands on her waist and boosted her up so she could swing her leg over the saddle. Ben handed her the reins, and she sat back. Things certainly looked different from this height. At least this was more comfortable than the saddles she usually rode, and now she looked forward to the ride with less fear and more excitement, although her hands did shake at the prospect of trying to control such a large animal. She breathed deeply, grasped the reins with a firm grip, and waited for Ben.

Ben mounted his horse and turned Blackie toward the fields beyond the house. Victory followed right along beside the black stallion. Ben had told her the two horses had both been sired by one of the older horses on the ranch and were of good stock. She believed it now as the mare trotted along beside Blackie.

She bounced up and down enough to make her teeth chatter, which made conversation all but impossible. Twice she'd caught herself slipping to one side on the saddle.

Ben slowed beside her. "Relax and grip her with your knees. Feel movement and go with it. The ride will be much smoother."

She tried to do what he said, but improved only slightly, and her teeth still shook in her head. Ben urged her to keep trying. Finally she began to match the movement more evenly, and the bouncing lessened to the degree she could at least carry on a conversation. She'd probably be sore in the morning, but having this time with Ben would be worth every ache and pain.

Soon the house and out buildings disappeared behind them, and they rode across open range. Such wide-open spaces were so different from the crowded streets of Boston. Here one could breathe and walk or ride about without running into hundreds of other people bustling about their business. This was freedom like she'd never experienced it, and she felt instinctively that Kansas was a place where she could live out the rest of her life.

She pointed toward the south. "What are those hills I see in the distance?"

"That's part of some red hills down toward our state line. Some really good scenery down that way. Pa took Gideon and me down there one summer, and we found some amazing caves and red cliffs. I'm sorry we won't have a chance to go down there while you're here."

"Me too." She'd love to see it all, but with limited time they would stick with what Mr. and Mrs. Haynes had planned for them. "I know Sweetwater Springs is the nearest town, but are there any larger ones around?"

Ben pushed back his hat and leaned on his saddle horn. "We're about halfway between Dodge and Wichita, around seventy-five miles or so either way. Neither of them is a large town, but Wichita keeps growing. That's where Pa takes the cattle to market. He'll drive part of the herd over there in a couple of weeks and sell them."

He swept his arm out across the air. "We have several thousand acres now, and I'll have my own spread to start us out. I plan to buy a few calves and cows as well as a good bull to get started. Pa's going to let me buy some of his stock, so we both know it's good and will produce more to bring a good profit."

"It looks like you have your future all planned, and it sounds wonderful." She wanted so desperately to be a part of that future, but so much depended on how Father reacted to the ranch and her being with Ben.

"What will make it perfect is for you to share it with me. I plan to talk with your father about us later after he's had a chance to really see what our ranch is like."

"I hope he'll like what he sees." She lifted a hand to her forehead to shade her eyes and get a better view of what lay ahead. Her heart beat faster when she recognized the mill from Ben's descriptions in his letters. "I see the mill up ahead."

"Yep, that's it. You see the wheel turning and the water spilling over it? Pa and I got it to working a little last week, but it still needs lots of repairs."

"It's wonderful. Let's hurry and get there." She nudged Victory to a faster trot, which made her bounce even more and rattled her head, so she slowed again. She had a ways to go before she'd really be comfortable in the saddle.

They drew closer to the structure, and the water splashed down into the stream running alongside the mill. The gurgling sound of water hitting water was the only sound at first, but then a few birds joined in a chorus to add their voice and a breeze rustled through the trees. A little ways behind the mill the first walls of the framing for the house stood ready for inspection. He must have done a lot of work on it in the past week, because what he'd written about it didn't sound like this much had been done.

She swung down from Victory and looped the reins around a nearby bush. Ben did the same and followed her to where he had marked off the area with rope.

Ben's heart pounded and his mouth dried up. She had to like what he'd planned. He'd done it all for her, but if she wasn't pleased, he'd start over again. "Well, what do you think?"

"I love the land and everything around here. It's so absolutely peaceful." She skirted around behind the mill and headed to the framework.

"Here, let me show you where things are." He held her hand and led her up the slight incline. "This is where the front door will be, and I hope we'll have a porch all the way across the front." He stepped through an opening. "And here is the parlor where we'll have a fireplace to sit by on cold winter nights."

"I can see it now with a fire blazing, you reading a book, and I'll be doing some mending or needlework." She turned to him with a grin. "Did I tell you Lettie is teaching me to mend and darn things? Now I'll be able to darn your socks and sew buttons on your shirts."

Anything she did for him would be special. Even if she didn't learn to sew, she had the dressmaker in town who could do that for her, and he could always buy his shirts and pants at the mercantile. Ben led her into the kitchen area. "We just passed through the dining room, and here's the kitchen. The stove will be over in this corner, and we'll have a pantry where you can store all kinds of things and a cupboard for dishes and utensils."

"I can't wait to get some recipes from your mother. Lettie said to bring some home, and she'd help me learn to cook them. I told her I didn't want to learn how to make all that fancy stuff Mama has her prepare. Good old country cooking is what Mary Beth said your ma fixes, so that's what I want to learn."

Because they were so far away from the main house, he fought the urge to take her in his arms. He didn't trust his feelings, and he didn't want to put Amelia in any compromising position. Just holding her hand sent heat up his arm and into his heart. Any closer and he might not have such control as he did now.

She released his hand and dashed through the openings between the boards. "Is this part where the bedrooms will be?"

He followed her but kept his distance this time. No use in putting temptation closer than it already was. "Yes, we'll have two to start out with. I put a storage room between them and hope to have space to add on more rooms if we need them."

Amelia stopped and stood very still, her shoulders and back stiff. "Amelia, I'm sorry. Even if we don't have children, we'll need other rooms like an office for me, a library or study and things like that. This will be your house, and you can put the rooms anywhere you like."

His heart ached for her concern. How could he have been so thoughtless as to imply they'd need more rooms for children? He carried hope that she'd be open to taking in children from an orphan train, but he'd wait a few years before suggesting something like that.

She didn't say much after that except to compliment his design. After another five minutes or so of wandering around, she headed back toward Victory. Ben wanted to kick himself for draining all her enthusiasm with misspoken words. But she had to know he loved her no matter what happened.

At the stream, Amelia stopped and stooped beside it. She dipped her fingers into the clear waters then yanked them back out. "Oh, my, I wasn't expecting the water to be that cold. It's like ice."

"That's one of the nice things about this stream. It's cool even in the summertime and will be great for wading on a hot summer day." He couldn't count the number of times he'd done just that in the past two years since Pa had bought the land. Wading in the stream's clear waters was one thing he wanted to do with Amelia, if not this summer, then all the ones that would follow.

She dried her fingers on her skirt and with his help mounted Victory. "If we want to have lunch with our families, we'd better head back now." Enthusiasm had disappeared from her voice.

He nodded and swung up onto Blackie. If he'd thought ahead of time, he could've had Ma prepare a picnic for them, and they could have eaten it in the space set out for their dining room. As it looked now, she was anxious to get back to the ranch. She rode off ahead of him, and he had to nudge Blackie into a faster pace to keep up.

One of these days he'd learn to think before he spoke, but that had always been a failing of his. The important thing for the next two weeks was to win her trust and make her believe in his love. Then on top of that, he had to win over her father, and that would be by far the more difficult of the two tasks.

His heels bit into Blackie's flank. "Race you back to the stables. C'mon, Blackie, lead the way." If he didn't put a little distance and speed between him and Amelia, no telling what he'd be tempted to do. He loved her too much to trust himself, and he'd already done enough damage for one day.

Chapter 26

*A*melia sat back on Victory with her mouth open. How could he have raced off like that, leaving her behind? After the trotting incident, she didn't dare speed up to Ben's pace. Victory did pick up her pace, and Amelia held on for dear life, keeping Ben's figure in sight. What in the world had possessed him?

When she arrived back at the stables, Ben waited with remorse written across his features. "I'm so sorry. I don't know what I was thinking. You're not experienced enough to race like me."

He helped her down from the horse. "Will you forgive me?"

She stared up at him for a moment. Nothing had happened, and she'd made it back here in one piece. "Yes, I forgive you...this time, but don't you ever dare to do that again."

"I promise I won't. I'll think before I act next time." He led the horses back into the stables and handed them over to one of the ranch hands there. "Zeke, would you take care of Victory for me? I'll be back for Blackie after we eat, so I can go join Pa."

"Sure thing, Ben." He tipped his hat to Amelia. "I hope you had a nice ride on Victory."

"I was, until this cowboy here decided he wanted to race."

Zeke jerked his head back. "You did what? Boy, she could have fallen off that horse and hurt herself bad."

Heat colored Ben's face a blazing shade of crimson. "I know, and it won't happen again. I promised."

He grabbed her arm and headed toward the house. "We always leave one of the men back here so Ma won't be completely alone in the house, and I wish it had been someone besides Zeke today. He'll never let me forget that race bit. I'll get a reminder every time your name is mentioned, and he's sure to let the others know."

Amelia said nothing and let him think about his misery for the moment. She appreciated his regret for what he'd done, but could she expect such spontaneous outbursts in the future? A realization hit her like a blow to the chest. She didn't really know Ben at all. Even though he'd talked about himself enough, she hadn't been around him that much to see his true personality.

Wonderful aromas floated through the open windows of the kitchen and shoved the doubts from her mind. Something about the fresh air had certainly whetted her appetite. She didn't ever remember being this hungry before.

Only the women were at home for the noon meal today. Mrs. Haynes explained, "Some days Matthew and the crew don't come in at midday, but eat on the range and come home for supper."

Ben held the chair for Amelia then Mrs. Carlyle. "That's right. I'm going to head out to meet them soon as I've eaten. You can explore around here if you like."

His grin chased away her misgivings about his misstep in racing this morning. "I'm sure we'll find plenty to do."

After the meal, Ben took off just like he had said, and Amelia helped Mrs. Haynes clear the table.

"Amelia, dear, would you like to help me in the kitchen this afternoon? Our men folk will be hungry when they return from a day with the herd."

"Uh, oh, yes, that would be wonderful. I want to get some of your recipes to take back to Lettie so she can teach me to cook them."

Mama and Mrs. Haynes both laughed. Mama picked up her plate and glass. "I think I want to join this session. It never hurts to learn new things."

The next few hours were spent with Mrs. Haynes giving Amelia pointers. By the time they were ready to put Amelia's biscuits in the oven, flour dusted her face and hair as well as covered her hands.

"While those are baking, I'm going to fry up these steaks." Mrs. Haynes sprinkled more flour over slabs of meat already covered in a wash she'd concocted from eggs and milk.

Amelia watched, envious of the ease with which Mrs. Haynes handled the meat and the hot grease in the huge black iron skillet. The meat sizzled and crackled, and the grease bubbled as the meat settled into it. Amelia shook her head. Would she ever be able to do this? Mrs. Haynes made it look so simple.

They had already made a batter for a cake, and it would

go into the oven next. That didn't seem right. Shouldn't the biscuits be last so they'd be hot when the meal was served? But then what did she know about making biscuits in the first place?

A few minutes later when Mrs. Haynes removed the biscuits from the oven, Amelia's mouth dropped open. They were browned to perfection. She'd done it.

The biscuit pan was set on the counter to cool, and the cake went into the oven. A few minutes later, Amelia picked up one of the biscuits. It felt like lead. When she tried to break it in half, the dough was stone hard.

Amelia held it out to Mrs. Haynes. "What...what happened?"

Mrs. Haynes wrapped her arm around Amelia's shoulders. "You handled the dough too much and toughened it before you baked them. It happens all the time to new cooks and sometimes even to experienced ones." She then reached over and uncovered another pan of unbaked biscuits. "I always have an extra ready for times like this. Mary Beth and Clara have both ruined their share."

Heat rose in Amelia's cheeks. She'd never be able to do this. Whatever gave her the idea she could learn to cook? Ben would starve to death with her as wife.

As though reading her thoughts, Mrs. Haynes patted her shoulder. "Don't worry about it any. It was like that for me when I first started learning. All you need to do is practice."

Mama hugged her. "If you really want to learn, Lettie will be the best teacher when we get back home. I'm sure Elizabeth has a good number of recipes for you to take back."

Amelia's heart raced. Mama was actually approving of this. Did that mean Pa might begin to soften too?

At dinner that night, Ben was pleased when Mr. Carlyle talked approvingly about his day on the ranch. "I had no idea so much was involved in running a ranch like this. Seeing all those cattle made me realize how fortunate we are when we serve beef on our table at home."

Pa laid his napkin beside his plate. "We do have a surprise in store for you. We have branding next week, and we're planning on taking all of you out to see it."

Mrs. Carlyle shook her head. "I don't believe I'll go, if it's all right. I don't like being out in the sun very long."

Ma smiled with sympathy filling her eyes. "I understand, Lenora. I didn't like that much sun in the beginning myself."

The rest agreed they would like to participate. Ben imagined the look that would be on the faces of Amelia and Mr. Carlyle as they watched. Branding was a hot, dusty, smelly operation, and the calves bawled when the hot iron hit their flesh. But if Amelia wanted to know what ranch life was all about, she had to be at the branding. Ma would be there, and Clara would too if not for her teaching.

Ma gazed around the table. "I hope you all loved the meal because Amelia helped me prepare it."

Ben's mouth dropped open, and Amelia bowed her head, her cheeks stained with red. She didn't know how to cook, or least she'd said she didn't. He noted the sparkle in Ma's eye; she must have been teaching Amelia today. "It was an exceptional meal. Thank you, Amelia." She glanced up at him and swallowed hard. An odd reaction to a compliment, but he dismissed it.

Clara and Grace Ann cleaned up from supper to allow Lenora time to visit with Elizabeth. The men were in Matthew's office. Lenora and Elizabeth sat in the parlor while Benjamin and Gideon entertained Billy and Amelia elsewhere.

"Thank you for not mentioning Amelia's cooking disaster," Lenora said. "She was embarrassed enough when it happened."

"Oh, I had plenty of mistakes of my own that nobody knew about. A lot of things got thrown away that no one ever saw. If she truly wants to learn, she'll catch on quickly."

Lenora gazed around at the furnishings of the house. The wood and fabric of the chairs and sofa blended well with that of the tables. Matching curtains adorned the windows and added to the homey feeling. "You've done a wonderful job of decorating. The house is quite nice and so comfortable."

"We've been here long enough for it to be the way I want it, and Clara has been a big help."

Lenora bit her lip, not sure where to go next in the conversation she wanted to have about Benjamin and Amelia. Finally she decided to plunge ahead. "Elizabeth, you know the problems I had in childbirth, and now Amanda is facing them. I'm afraid it will be Amelia's lot also. I'm concerned with how that might affect any relationship Ben and Amelia may have." No "may" about it; they were in a relationship, and anyone knowing them would be very much aware of it.

"Yes, I remember, but Isaac loved you and worried about you those times. Charles will do the same for Amanda, and knowing my Ben, he will be just as concerned about Amelia. Losing the babies was hard on Isaac and Charles, but their love remained steadfast. If Amelia can give Ben only one child, he'll be happy with that."

Isaac had said more than once that having the two girls was blessing enough for him, but often Lenora wondered if he missed not having a son, especially since one had come and then been taken away before he could live. Would that happen to Amelia? She didn't want that kind of hurt for her daughter.

Lenora shook her head and blinked her eyes. "Here we are talking like a wedding is already planned when her father is still against such a union. Now that I've been out here and seen your life, I realize Amelia would be happy on the ranch. I'd miss her so much, and so would Amanda, but I don't think either one of us would begrudge her if she's found her one true love. Still, I'm not sure I want her to leave us."

"Matthew and I have had our doubts about the relationship as well, but Ben seems so confident that God is working it all out. I would love to have Amelia as part of our family. It would strengthen the bond our families already have."

Amelia would be happy with Elizabeth and Clara here to guide her, but she'd be so far away from home. "It looks like I'm going to have to do quite a bit more praying about this matter. If my heart isn't willing to change right now, then perhaps I should pray for God to make me willing to be willing. Does that make sense?"

Elizabeth hugged Lenora. "Perfect sense to me. I had to pray that same thing when making the decision about letting Mary Beth stay in Boston."

Lenora sat back with a slump against the back of the couch. "I hadn't even thought of that. Here I am going on and on about Amelia when you've already made the decision and let Mary Beth find her happiness in Boston. She's as far from you as Amelia would be from me." How thoughtless to pity herself when her friend had already walked that path and accepted her daughter's choice.

Perhaps it was time to think of Amelia and not of selfish desires for Isaac and herself.

Chapter 27

The day of the branding arrived, only two days before they were to leave. Where had the time gone? She and Ben had had some time alone over the last twelve days, but not nearly enough to suit her. He was busy with his duties on the ranch, and she was kept occupied with Mrs. Haynes and Mama as they visited friends of the Haynes family on other ranches. Everything Amelia had seen she liked so far, but today would be a real test.

After a final check of her boots and riding attire, Amelia made her way downstairs to meet Mrs. Haynes. They headed for the corral where Ben waited with the horses.

Once again Ben gave her a boost up into the saddle on Victory. He grinned up at her, his brown eyes serious. "Are you sure you want to do this today? It can be brutal if you've never seen it before."

From the descriptions she'd heard, she didn't doubt it, but she wanted to know everything about running a ranch. "No, I'll be fine." The stiffness and aches in her legs and back had given way to occasional aches and pains, but she enjoyed being on a horse.

When they reached the area for the branding, a fire blazed and several long-handled irons with the Rocking H brand lay heating in the flames. Three cowboys along with Ben culled out the calves and then proceeded to rope each one individually.

Steve looped a rope around a calf's neck and pulled it tight. Then he jumped from his horse and had the legs tied in just seconds. Amelia's mouth dropped open. How had he done that so fast? The calf lay bawling on its side, and another cowboy approached with a branding iron. When the stench of burning hair and flesh filled the air, Amelia winced then screwed up her nose and covered it with her hand.

How awful for that poor calf to have that red-hot iron pressed into his hip, and that smell was bad enough to make a person sick. Indeed her stomach had begun rolling, and she swallowed to stop the waves of nausea.

She glanced over and found Ben watching her with narrowed eyes. Her shoulders straightened and she held her head high. Pa rode up to her.

"Are you all right, Amelia? This isn't a pretty sight, and I'm glad your mother stayed away. Perhaps you should join her. This is no place for a lady of refinement."

She waved him away. "No, Papa, I'm fine. But when the iron hit the second calf, Amelia's insides rebelled completely. She jumped from her own horse and promptly emptied her stomach of its breakfast. Ben immediately ran to her side.

He wrapped his arms around her and patted her back.

"It's OK. The smell is pretty bad, so you needn't feel bad. It happens to the best of us."

Heat filled her cheeks, and she lifted tear-filled eyes to his. "I'm so sorry. I just couldn't stop it from coming."

"Would you rather go back to the house now?"

She wanted to be brave and stay, but her stomach wouldn't obey. "Do you ever get used to it?"

"After a time we don't notice it so much, but it still has an odor hard to ignore. Come on, I'll get Ma to ride back with you."

He helped her back onto her horse and turned to his mother. "Ma, Amelia's not feeling well. Will you accompany her back to the house?"

Papa rode up beside her. "That won't be necessary. I'll take my daughter back. I've seen all I need to see, and I want to check on Mrs. Carlyle anyway."

As they rode away another calf bawled its objections, and Amelia held her breath so as not to catch the whiff of the branding. When they rode out of earshot, Papa put one hand on his hip and sent a glare her way.

"Are you satisfied now that ranching is not the kind of life for you?"

"I admit it is a hard life, but I love the wide open spaces, and I can ride a horse now without hanging on for dear life. It's really not bad."

"How can you say that after all you've seen and done the past two weeks? Mrs. Haynes has to do all her own cooking, with Clara's help, but still she does it, and she has to take care of all the chores around the house to keep it clean and tidy. You're not prepared for that kind of life."

His harsh tone did nothing to convince Amelia that

she wouldn't like living on a ranch. "I can learn to do all those things. Mrs. Haynes has been teaching me." It was best to keep quiet about already asking Lettie to teach her the basics of cooking. That might send Papa over the edge.

"Dabbling in cooking is one thing; having to cook day after day is another. You were not raised to live this kind of life. Your mother and I have worked too hard to give you the things that will make life easier for you. I believe you are better suited to a life in Boston."

Amelia bit her tongue to keep from a retort that would anger her father. How could he be so blind as not to see the love she and Ben had for each other? Theirs was the kind of love that could endure the hardships of living on a ranch. And he had even managed to convince her that the number of children they had, if any, didn't make a difference in his love.

The clatter of horse's shoes pounded the hard-packed earth behind them. Then Mrs. Haynes rode up and pulled in her reins. "Matthew reminded me that with all the rest of us eating at the chuck wagon back there, you would need to have someone to get your noon meal. I'm going with you to prepare something so you won't have to worry about it."

Papa nodded and smiled at Mrs. Haynes. "That's very nice of you, Elizabeth. I'm sure Lenora will appreciate it."

Amelia hadn't given any thought to food, and the way her stomach still felt, she didn't want anything right now. She appreciated Mrs. Haynes's thoughtfulness, but she could probably have found something for them to eat. "I'm sorry you had to leave the group, and I'm sorry I made a spectacle of myself back there."

Mrs. Haynes laughed. "Don't worry about that. I did exactly the same when I first came out here. Clara did too, as well as Mary Beth. We let Grace Ann go last year, and she cried the whole time for the calves. It's all a part of living on a ranch."

Papa commented, "You and Matthew have done quite well for yourselves. He said the herd had a good number of calves this year."

"That's right. He's selected several of the best ones to give to Ben for his own stock. Ben has a piece of land that's his now, and he's going to begin building his own herd through the summer. Matthew is very proud of him."

"I see." Papa cut a glance her way, a hard glitter in his eyes. "That will take a while, I presume."

"Yes, but he's smart and has a keen mind for business and loves ranching, so he'll be as successful as Matthew has been. It wouldn't surprise me any to see him go on beyond what we have done."

Amelia's heart swelled with pride at Mrs. Haynes's confidence in Ben. With the plans he had already shared with her, Amelia saw Ben as a prominent man in the ranching business someday. Too bad Papa couldn't see the same success for Ben. If that didn't convince him, then she had little hope of being Ben's bride anytime in the near future.

Ben's concern for Amelia grew as the day wore on. Would the sight she'd witnessed this morning turn her off to ranching? He could reassure her that she wouldn't have to take part in such activities, but would it be enough?

After the last calf had the Rocking H brand on his

backside, the ranch hands doused the fire and made preparations to head back to the bunkhouse. He helped the cook load up the chuck wagon and put away supplies. Then he glanced up at the skies, and a frown creased his brow.

What had been a good cloud cover from the sun for their work now loomed dark and gray overhead. He spotted lightning in the distance and detected the scent of rain in the air. They sorely needed the moisture, but he would rather it wait until they were at least undercover. He hated riding Blackie in heavy rain, even if he wore his slicker.

Pa mounted his horse. "Let's get going, boys. That rain won't wait on us."

Ben swung up on Blackie just as a hard gust of wind hit him and threatened to take his hat. He secured it then reached for the oil skin coat behind his saddle. Even if it was rarely needed, none of them left the ranch without protection from the elements.

Dust swirled about the horses, and the grasses swayed in the wind. At least they were headed in the same direction as the wind and not into it. That made riding somewhat easier, but the thunder now roared more quickly after the lightning strikes to indicate it had drawn closer.

Pa picked up the pace to a near gallop, and they reached the bunkhouse just as the first large drops of rain splattered the ground. They led the horses into the stables and quickly unsaddled them. After being out all day, they needed tending, and Pa never neglected his horses.

Half an hour later, the men made a run for their shelter, and he and Pa ran for the house. Cook had managed to get the chuck wagon into the barn, and Ben spotted him scurrying for cover too.

The rain fell harder and soaked Ben to the skin by the time he reached the front porch with Pa. A chill wind accompanied the downpour and sent shivers through Ben. He and Pa tramped into the house, their clothes dripping on the floor.

Clara hurried toward them. "You boys best get out of those clothes right away then get back here by the warm fire." She grabbed their hats to dry them and shooed them out of the room. At least she and the children had made it home before the deluge.

While Ben toweled dry and donned fresh clothes, the wind began a howling that rattled the window panes. The clouds hadn't looked like ones that might produce a tornado, but out here, they couldn't be too careful. If things grew bad enough, Pa would move them all to the storm shelter to wait it out.

Here it was the last few days for Amelia and her parents, and a storm had to come. He prayed it held only thunder and lightning and no twisting winds that could destroy everything in their path. He'd been through one of those once before and didn't like the idea of doing it again.

Ben ambled downstairs and joined the others in the parlor. Billy played with blocks near the fireplace, and Grace Ann had curled up in a chair with a book. Mr. and Mrs. Carlyle sat on one side talking with Pa. Amelia spotted him and rushed to his side.

Her eyes opened wide, and her face had grown pale. "The storm sounds horrible. Will we be safe here?"

He held her hands. "Yes, if it gets worse, we will all go down into the storm cellar. It's out beside the house." If only he could take the fear out of her face, but he had no idea how much worse the storm might become.

Mama appeared, wiping her hands on a dish towel. "Supper's ready. This storm isn't letting up, so we may as well eat."

Everyone gathered around the table, and Pa offered a prayer for safety during the storm. They ate mostly without conversation as the wind howled and the house groaned. Papa had built it strong and sturdy, and it would survive a thunderstorm, but he wasn't too sure about Mrs. Carlyle. The pinched appearance of her face spoke not only of her fear but also of the lingering headache she'd complained about earlier.

At the end of the meal Mr. Carlyle laid his napkin on the table. "Matthew, Ben, may I speak privately with the two of you?"

Ben stiffened and glanced at Amelia, who stared back wide-eyed. He shoved back from the table and followed his father and Mr. Carlyle into his father's office.

Once the door closed, Mr. Carlyle stood with his hands behind his back and glared at Ben. "I know my daughter cares about you, and you appear to care a great deal about her. I take it you want her to come out here to live?"

Ben swallowed hard. Bracing himself for the refusal, he said, "Yes, sir, I would like to marry your daughter."

"I expected so, but let me ask you something. Since you expect my daughter to give up all she has known in life to come out here, and she appears to love you enough to be willing to do that, do you love her enough to give up what you have here and move back to Boston to find work there as her husband?"

Ben's heart lurched in his chest. Give up ranching to take a position somewhere in Boston? "I don't know. I hadn't even considered it." The thought had crossed his mind, but he'd shoved it away and gone ahead with his own plans.

"Don't you think that's rather selfish? You expect her to give up everything for you, but you haven't considered giving up everything for her." He turned and grasped the door knob. "Think about it, young man. There are two sides to every dilemma." He strode from the office, closing the door behind him.

Ben stood speechless beside his father for a moment then turned to him. "What in the world would I do in Boston? All I know is ranching."

Pa shook his head. "No, son, you know ranching *and* business. Those courses you took at the university have given you a keen business sense. Your uncles would welcome you into the family company in Boston."

"But...but...I want to have a ranch and a home for Amelia here." Now that simple statement did sound selfish to his ears.

Pa placed his hand on Ben's shoulder. "I think Mr. Carlyle has given you something to seriously consider and pray about. Before asking Amelia to commit her life to you and your dreams, make sure they're her dreams too."

Pa left the room and rejoined the family. Ben slumped into his father's chair. *Lord, what am I supposed to do now?*

Chapter 28

*A*melia watched the door to Mr. Haynes's office, her heart pumping blood faster than Blackie raced that first morning. The grim expression on Papa's face and then Mr. Haynes's when they had come from the office sent currents of fear up her spine. The two men continued to talk for a moment until Ben appeared in the doorway. His expression turned her ice cold.

Papa turned and strode to Mama's side. "I think if this storm lets up, we'll head back to St. Louis on tomorrow's afternoon train."

Amelia gasped and stared at her father. "But Papa, we have two more days left. We can't leave so soon."

"We'll see what the storm does, and if it passes, we're leaving."

Ben locked gazes with Amelia. Still so much to be said. What had happened in that office?

Papa reached for Mama's hand. "I believe we need to go to our room and prepare our luggage for tomorrow."

He gazed at Amelia with eyes that pierced her soul. "And I suggest you do the same, Amelia."

She said nothing but bowed her head and nodded. The storm outside may have done no physical damage, but some hidden storm inside had splintered her heart and life here in the house.

Ben jumped to his feet and followed Papa to the stairway. He touched the man's shoulder.

"Mr. Carlyle, may I have a word?"

"What is it? We have things to do."

"I understand, but please reconsider and stay the full time. There are still things I want Amelia to see."

The veins in Papa's neck stood out and his chest swelled. "Young man, have you thought about what I asked a few minutes ago, and would you be willing to do it?"

Ben's jaw tightened. "I don't know."

Papa narrowed his eyes. "Until you do, I want you to have no further contact with our daughter. Do you understand?"

All air left Amelia's lungs, and she could scarcely breathe. What had Papa done? What did Ben have to do? A sob escaped her throat and she pushed past her parents, racing up the stairs before tears could fall.

"Now see what you've done? We'll be leaving as soon as possible tomorrow, storm or no storm." He turned on his heel. "Come, Lenora; we must get packed."

His words followed her to her room where she fell across her bed. When neither Mama nor Papa came in to explain, Amelia sat up and wiped her eyes. Something had happened in that office, and it had turned her father even further away from allowing a relationship between Ben and her. She had to speak to Ben tomorrow and find out what Papa had said.

The next morning Ben wanted to get Amelia aside to explain. He'd spent the night praying and thinking, but he had come to no conclusion. For some reason, God wasn't giving him any answers.

When she came down to breakfast, her parents accompanied her and sat her between them at the table. Ben's gaze locked with hers, and she held a look begging for an explanation. He must find a few minutes alone with her.

Even Billy and Grace Ann sensed the tension and remained unusually quiet this morning before they left for school with Clara.

With the weather clear and sunny, after breakfast Mr. Carlyle sealed his statement of last evening. "Matthew, if you would be so kind as to hitch the surrey, we can be back in town to catch the train to St. Louis. Elizabeth, there's no need for you to come."

"Whatever you say, Isaac." Pa sent him a look that told Ben he wanted to talk later. Ben had no answers for the questions Pa would ask.

Mr. Carlyle managed to keep Amelia close to his side, never giving Ben the opportunity to get near her. Her father lifted her up to the backseat and then helped his wife to sit beside Amelia. She bit her lip and blinked back tears that glistened in her eyes.

The look on her face created a lump in his throat. This couldn't be the end. He still believed Amelia was the girl

God had chosen for him, and somehow, He would put them together.

The surrey left the yard and headed down the road to town. He followed them to the gate then stood and watched the surrey until it became only a dot in the distance.

He strode back to the corral and leaned on the fence. He swallowed the lump in his throat and gazed up to the blue sky dotted with clouds. "God, what am I to do? I love her and want to marry her. There has to be a way we can be together despite what her father says."

What are you willing to give up for her?

Ben shook his head. Where had that come from? Then the words of his own prayer came back to him. That was what he had to do, but could he give up everything he'd worked for, planned for, and dreamed about for so long? Until he could answer that question, he didn't have any hope of winning Mr. Carlyle's support, but the thought of doing it, even for Amelia, tore his soul in half.

Mama stepped up behind him. "Your pa told me about Isaac Carlyle's question last night. Have you prayed about it?" She placed her arm across his shoulders.

"Yes, but I don't have any answers. I'm not sure I can give up everything here at the ranch. I love her, but I see her here as my wife, helping me with our own ranch." The picture of himself in Boston going to an office every day and working with his uncles wouldn't come.

"Until you can honestly say you'd give up everything for her, can you say you truly love her and want what is best for her?"

Her words sliced through him, cutting his dreams into

little pieces. What good was life without Amelia? What good was his life not on the ranch?

Ma hugged him. "I'll be praying for you, as will Pa, but you shouldn't write to Amelia and give her any hope until you can honestly answer Isaac's question one way or the other."

With a pat on the back and a smile, she strolled back to the house, leaving his soul more in doubt than it ever had been.

The countryside rolled past the train windows in a blur. Until she could control her tears, she didn't dare question Papa. No matter what she tried to imagine, nothing could warrant the decision her father had made to return home early.

Finally her tears lessened, and she used her handkerchief to dry her cheeks. She moved across to an empty seat to speak to her parents. After turning the back of the bench so she could face them, she sat down and drew a deep breath.

"Papa, what did you mean when you asked Ben about being willing to do something?"

"That is something Ben will have to explain for himself. I do not want to discuss it any further. Until I hear from him otherwise, he will have no further contact with you. I made sure his father understood that."

"But how can he tell me anything if we're allowed no contact?"

"When he writes to me with his decision, I will let you know. Until then I want to hear nothing more about it."

A glance at her mother, who stared out the window, told Amelia she'd have no help from Mama. Of course she wouldn't go against Papa because he was her husband, but neither one of them considered their daughter's feelings and what she wanted from life.

For the remainder of the trip, nothing more was said about Kansas. Every time Amelia tried to mention it, Papa refused to listen and Mama backed him.

When the train finally arrived back in Boston, a spring rain storm dampened her spirits further. No matter what Papa and Mama said, Amelia would go on with her plans to learn to cook. She had the recipes from Mrs. Haynes in her bag and would give them to Lettie for cooking lessons. Without that diversion, the months ahead loomed long and lonely.

To appease Papa, she would even attend events with different young men, but it would never ease the ache in her heart for Ben. Until she heard from him, or Papa did, she'd pray every day for things to be resolved so that she and Ben could be together.

Chapter 29

*E*ight long weeks had passed since Papa's proclamation, and Amelia had cried until she had no more
tears to give. A little brown wren sat on a tree limb not
far away and sang notes that fell flat on Amelia's ears. No
song, no sun rays, no blue skies or warm weather could lift
the heaviness in her heart and break through the clouds
of sadness. She picked at a piece of raised design on the
brocade-covered chair. This room had become a prison by
her choice. She left only for meals or when Mama insisted
on Amelia's company on a shopping trip or a dress fitting.
The only bright spot in her days was the time she spent
with Lettie in the kitchen. At least Mama hadn't put a stop
to that.

Mary Beth stopped by, and they talked about the
wedding coming on the first of September. Amelia could
muster no real enthusiasm for the event, and Mary Beth
understood, not pressing for participation in all the activities. Amelia had offered to drop out and not be a maid,
but Mary Beth had refused to listen, and for that Amelia

was thankful, because if she dropped out, Papa most likely wouldn't let her attend the wedding at all. Then she'd have no chance of seeing Ben again.

Mama stepped through the door and strode to Amelia's side. "We're going to your grandmother's house. She's invited us for lunch, and Amanda will be there as well."

"I don't want to go. I'll have to pretend that everything is all right when it isn't. You go and have a nice visit."

"That's nonsense. Now get yourself ready. Toby will have the carriage down front in half an hour. If you're not ready, you'll go just like you are. Understood?"

Amelia heaved a sigh and nodded. "Yes, Mama, I understand."

"Good. This visit will do wonders for that sour mood of yours." With that she swept out of the room, her petticoats swishing around her ankles.

After a few minutes, Amelia pushed herself from her chair and sat at her dressing table to tuck in loose strands of hair and make herself more presentable. When Mama called exactly thirty minutes later, Amelia made her way downstairs and out to the carriage.

The bright June sunlight offered warm temperatures, but Amelia's heart and soul bore the bitter cold of winter, and no amount of sunshine could thaw them. Mama said nothing on the trip to her grandmother's house, but a smile played about the corner of her mouth. Amelia sensed something afoot, but she didn't have the energy or inclination to question as she would normally have done.

When they arrived, Amanda sat with Grandma in the parlor. Both wore huge smiles on their faces that did nothing but irritate Amelia. She'd been a mopey, rude young woman the past weeks, but she simply didn't care who bore the brunt of her mood.

Her grandmother hugged Amelia and asked her to have a seat next to her on the sofa. Because she loved her grandmother, Amelia sat. Grandma clasped her hands in her lap. "I think it's time for a good heart-to-heart talk."

Mama sat across from them next to Amanda. "I agree. I had a difficult time getting Amelia to come with me, but she may feel differently after this."

Amelia furrowed her brow and bit her lip. What were these three up to now? Did they think they were going to cheer her up with some stories and anecdotes? Anger wrapped itself around her heart like a vise, and she wished more than ever that she'd remained at home.

Grandma's voice snapped Amelia to attention at the mention of Ben.

"Now it seems to me that all your problems started with this young man, Benjamin Haynes."

Amelia said nothing. She'd done all her talking, and Mama and Papa hadn't listened to any of it. If they were going to try to talk her out of her love for Ben, she'd be out of the house in less time than it took to tell it.

Grandma pursed her lips. "I sense you are not happy to be here. You may change your mind when you've heard us out."

Amelia doubted it, but the least she could do was to listen to what Grandma had to say. "Go ahead. Whatever you say won't change my mind."

"First of all, your mother tells me you haven't been yourself since your return from Kansas. Have you prayed about the situation?"

Amelia choked back a retort. To be truthful, she'd have to admit she hadn't prayed about it much at all since her return. She just assumed all was lost and vented her anger on whoever happened to be in her way. Prayer wouldn't really help things anyway. What was done was done. "What good will prayer do?"

"Much more than you can imagine." She reached over and covered Amelia's hand with hers. "We're not out to change your mind about Ben, my dear child. We're here to try and help you and Ben to work things out with your father."

Amelia bolted upright. Had she heard her grand- mother correctly? "You want to do what?"

"I said we want to help you and Benjamin. Your mother and I have discussed it at length, and Amanda has added her own opinion. While your mother didn't approve of my suggestions at first, she has since seen how much you care about Benjamin. We are of the same opinion and believe you and Ben do love each other and should be allowed to marry."

How could this be? Amelia glanced at her mother. "Papa was so adamant and said that was his final word on the subject when I tried to talk to him on the train, and you seemed to agree with him."

Mama bit her lip. "I remember. Your grandmother and I didn't want to get your hopes up until we could work out some solution. Matt and Elizabeth Haynes will arrive in a few weeks to help Mary Beth with the final preparations for the wedding, and we wanted to make sure we could resolve the problem while they are here."

Mama moved to kneel beside Amelia. "We believe

Ben could provide a good life for you in Kansas, and we'll find some way to make Papa see it. We just wanted you to know that we're on your side and are willing to do whatever it takes to make your dreams come true."

Grandma braced her hands on her thigh, ready to stand. "I believe lunch is ready, so let's eat and we can talk more."

Amanda held up her hands. "Wait just a minute, please. I have a wonderful announcement. The doctor says I am fully recovered from my experience New Year's Eve. So by next spring, Charles and I are hoping we'll have a baby Bishop to welcome into the world."

All the horror of that night rushed through Amelia's mind, as well as the story of the women in Mama's family. If Amanda had a successful pregnancy the second time, there was hope for Amelia too. She rushed over and hugged her sister. "I'm so glad. It'll be wonderful to have a little niece or nephew." What had started out as another gloomy day full of self-pity and despair had turned into one of hope and promise for the future.

Ben's heart lay like lead in his chest. Nothing helped. Over the last two months since Amelia left, his prayers for Amelia's father to change his mind fell flat, and now his faith had hit the lowest point ever. Only one thing he could do, and that was to answer the question that had plagued his mind since he first heard it in his heart: What are you willing to give up for her?

He pulled on his reins and searched for Pa. Ben spotted

him nearby and rode up to him. "Pa, I need to talk with you about something."

"All right, let's go over to those trees so you can tell me what's on your mind."

A few minutes later Ben leaned forward on his saddle. "I've made a decision, and I want to seek your help."

Before Pa could comment, Ben plunged ahead. "I've decided I can't live without Amelia, and if takes giving this up and moving to Boston, then that's what I have to do."

"I see. Your ma and I have been praying for you to do this, but why has it taken you long?"

Ben pushed his hat back on his head; he had questioned why himself. "I'm not really sure. I prayed about it, but deep down I wanted God to tell me I didn't have to do that. Now I can see that is the only choice I have if I want Amelia as my wife."

Pa gripped his saddle horn with both hands. "I'll write to your uncles, and we can discuss a position for you in the company when we return to Boston for Mary Beth's wedding." He hesitated a moment then continued. "I don't know if this is the right thing, but I'm proud of you no matter how things turn out. Now let's get back to the herd." He turned his horse and trotted away.

Ben breathed deeply then exhaled. Now that the decision was made, his body relaxed and his heart lightened. He'd do anything for Amelia. All he wanted was for her to be happy, and her father would have to see that now.

Isaac left his study door open so he could hear when Lenora and Amelia returned from their outing. When he'd questioned Lenora that morning, she'd been rather vague, only saying she and Amelia would visit his mother. Something was going on, but he couldn't put his finger on it.

The front door closed, and he heard voices. Amelia said something about going upstairs to take care of writing a letter. Her voice sounded much lighter and happier than it had in weeks. Perhaps his mother had been able to talk Amelia out of her feelings for Benjamin. That wasn't likely, but something had happened.

He returned to his books when he heard a knock on his door. Lenora stood there with a very determined look on her face. "Come in, dear," he said. "How was your luncheon with Mother?"

"Very nice." She strode across the room and stood before his desk. "Isaac, we have to talk about Amelia and Benjamin Haynes."

"What is there to talk about? That's over and done with. I thought you realized that." Why was she bringing this up now? He'd made his wishes known, and he expected them to be followed.

"Well, it's not over, and it's not going to be over." She leaned her palms on his desk. "I want to know exactly what it is that you have against Benjamin Haynes. He's a fine young man and would take very good care of our daughter."

He pressed his fingertips together. She didn't understand his reasons at all. "My dear, I don't disagree with that. Any son of Matthew Haynes would be a fine young man. It's not him I object to. It's the fact that he lives in

Kansas, and that's too far away from Boston for Amelia to live. You'd miss her too much."

Her mouth dropped open. "Isaac Carlyle, is that the only reason for your objections?"

"If he lived here, I probably wouldn't object to a marriage between the two of them."

Lenora pulled a chair up and sat down hard, her eyes blazing. What had he done to arouse her anger? He'd done all this because he didn't want to see her hurt.

"I can't believe you. Of course I'd miss Amelia if she moved to Kansas, but the more important thing is that she'd be happy with a man she loves with all her heart." Then her eyes narrowed. "Is that what you asked him to do? Move here? I'd rather see her in Kansas, married to Benjamin and happy, than to see both of them miserable here in Boston."

"What makes you think they would be miserable here? If Ben is with her, Amelia should be happy."

Lenora pounded the arm of the chair. "But what about Ben? What if he is called to a life of ranching? Would you ask him to sacrifice his dreams for our daughter?" She leaned forward, the fire still raging in her eyes. "Look at Elizabeth and Matthew. They let Mary Beth stay here in Boston for the social season, and now she's going to marry and stay here. They aren't doing all they can to prevent it. They welcome Andrew as a son."

"That's different. She's making a good marriage, and they have four other children at home to occupy their time." He narrowed his eyes at her. "Why this sudden disagreement? You've never argued with me before about our children."

"I think it's about time." She stood and planted her fists on her hips. "You and I married because we loved each other, and I still love you, but sometimes you can be so stubborn. You've always been one to advocate following God's will for one's life, and here you are refusing to let Amelia and Ben discover and follow His will for their lives. You can't play God. Now I suggest you do a little praying and turn complete control of Amelia over to the Lord." She turned and marched from the room, her back straight as an arrow. The door closed with a thud after her.

Isaac leaned his head on his hands. He only wanted what was best for all concerned, but had he been too busy with what he wanted to see that he had missed what really mattered? Had he put himself in control as Lenora said?

Lord, I'm going to need some guidance here. It looks like what I want and what I believe is right isn't what others see and believe. Show me what You want me to do. Lead me to make the right decisions for my daughter. I love her with all my heart, but like Lenora, I do want her to be happy.

He laid his head back and rested it on the back of his chair. Why did bringing up daughters have to be so difficult?

Chapter 30

Nothing had really changed in the weeks since Mama had talked with Papa except that he no longer scowled every time she mentioned Kansas. A few times at dinner or breakfast, Amelia had said a few things about their trip, and Papa had not changed the subject. That was a step in the right direction, but they still had a long way to go.

Amelia followed Grandma's advice, and every morning now she prayed for her father, for Ben, and for the situation between them. She even offered up random prayers during the day as she thought of Ben.

Disappointment had come when he didn't accompany his mother back to Boston this week. He had work to do in Kansas and would not arrive until the rest of the family did in August. Mrs. Haynes, along with Mary Beth, Mrs. Farnsworth, and Isabella, were due any minute for a planning session and a luncheon.

Lettie had resumed teaching Amelia a few things about cooking, and she had learned to sew on buttons and repair seams. Doing those things gave her hope that the rift with her father and Ben would be resolved in a positive way. Mama continued to say to be patient and wait on God to work. That patience, which was not strong for Amelia anyway, had stretched way beyond what seemed to be logical. Sometimes she wondered if God had forgotten her.

She headed downstairs and was greeted by Mary Beth and her mother entering the foyer downstairs. Mrs. Farnsworth and Isabella followed close behind. Amelia hugged Mary Beth. "I'm so glad to see you. I only wish Ben was here in Boston."

"I know you do, but he'll be here in a few weeks, and you'll be with him at the wedding." Mary Beth turned away to greet Mama.

Mrs. Haynes handed Mama an envelope. "This is for Isaac. Ben asked me to give it to him."

"Thank you, Elizabeth." She handed it to Murphy. "Will you take this in to Mr. Carlyle's office and place it on his desk?"

Murphy nodded and strode away with the envelope in hand.

Amelia's heart leaped to her throat. Why was Ben writing Papa a letter? Was this what Papa had been waiting for? She wanted to race after Murphy and grab the letter from him, but she willed herself to stay with her guests.

Amelia led them to the library where they could visit while the older women talked. She had just learned that Mama, Mrs. Haynes, and Mrs. Farnsworth had all been close friends in school. Their involvement in the wedding brought them together today, and from the sounds of laughter and animated conversation from the parlor, they were enjoying their reunion.

Amelia sat down across from Mary Beth and Isabella, who had chosen the sofa. "I had no idea that Mama and Mrs. Farnsworth had been friends at school."

"Ma told me as soon as I started seeing Andrew that the three of them had been very close, almost like sisters. I think that's why they were both so excited about our betrothal." Mary Beth giggled. "Sometimes when they're together, it's almost like seeing them as young schoolgirls again the way they carry on and have such a good time."

Isabella smoothed out her skirt and brushed away at imaginary lint. "I think you're the luckiest girl around to have Andrew. I've seen the way he dotes on you, and the stars in your eyes say you feel the same for him. I wish I had someone to look at me like that."

Mary Beth glanced over at Amelia. "I would think one of the young men from our coming out would show some interest."

"Well, Philip Barlow did ask my father for permission to call on me. I hope you don't mind, Amelia."

"Of course I don't mind." Amelia didn't have anything against Isabella, but so many times she'd observed Isabella with other young men, and her interests were always the same, what Isabella wanted and what would be beneficial for her. Philip would be a good match for her friend.

Later, after the luncheon, they gathered again in the parlor to discuss the wedding plans. Mrs. Haynes consulted a list she had drawn up. "All right, girls, you are to go for your final fitting of the dresses on Thursday of next week. Mrs. Barnes will have them ready for any last-minute adjustments."

Amelia looked forward to that time. The pattern and color chosen by Mary Beth suited the coloring of both girls. The green of each dress reminded her of the new leaves of spring, fresh and light. The several fittings they'd had thus far had been fun.

Several other events were mentioned, but Amelia didn't pay much attention. Mama would fill her in with the details later. She could think only of Ben and the envelope now resting on her father's desk. Would the contents make a difference in Papa's feelings? She'd know this evening if she could keep her patience. How she wished it was her wedding to Ben that they were planning.

Before she realized it, the time had gone, and her guests prepared to leave. After they departed, Mama decided to go upstairs for a rest, but Amelia didn't want to spend any more time in her room. She passed her father's study and fought the urge to go in and confiscate the letter.

Instead, she retreated to the drawing room and proceeded to play the piano. So many times when her heart was troubled or her mind filled with unrest, the soothing notes of Mozart's *Piano Concerto 21* or Beethoven's *Fur Elise*, always seemed to calm her spirits and bring peace.

When the last notes of *Fur Elise* faded, someone behind her clapped his hands. She whirled around to find Papa in the doorway applauding.

"Beautiful, my dear. Your playing has grown better each year."

"Thank you, Papa. I didn't know I had an audience."

"I know, and that's what gave your music even more

beauty and meaning." He turned to go, but paused and peered at her as though making a decision. "Come into my study. I must have a talk with you."

Fear knotted her stomach and sent a lump to her throat, but a ray of hope wiggled its way into her heart. Perhaps Papa wanted to tell her he'd changed his feelings. Whatever he might have to say couldn't be worse than what happened in Kansas.

Isaac sat down behind his desk. Listening to Amelia play the classical pieces she loved reinforced his belief that she belonged here in Boston and not in Kansas. Lenora would be angry, but she'd get over it and realize it was for the best. He'd prayed about the situation, and the music he'd just heard gave him the answer.

Amelia entered the room and approached his desk. At his nod, she sat in the chair nearby. He cleared his throat, seeking words to say what he believed for her. "Amelia, your mother and I talked about your relationship with Benjamin Haynes. I have to say I cannot agree with her. I have prayed about the situation and have my answer. I cannot allow you to marry him. You may disagree and be angry at the moment, but you'll see in time that I'm right."

Her face blanched, and she sat perfectly still. Then her eyes smoldered with anger, and her lips pressed together in a firm line. She stood and looked him straight in the eye. "I'm sorry, Father, but you can no longer tell me what to do."

How dare she question his authority. "I can, and I will."

"No, you won't. I'll move in with Grandma Carlyle tonight, and then when Ben comes with his family for the wedding, we can be married too, and I'll go off to Kansas with him."

Her voice remained steady with a deadly calm that sent fear to his heart, but he had to stand his ground. "I will not allow you to move. I'll fight you every step of the way."

"You cannot and will not control my future. The only one in control of that is God, and if He gave you the answer you just used, then maybe we aren't praying to the same God."

"Amelia, sit down, and don't talk such nonsense." What had come over Amelia? She'd been rebellious before, but never this outright refusal to follow his orders.

Her face grew red, and she took deep breaths to control her anger. Then she exploded and hit her hand on his desk. "You are not God, and I will follow my heart. I cannot just stand here and let you ruin my life and destroy my future. I'm going to leave and I'm going to marry Ben, and you can't do anything to stop us. If you try, then you'll be out of my life forever." She whirled around and stormed from the room, her feet pounding with each step.

Isaac fell back in his chair, his heart deflated and hurting. Had he just lost the one daughter he wanted to protect? He cried out in anguish, "God, what just happened here? I believed I had the right answer, but I ruined everything. How can I make her see what is best?"

Is it the best?

Isaac jerked his head around. Where had those words come from? He buried his face in his hands. "God, what do You want me to do? How can I make this right?"

Again a voice whispered in the air. *Let her go.*

That couldn't be the answer. Surely God didn't want

that. The longer he sat, the darker the shadows grew, not only in the room but also across his heart.

The aroma from the dining room signaled dinner would be served soon. He pressed his fingers to his eyes. He'd do whatever it took to regain Amelia's trust. He'd wounded her deeply, or she would never have lashed out as she had. It may take some time, but he had to figure it all out before it was too late. "God, I can't let her go."

Then he spotted the envelope on his desk with his name on it. Why had he not seen this earlier? He slid his fingers under the flap to break the seal. His eyes went to the bottom of the page, and when he saw Ben's name, he quickly read the rest. A band tightened around his heart at each word. Perhaps he had misjudged the boy after all.

Amelia flung herself across the bed and sobbed until her throat ached and her body went limp. How could Papa have issued such an ultimatum? Now she'd backed herself into a corner and didn't know what to do. If she apologized, she'd end up doing what Papa wanted and lose Ben, but if she didn't, following through with her threat would bring heartache to everyone. Running away wasn't the solution, but what was?

Footsteps crossed the rug, then Mama settled at her side, placing her hand on her head. "Amelia, my sweet child, I heard what happened in the study. You don't want to run away to Grandma's house, and you don't want to marry without your father's consent. Anger causes us to say things we don't really mean, and backing down from them is hard. The best thing to do now is to stay here, be patient, and let me continue to work on your father."

Amelia sat up and swiped her fingers across her cheeks. "He'll never change his mind. He was furious with me, and I...I just blew up at him. I shouldn't have, but I couldn't help it."

"If you apologize to him and respect his wishes, it will go a long way toward changing his attitude. You also need to forgive him for issuing such an ultimatum."

Amelia couldn't do that now, and maybe not for days or weeks. This was something she'd have to work through.

After a few minutes, when Amelia didn't respond, Mama leaned over and kissed her forehead. "You have as many feelings to work through, as does your father. I will be praying for you both." She rose from the bed and slipped from the room.

Sobs filled Amelia again. What she'd done had been wrong, but she couldn't seek forgiveness from him, nor could she give it. Only God could change the way things were, and so far He hadn't. The situation had only grown worse.

Ben stood with his father, surveying the nearly complete house. "You've done a fine job, son, and I'm proud of you."

He bent and picked up a stone and threw it toward the stream, where it hit with a splash sending ripples over the still waters. "I hope whoever lives here will appreciate the work we put into it."

Ben gazed at his house made of sturdy pine boards and stone dug straight from the Kansas earth. He'd used a sloped roof like Pa had done on the main house in hopes of adding rooms later. The porch stretched across the front, ready for a rocking chair or two. His heart ached because he would not be here to share it with Amelia. If things went well in Boston with his uncles, Pa would sell the property. If not, Ben would return and live here alone. The dream of Amelia and him sitting on the porch in the evening, watching the sunset or listening to the music of the paddle wheel turning in the water ended with his decision to live in Boston.

He and Pa walked back to where they had tethered their horses, and Pa swung up into his saddle. "What are you going to do if Isaac Carlyle doesn't accept your decision?"

"I'm not really sure, but it's what he indicated he wanted. I love her as much as you love Ma." He'd seen enough of the relationship between his parents to want it for himself and Amelia. Everything Ma and Pa did for each other was out of their love not only for each other but also for the Lord.

Ben continued, "Amelia told me she couldn't cook or sew, but that won't matter now. She'll have others to do it for her."

"That she will, but I have the feeling Amelia isn't one to sit around and let servants do all the work. She just might surprise you."

"I'd appreciate that, but one thing has been bothering me. Mr. Carlyle doesn't want Amelia to leave Boston and come to Kansas because it's so far away, but you and Ma are not keeping Mary Beth from marrying Andrew because he lives in Boston and not Kansas."

"It's different for us because we moved away from our parents. We understand the importance of a young couple going where they think it will be best for them to live. Mary Beth has always liked Boston, and now she'll live there with her husband."

If only Mr. Carlyle could see things the way Ma and Pa did. The way the man felt now, he and Amelia didn't have a chance if Ben didn't return to Boston and the family business, and even that wasn't a certainty. He'd asked Mr. Carlyle not to say anything to Amelia about the letter and the decision. Telling her of his move back to Boston to be with her had to come from Ben and no one else.

Chapter 31

*F*or two weeks Amelia avoided her father and spent a great deal of time with her grandmother, only going home to sleep and eat breakfast after Papa left for his office. She had written Ben to tell him to send letters to her at her grandmother's address. A new one had just arrived in the day's mail delivery. She tore open the envelope and held the letter with shaking hands.

> *Dear Amelia,*
>
> *I was so sorry to learn of your disagreement with your father. I know how angry I was with him when you left Kansas. I love you, and I know you love me, but after much prayer and talking with the Lord, I've decided we can't go on against your father. Our marriage would be miserable, and you'd never be happy.*
>
> *I will be in Boston in a few days after you receive this letter. We'll see each other and*

talk more about this face-to-face then as I
have some important news to share with you.
Until I see you, I remain faithfully yours,
Ben

She laid the letter aside. Ben was right even if she didn't like it. Mary Beth had said Ben was coming early, ahead of the family, and would arrive on Monday. They could meet here at Grandma's house and talk, but what good would talk do? They had to act, make something happen.

Grandma entered the room. "I think it's time we had another conversation. I've let you come over here for the past two weeks because I knew you had things to work out in your mind, but it's been long enough. If your thoughts are not yet clear, I think you may need a little help."

Amelia picked up the letter and handed it to Grandma. "This is what Ben thinks."

Grandma read the paper and set it on the table. "He's a wise young man. Listen to what he has to say when you see him again."

"I want to, but this whole mess is more than I can handle. I don't know what to do."

"You asked your mother and me to be on your side, but are there really sides we must take? You and your father are in opposite corners, but both of you are right in your feelings but wrong in the way you are expressing them. Your father doesn't want you to move so far away from your home here and lose you. He's acting in the only way he knows to keep that from happening. You want to marry Ben and leave Boston, and you're doing what you think is right in going against your father's wishes."

Amelia studied her hands then clasped them together. She hadn't truly considered Papa's reasons for his attitude. Maybe he hadn't been trying to control her life after all. He kept saying he wanted what was best, but for whom?

"He's already lost me, and I think he sees that now. I don't want it that way, but I can't forgive him or apologize."

Grandma reached for the Bible on the table by her chair and opened it. "Here in the sixth chapter of Matthew, verses fourteen and fifteen, Jesus talks about forgiving. 'For if ye forgive men their trespasses, your heavenly Father will also forgive you. But if ye forgive not men their trespasses, neither will your Father forgive your trespasses.' That simply means you must forgive others their sins just as our Lord forgives ours, or our petition for forgiveness is in vain."

Amelia let the words soak in. Her heart ached in the worst way as though it had been ripped apart. Only God could put it back together, but it would take effort on her part to be obedient to what He required of her. "I will think about this and pray about it. I do know what is right, but I can't do it now. I'll wait until Ben is here and we can pray together."

On Monday, after a long weekend on the train, Ben's heart thumped in his chest as they entered the station in Boston. All through this trip he'd sat alone, read his Bible, prayed, and rehearsed his speech to Mr. Carlyle and what he'd say to Amelia. Mary Beth said she'd meet him and take him straight to Amelia at her grandmother's house. He had only met Mrs. Carlyle once at his grandfather's funeral, and he'd been impressed by her kind spirit and her strong faith exhibited by the words spoken to his grandmother at the services.

His letters to Amelia through Mary Beth and then to her grandmother's had not been the way he would have liked to communicate. It was too much like deception, but he didn't have any other choice if wanted to keep in touch with her. Each letter had been saved and read over and over again as she expressed her love and how much she missed being with him. They gave him assurance that his decision was best for both of them.

The train stopped, and Ben gathered his belongings. Soon he'd see Amelia and she'd know of his decision to stay in Boston after the wedding. His uncles planned to meet with him tomorrow and go over the details of his position with the company.

Ben searched through the horde of people and spotted Mary Beth waving at him. He grinned and returned the greeting. He elbowed his way through the crowd to reach her. When he had finally pushed through and stood before her, she stepped away, and Amelia smiled up at him.

At first he could not speak then he gulped and held out his arms. "Amelia, I can't believe it."

She stepped into his embrace and wrapped her arms around his back. "Believe it. I couldn't wait another minute to see you."

Mary Beth smiled and her eyes danced mischievously. "The carriage is waiting for us, and as soon we get your bags, we'll be on our way. I asked our driver to stop at our place and drop me off, then you and Amelia can go on to her grandmother's house."

With one arm around Amelia, Ben retrieved his bag and followed Amelia out to the carriage. Once settled inside, he could finally say what he'd bottled up for so many months even if Mary Beth sat across from them. She'd understand since she loved Andrew as much as he loved Amelia, if that was possible.

He held Amelia's hand. "I've missed you so much. My love has grown stronger in the days we've been apart."

Amelia squeezed his hand, and the love that shone in her eyes brightened his hopes and filled his heart with more assurance that God ordained and blessed their love.

"My life has been miserable without you. No amount of talk from Mama or Grandma has helped with Papa. We've let him be for the past two weeks since I lost my temper."

"That's something I'm glad I didn't have to see, and I hope I never do." Amelia had always been somewhat of a rebel according to Amanda, but she'd always been good-natured and easy to get along with. Lashing out in anger had never been in the picture. Ben still found it hard to believe that she had behaved in such a manner.

"I'm ashamed of it now, and I've made a decision for something I know I must do before we do anything else." She paused then said, "We must go see Papa first so I can seek his forgiveness and let him know I forgive him for what he said to me."

Ben shook his head. "This is crazy. I had the same idea, because I need to let your father know I understand his feelings, but also tell him what I plan to do. We can do it now as soon as we take Mary Beth to Grandmama's."

His sister clasped her hands and smiled. "I knew

bringing her to the station was the right thing to do, and now you both have the same idea. This is delicious."

The carriage stopped, and Mary Beth stepped out and directed the driver to take them to Amelia's house.

Once they were alone, Ben struggled with the words he needed to say to her father. They kept tumbling over one another and sat as a scrambled mess in his heart.

When they arrived at her home, Amelia held tightly to Ben's hand in hopes of drawing some of his strength into herself. Neither of them had told the other what they planned to say, and now doubt filled her soul. This is what the Lord wanted her to do, and He'd give her the words to say.

Maeleen's eyes opened wide, and her mouth dropped opened. "Miss Amelia, Mr. Haynes. We weren't expecting ye. Come in."

"Is Papa at home, Maeleen?" It was a little before his usual time, but he sometimes came home early. If he wasn't, they'd wait.

"Yes, in his study, he is. He arrived only a few minutes ago. Do ye want me to tell him ye be here?"

"No, we'll go on in." She grasped Ben's hand, and together they approached the study. When Amelia knocked, her father told them to come in. When he saw them, he jumped up from his chair. The look of surprise followed by narrowed eyes and pursed mouth sent a shiver through Amelia. If she hadn't been holding on to Ben, her legs would have failed her completely.

Then Papa smiled and came from behind his desk. He

wrapped his arms around Amelia. "My sweet daughter, how I've missed you these past days." His tone was less harsh than expected, and he hadn't told them to get out or leave. *Lord, it's in Your hands.* She squared her shoulders and breathed deeply. "Papa, I've come to apologize for my unseemly behavior. The Bible tells us to respect our parents, and I did not do that when I struck out at you with words of anger. Please forgive me."

Papa slumped down into his chair. "I accept your apology, Amelia. I love you too much not to."

Relief flooded through Amelia. Now if Papa listened to Ben, all would be right.

Ben cleared his throat. "Mr. Carlyle, I've come to seek your forgiveness also. I should never have gone behind your back and kept in touch with Amelia, but I love her with all my heart and couldn't bear not hearing from her. I know you don't want her to live out in Kansas, so I've secured a position with my uncles in our family business. I'll not be returning to Kansas after the wedding."

Amelia gasped, and her heart turned somersaults in her chest. "You've done what? What about the house and all your plans for your own ranch?"

Ben grasped her hands in his. "I tried to tell you on the way here, but the words stuck in my throat. Without you my life is meaningless, and if you can't be in Kansas, then I'll move here to be with you."

Tears filled Amelia's eyes. "I can't let you do that. All your hopes and dreams are in Kansas, not some investment company here in Boston." She turned to her father. "Papa, you can't let him do this. He'll be miserable here."

Papa reached for the Bible on his desk. "I've been

reading God's Word and praying a great deal since that day you left in such anger. I must ask for your forgiveness too, Amelia." He turned his gaze to Ben. "And for yours, young man. I let my own selfish desires attempt to dictate what the two of you do with your life. For that I am deeply sorry. The very thought of losing you, Amelia, has troubled me deeply."

Amelia swallowed a sob and ran to her father's side. She bent to wrap her arms around his shoulders. "Oh, Papa, I do forgive you. I'm so sorry I hurt you."

He reached up and stroked her arm. "Oh, but I fear I harmed you and Ben more than you did me. You simply opened my eyes to see what I'd really done. It's taken me these days of your absence to realize that the only way to show my love is to let you go your own way. Ben has proved his love for you by being willing to sacrifice his plans to be with you."

Amelia stood and stepped back beside Ben. "Does this mean what I think it does, Papa?" Her heart pounded, but her breath stopped as she waited to hear his answer.

"Yes, it does. I can no longer, in good conscience, stand in the way of your happiness with Benjamin. Son, you don't need to give up your dream of a life in Kansas. Knowing that you are willing to do anything for my daughter is enough for me. I give you both my blessings for a happy marriage."

Amelia's breath escaped in a whoosh, and she turned to hug Ben. His jaw clamped tight with disbelief, but as the truth set in, he returned her embrace, and a smile replaced the frown.

His lips brushed her hair. "Mr. Carlyle, I can't begin to

tell you what this means to me. I'll speak with my uncles today if you're sure this is what you want."

Papa stood and then came around the desk to shake Ben's hand. "It is, son. It's taken awhile, but I see my daughter's happiness is more important than my selfish desires, and I'd rather have her in Kansas loved and cared for than to have her here at home, miserable and alienated from me."

Mama strode across the room to Papa. "Isaac Carlyle, those are the sweetest words I've heard you say in a while." She embraced Papa.

A miracle had happened in this room, and love filled it to overflowing. Papa raised a hand and waved it. "Go on, you two. I'm sure you have plans to make."

Ben reached down to hold her hand. "Thank you, sir." He grinned at Amelia. "Let's go. I have a few things to say to you."

Amelia's heart filled so full, it might burst at any moment as she followed him to the foyer. Under the crystal chandelier in the middle of the hallway, Ben gripped her hands. "With all the new territories opening up, I don't know what the future will hold for us or where we might go, but I do know that I want to face it with you by my side. Miss Amelia Carlyle, will you do me the honor of becoming my bride?"

Amelia's heart took flight and soared to the heights of heaven with love for Ben. She threw her arms about his neck. "Yes, yes, yes. I'll marry you."

Mama and Papa laughed from the doorway to the study. Papa's voice boomed across the foyer. "Well, kiss her. You've certainly earned it."

Amelia gazed into Ben's dark eyes filled with as much love for her as she had for him. He grinned and lowered his face to an inch from hers and whispered, "They don't need to know this isn't the first time I've kissed you." Then his lips touched hers, and all the months of waiting found their meaning. Tested and tried, their love had endured. Not only that, a home stood waiting for her—a home she now knew she was prepared to handle. This was the beginning of her journey to being the wife of a rancher in Kansas, or wherever the Lord led, and what a journey it would be.

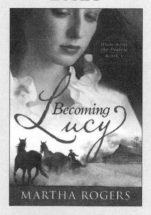
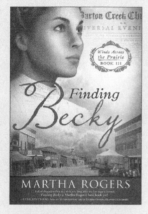